IT MUST BE FATE
A Royal Crown Academy Epilogue

KHAI HARA

AUTHOR'S NOTE

Be forewarned—this epilogue introduces new characters and sets up new storylines for the next gen series that do not get in-depth coverage and/or find complete resolution in this epilogue.

If partial cliffhangers make your eyelids twitch and your blood pressure rise, I'd suggest holding on reading *It Must Be Fate* until the next gen series is out. There's a lot of good stuff in here but also a hefty dose of mystery. I can't give away all the next gen secrets just yet
:)

If not, happy reading. I look forward to you discovering the children of some of my favorite psychos.

*To the end of one generation
and the start of another.*

*And for Amanda, Anushka, Kreena, Lena Monique,
Miya, Simran, and Vrushti.
No one rides for the RCA family like you do.
I can't thank you enough for it.*

The summer after graduation

Chapter One

Bellamy

"Alright girls," Thayer exclaims, getting up and immediately stumbling. "Oops."

She tries righting herself and is unsuccessful before ultimately deciding that staying seated might be the safest option for everyone involved. Dropping back onto the floor, she raises her glass to get our attention.

"I think we're at the point in the night where we're sufficiently drunk that I can suggest we play *Truth or Dare* and you'll actually say yes. Who's with me?"

I hear an excited squeal leave my mouth and join the sound of Sixtine and Nera's. They immediately jump to their feet and dance around the room to the beat of the loud party music blasting on the speakers.

There are four of us in the room but the volume of noise we're unleashing on the floors can closest be compared to a stampeding herd of rhinos running desperately from a lion.

Our poor downstairs neighbors.

Ah, well, I think to myself, the flash of guilt extremely brief, *it's our last night together.*

Even though we graduated from RCA in June, we ended up extending our lease at The Pen through the end of summer so we could spend more time together. Sixtine's parents had helped us keep our apartment far beyond the usual deadline, until the school had no choice but to kick us out because new students were moving in.

Until the very last moment.

And that moment is tomorrow.

After tonight, we'll likely never live together again.

We're sitting cross-legged around our coffee table, our couch wrapped and set on its side against the wall, ready to be picked up by the movers. Boxes containing all our possessions are strewn across the space.

When I look around me, it's hard not to get choked up by the memories of the best year of my life, and the fact that after tomorrow, everything will change.

We're good with change, as individuals and as a group.

I know that.

Since we came into each other's lives, all we've had is change. Thayer and I moved to Switzerland. We met Sixtine and Nera and became instant best friends.

I went from hating Rogue to dating him.

Thayer went from dating Carter to falling in love with Rhys.

Phoenix didn't speak to Sixtine for two years then dated her and married her within the next one.

And Nera… Well, she said 'fuck it' to teenagers and started dating her professor. Then she won a gold medal at the Olympics and became a global Nike ambassador overnight, for God's sake.

We're *great* with change.

And it's all good change, because we each found the love of our lives.

Rogue and I are moving back to the U.S. so he can step into his role as CEO of Crowned King Industries.

Thayer is moving to London where Rhys just signed a contract with Arsenal, his dream team. Sixtine and Phoenix bought their second home, this one in Kensington, where they'll live while they both go to college to study pre-law.

Tristan and Nera are going traveling for a while with no end date or destination in mind, just seeing where the journey takes them.

After tonight we're all moving on to even more exciting chapters in our lives, but there's something about no longer living with my friends that makes me emotional. We're never going to have this moment in time again together and I really cherished it.

It changed me, it shaped me, it meant the world to me.

Neither Thayer nor I ever imagined how much our lives would be capsized when we moved here. It was the *best* decision we ever made and that's in large part because of the friendships we found here.

And this apartment bore witness to almost all of it.

Eating breakfast at the kitchen island, bleary-eyed and gossiping about the night before. Watching reality tv on the couch. Going endlessly back and forth between each other's closets to find the perfect outfits for every occasion, whether it was going to class or going out. Hugging each other in our rooms when our families disappointed us. Crying on each other's shoulders when the boys broke our hearts.

These walls were constant during the highs and lows of the past year. They housed us, our emotions, and our memories.

So, we decided to give The Pen what it was owed – a proper farewell, one worthy of all the time we spent here together.

Last week with the date quickly approaching on our calendars, we'd opted to throw a girls-only, 'final sleepover' themed night.

Booze in ample quantity.

Snacks in ampler quantity.

And no boys.

This wasn't about them. It was about *us*.

They'd been banished back to their mansion with a mandate that they weren't allowed to text or call unless texted or called first.

They'd taken the news about as well as could be expected.

Poorly.

"You know you have to sleep in my bed every night," Rogue grumbled, wrapping an arm around my waist and pulling me close. "Contractually."

I grinned up at him. "Show me the paperwork."

"Let me marry you and I'll have the officiant put it in the vows. I can have someone here within the hour to make it official."

I patted his chest. "After I graduate college."

"One thousand three hundred and ninety eight," he answered.

"What?"

"That's how many days until your college graduation," Rogue said. "I counted."

I curled my hand around his nape and pushed up onto my toes. His face came down to meet mine halfway as I reached to kiss him. He mumbled a heated 'fine' against my lips when I pulled back minutes later.

Behind me, Phoenix groaned dramatically. "You'd do this to me during our honeymoon?"

I could practically hear Six's eyes roll back into her head. "*Fiji* was our honeymoon, babe."

"The honeymoon phase is over that quickly for you, huh?" he pouted, crossing his arms. He was going to make a great lawyer one day.

She disarmed him with a soft look and equally tender smile. "No one's loved anyone in this room longer than I've loved you, Nix," she reminded him.

"That's not true." He wrapped his arm around her neck and pulled her into the crook of his shoulder as he fingered a strand of her red hair. "I saw you first, remember?"

"Come on, Rhys," Thayer implored. "Distance makes the heart grow fonder and all that. And honestly, I'm being generous by calling it 'distance', it's just one night."

He crossed his arms, his eyes raking slowly down and back up her body. "I don't need to miss you to want you, love. Never have, never will."

I watched the man physically melt when she gave him a brilliant smile in answer to his sweet words.

Tristan, meanwhile, outright refused.

"Out of the fucking question," he said, shaking his head. "I spent *four months* sleeping without you, Nera. I just got back into your bed, I'm not giving you an opportunity to find a way back out of it."

"Baby," she purred, hugging him around the waist. "I'll let you…"

I didn't hear the rest of her sentence because she pressed the words right up against his ear, but the way his shoulders relaxed in response told me he would also give in. She was just going to need to put in some extra convincing, but I knew she was more than willing to do it.

One thing about The Pen? The walls are thin.

Very thin.

"Earth to B?" Thayer calls out, waving a hand in front of my face and snapping me out of the memory. "You looked like you were in a trance just there. What were you thinking about?"

I laugh, smacking her hand aside.

8

"Just the boys and how dramatically they took the news that we wanted to spend *one* night without them."

"For real, so dramatic. Except maybe for Tristan," she quips back. "You really made that man suffer, Nera," she adds, turning towards the woman in question.

"Hey!"

"Not a criticism," Thayer adds, putting her hands up. "I've seen the man shirtless, you're literally God's strongest soldier. How you managed to resist the fanny flutters for that long is beyond me. You should teach a class or something."

With no throw pillow nearby to toss at Thayer, Nera picks up a loose roll of toilet paper lying in a pile of random items we still need to put in a 'miscellaneous' box and lobs it at her.

Her target ducks just in time and the roll bounces off the wall before hitting the ground.

"Missed!"

"Have you been watching *Love Island* without us again?" Six asks. "'Fanny flutters' sounds suspiciously un-American."

"Guilty," Thayer answers, putting her hands up for the second time in less than a minute.

"*Anyway*," Nera says before turning towards me. "Are you up for *Truth or Dare*, B?"

"Absolutely."

***

Chapter Two

Thayer

"Okay, ladies," I announce, standing up next to the coffee table. For a moment, I sway, the ground moving dangerously underneath my feet.

The floors have been super weird tonight, I think to myself as I bring the bottle of tequila to my lips and take a swig. *Not sure what's up with them.*

All three of my friends' faces are upturned, listening intently to what I'm about to say, and I'm just so happy we were able to do this.

One last night, all together.

"We're going to play using the typical *Truth or Dare* rules, but with an added 'mercy' option. If you don't want to do the dare or tell the truth, you can take a shot of tequila instead." I brandish the bottle between us. "It's not actually a merciful option, you'll definitely pay for it in the morning, but it's a fun excuse to get a little drunker," I add with a grin.

"We're all in, it's our last night," Nera says. "But don't sit back down just yet, Thayer, you're up next."

I spread my arms to each side. "Hit me."

"Truth or dare?"

"Dare," I say, tipping my chin up.

As if I would pick anything else.

She nods at the bottle. "Take a shot."

I pout. "That's it?"

"Let's ease our way into it. Did you forget that we're moving tomorrow?"

"Ugh," I say with a groan, pouring an actual shot this time and throwing it back. My throat burns as the liquid shoots down my throat and I wince. I bite into a nearby lime wedge and enjoy the acidic kick on my tongue. "Don't remind me."

I didn't think our last night would make me so emotional.

It crept up on me over the last couple of days as we'd put the common areas into boxes. We'd reminisced about the pieces we'd each brought into the apartment as we packed them.

My tone makes Six reach out and squeeze my hand.

"No being sad tonight," she says, her kind voice firm. "Your turn to ask a question."

"B," I say with a sly smile. "Truth or dare."

"Truth."

"Hmm," I answer, thinking up something. "Are you excited to move back to Chicago?"

"Yes and no," she says. "I can't wait to live with Rogue and see my mom and go to college. I'm literally counting down the days until I can eat a hot dog and wear pajama pants outside without feeling like the entire world is judging me. But," she pauses, looking around at us. "I'm going to miss you guys. I'm going to miss the whole group hanging out together and my FOMO is going to be *violent* when I'll see you all hanging out without us."

"Maybe I'll come back to Chicago soon, you never know."

"Babe," she says, patting my hand. "Your man just signed a huge contract with one of the top clubs in the world. You're going to be speaking with a British accent before you ever come back to live in the US."

The familiar rush of delight swells through me when I think of the contract Rhys just signed with Arsenal. It's been his lifelong dream to play for the club his parents were diehard fans of and I couldn't be more that he made it come true.

"Don't worry, just tell Rogue," Nera offers. "He'll buy you a jet and bring you to London every weekend if it means you'll be happy. I'm sure he'd figure out a way to fly it himself too if that's what it took."

"You're not getting rid of us that easily, B," Six says.

"Good," Bellamy answers. "Come on, you're up Six. Truth or dare?"

"Truth," she puts her hands up when I groan at her choice. "I am who I am," she says with a laugh.

"Fine," I tell her, "but then you have to give us a dirty truth."

Bellamy nods in vigorous agreement. "Where's the kinkiest place you and Phoenix have ever had sex?"

She clears her throat and then blushes a violent color of red. "Um, do you mean...physical place or like...orifice?"

Nera bursts out laughing.

"Oh my god," Bellamy says with a shriek, covering her ears but also grinning like a fool.

"*Excuse* me?" I exclaim.

Nera wipes a tear from the corner of her eye and says, still laughing, "I guess it's a valid clarifying question."

"I just didn't know she was that kinky," I say. "I feel like I need to step up my game."

"To be clear, I was asking about the physical place," Bellamy answers, still giggling.

Six plays with a napkin on the coffee table, spreading it with her fingers to occupy her hands. Her cheeks are flamed pink.

"Six, you're scaring me, babe. What the hell are you about to say?" I ask, wide eyed. All three of us lean forward, the silence growing still as we wait for her to fess up.

"It's not *that* crazy and it's not like we planned it, it just happened."

"Where?" Nera nudges.

"I just," she says, pausing, before whispering the rest of her sentence so softly, I almost miss it. "I just...well, I finally convinced Phoenix to come horseback riding with me."

There's two seconds of heavy, thick silence.

"*What?*" I shriek.

"Did you just say..." Bellamy rolls back onto the ground in peals of laughter.

"I'm sorry, you two fucked on top of a *horse?*" Nera asks, incredulously.

Six slaps a hand over her mouth to muffle the laughter bursting from her lips at our shocked expressions.

Meanwhile, I feel like I'm doing math trying to figure out how that would even work.

Bellamy echoes my thoughts, grabbing her stomach and grimacing from the pain of laughing so hard.

"What are the mechanics of that, Six? How do you…get on?" she scrunches her nose. "Is it even hot or like, really fumbly?"

"It was back home, right before the wedding–"

"I can't wait to see how the *horse* comes into play here," Nera cuts in.

"—and I was at the stables, brushing one of the stallions when Phoenix came up behind me and started kissing my neck."

"I love when they do that," Bellamy says with a lovestruck sigh.

"Right? Well anyway, I told him I was going for a ride and again I asked him to come along," she continues. "You don't understand how many times I've asked him to come horseback riding with me. He's *never* said yes, so when he said he'd come but only if we rode the same horse, *bien sur* I said yes."

"Naturally," Nera quips, nodding encouragingly.

"So he took me on a walk—"

"'He took you on a walk'," Bellamy deadpans.

"It started out totally innocent!" Six promises. "At first we were both sitting facing the same direction and I was showing him the path I like to take in the forest and then," she pauses. "Well, and then…"

She trails off, seemingly unable to finish her sentence.

"Then you traumatized a horse," I cut in helpfully.

Bellamy and Nera burst out laughing again while Six's face pales.

"*Oh putain*, do you really think he's traumatized?"

"Who are you?" I ask, in wonder.

"An icon, that's who," Nera answers.

"Did the horse stay in place or did it move?" Bellamy asks.

I whip around and point at her. "*Excellent* question."

Six grimaces. "Not at first," she says. "But, you know, the rhythm of us…*doing it*…made him think we were telling him to walk, so he did."

"You have to stop," I beg. "I think I'm going to pee my pants." I have sharp pains stabbing at my stomach from how hard I'm laughing.

I couldn't ask for a more perfect last night as roommates than this; laughing at each other's obscene stories together.

"And to answer your question, yes," Six finishes with a final blush. "As disturbing as it sounds to admit out loud, it was *so* hot."

"Really?" Bellamy asks, leaning forward.

"Oh, yeah. I had my legs wrapped around Nix's waist and he used his hands on my ass to guide me," she shivers as she relives the memory and I add trying to have sex on top of a horse with Rhys to my list. "Then he flipped me around."

"Gosh, I thought I had a good answer — the forest," Nera adds in response to Bellamy's raised brow, "but I think you put us all to shame."

"*Avec plaisir*," Six does a small bow, flourishing her hand mockingly in the process. "Your turn, Nerita."

"Truth."

"Hmm, let me think," Sixtine says, tapping her chin pensively with her finger. "Do you think you and Tristan would still have fallen in love if you hadn't met at that hotel first?"

Nera smiles softly, cheekily almost, like she knows something we don't.

"No question. It might have taken us longer to get together, but I know we would have in the end. That pull was there from the first moment; whether it happened in a bar or a classroom wouldn't have mattered."

"I completely agree with you," I say.

It's hard to disagree. The connection between them crackles to life with unstoppable force when they're in the same room, like two magnets hurtling towards each other at speed without care of what might be in the way.

"Do you think the boys are being nice to him?" she asks, worry flashing across her face. "You know how those three can be."

"Oh he'll be totally fine," Bellamy answers, waving her concern away. "They kept Tristan's secrets from us for months. Rogue only just told me what he did to Coach Krav."

"He was never heard from again, right?" Six asks.

"He is alive," Nera answers, swallowing nervously. "I didn't ask for specifics and he didn't feel the need to tell me the gruesome details of what happened, thank god, but he's alive."

"I would not shed a tear should he find himself *unalive* one day," I say with a disgusted sniff.

He hurt our friend and physically scarred her, so I have less than zero empathy for that abusive animal. Whatever Tristan did to him that night, I hope it hurt.

I hope it *continues* to hurt every single day.

"I'm glad Rogue helped Tristan when he called him," Bellamy adds, warmth coloring her tone when she mentions her boyfriend. "I love that loyal side of him."

One of the best parts of the last year has been the real Rogue slowly revealing himself to the rest of us.

Turns out, he's a good friend.

If you'd asked me a year ago, I'd have said that I'd rather eat an entire piece of chalk without a drop of water than say those words out loud.

Today, I see he has the best heart and is fiercely protective of his new family. What won me over to him once and for all was seeing the things he did for our friends, the lengths he went to to look after us.

He's become like a brother to me and it's *because* we're that close that I tease him incessantly.

And there's no better way to tease Rogue than to mess with what he cares about the most.

Bellamy.

It's time to make this game more interesting.

***

Chapter Three

Sixtine

"Bellamy," Thayer purrs, and I know that voice.

It's her troublemaker voice, the one she uses when she's about to get up to no good.

We should all be very afraid.

"Truth or dare?" she asks.

"Truth."

"Dare? Okay, great choice. Let me think," Thayer adds, tapping her chin while deep in thought.

Bellamy laughs and shakes her head, letting her impish best friend do as she likes.

"Fine, dare. But make it good."

"Don't you worry about that, babe," Thayer tells her with a grin. "I saw this trend on TikTok that I want to try. Basically, you send a picture of a bouquet of flowers to Rogue and say 'thank you for the flowers'. He'll text you back freaking out about who could have sent them to you since they won't have come from him. We mess with him for a little bit and tell him it was a prank."

Bellamy groans. "He'll just get angry."

"There is a high likelihood he'll ruin girls' night," Nera agrees.

Rogue *is* extremely likely to barge through our front door swinging, wrecking destruction first and asking questions later, if she texts him that.

But a dare is a dare and I don't mind the show. Especially if it means Rogue will bring my husband along with him.

I don't think I'll ever get tired of calling him that.

Plus, it wouldn't be our last night in this apartment if one of the boys didn't attempt breaking down our front door.

"To be fair, Rogue getting angry does feel like a rite of passage at this point," I answer her, pulling my phone out and opening a new tab.

Thayer leans forward from her kneeling position so that she's on all fours, her face only a few inches away from Bellamy's.

She wiggles her eyebrows at her. "And think about how much you like it when you guys make up."

Bellamy's eyes darken. A mischievous gleam shines in her gaze as a slow grin stretches across her face.

"You're not wrong. Okay, what do I do?"

I look up from my phone. "The bouquet will be delivered in ten minutes. That gives us just enough time to get a refill on drinks."

"I love it when you get all scarily efficient," Thayer praises.

"Call me the enabler of all your terrible ideas," I reply.

She throws an arm around my shoulders and smacks a wet, tequila-soaked kiss on my cheek. "And that's why I love you!"

She skips over to the kitchen island with a giddy laugh, busying her hands with glasses and champagne bottles and snacks. Doing a million things at once and not finishing any of them.

She's energy and excitement, exuberance and loud, crazy plans. The complete opposite to my quiet reservedness in almost every way, which is exactly why *I* love *her*.

Rhys has met his match in every way with her. They're the very definition of two halves of the same soul; always in motion, laughing and enjoying life together.

I'm glad that they found each other and I'm even happier that they'll be moving to London with us after graduation. Nera and Tristan might come as well once they're done traveling so I'm excited that we'll still be able to do smaller squad sleepovers and see each other all the time. I'm not ready to give that up yet, if anytime soon.

The doorbell rings and a massive, three-tiered bouquet greets us at the door.

"Uh, Six," Nera says, arms shaking under the weight of the flowers. "You might have gone a little overboard."

"I've seen the bouquets he's sent her in the past and they haven't been your traditional dozen red roses. If we want this to work, we need this bouquet to put Rogue's to shame and that's no easy feat."

"I like your thinking," Thayer says with an assertive nod.

"Okay, Nera, what's my art direction for this photo?" Bellamy asks, standing hands on hips in front of the bouquet. "Do I just send a pic of the flowers and say thank you, baby?"

"That's the trend," Thayer confirms.

"I think we should put you in the photo. I mean you look so adorable right now,' Nera says.

She really does. She's wearing a cute lemon-patterned pj set, her hair is up in a messy bun and her cheeks are flushed pink because of the alcohol.

"Here," Nera continues, grabbing Bellamy's hand and forcing her to sit back on the ground. She poses her legs and pushes a strand of hair behind her ear. Then she hands her the bouquet and directs her on how to hold it. She steps back to look at her handiwork. "I'll take the photo from about this angle. The framing looks great with the background and lighting. Just one more thing…"

She leans back towards Bellamy and fingers one of the slim straps of her top. Nera pulls it down so it falls on her arm, revealing her bare shoulder.

"That finishing touch is going to finish *him* off," I point out.

Nera laughs and then takes a few snaps.

"Don't move, B," she instructs. "Six, Thayer, what do you guys think?"

She holds up the phone between us and we look over her shoulder.

"I think if you turn down the brightness, this one has the best framing."

"Oh my god, you look *stunning* here."

"This smile is even better."

We show her our favorite and she agrees. She's smiling broadly at the camera, mirth in her eyes and on her lips like receiving the flowers delighted her.

"Okay, so just 'thank you for the flowers, baby, I love them' with a kiss emoji? Is that it?" Nerves rattle her voice as she places the phone on the table between us.

"Yup!" Thayer answers. "It's going to be funny. He'll huff and puff and get over it. Come on press send."

She shakes her head. "I can't do it."

"I'll do it," Nera says helpfully, leaning over and pressing the blue arrow.

I watch the message leave the text box.

"*Oh mon dieu.*"

"*Oh my god*," Bellamy echoes.

"It's going to be *fiiiin*—"

Thayer doesn't get to finish her sentence because Bellamy's ringtone interrupts her.

Four heads snap down at the same time and watch as Rogue's name flashes across her screen.

Simultaneous panic hits each of us.

Bellamy's wide eyes find mine. "What do I do?"

I pick up the phone and hand it to her. "Answer it!"

"Why didn't I think about the fact that he'd call? What do I say?"

"Um, just go along with it. Let him do the talking. *Don't* tell him it's a prank just yet," Nera answers.

"Be cool, be cool," Thayer urges.

"This is your fault," Bellamy accuses.

"Let's remember you haven't actually done anything wrong, it's just a prank."

The prank seemed funny five minutes ago, but with how quickly he called her, I just know he's mad. And his anger is explosive to say the least.

"Answer the phone before he comes down here and burns the whole Pen complex down," I urge.

"*Loudspeaker*," Thayer whisper-hisses as Bellamy presses accept.

"Hey, babe," she answers, managing to keep her tone breezy even as her face reflects pure anxiety. "Thanks again for the flowers, you're so sweet."

"Hey."

Rogue's voice doesn't sound anything like what I expected. I share a startled look with Nera, confirming she's caught off guard as well.

There's no anger or aggression as I'd assumed there'd be. No, his voice is quiet.

Hollow.

Barely above a whisper and without any of the usual arrogant swagger. Even just with one word, one syllable, we can all hear it.

Bellamy more than the rest of us.

"You okay?" she asks, worry tightening her own voice.

"No. Do you have something you want to tell me?"

Bellamy bites her cuticles nervously, wide eyes meeting ours. I can tell she's doing her best to hold up the pretense of the prank but his voice is making her waver. "What do you mean?"

"Are you fucking someone else?"

I inhale sharply and she sucks in a shocked breath through her teeth.

"Is that what you're doing tonight? Are you with him?"

Rogue is missing the joke entirely. I'm surprised there's a world in which he'd ever believe that she'd do that to him.

Her mouth drops open in disbelief. "What?"

"I didn't send you those flowers. Have you been cheating on me?"

His words are raw with pain.

Bellamy jumps to her feet.

"I can't do this guys, I'm sorry," she tells us, face ashen. "Baby, we're playing *Truth or Dare* and this was my dare. It's a prank we saw on TikTok. Six ordered those flowers, they're not from someone else."

The line is silent for a couple seconds.

"Rogue?"

"You're really with the girls?"

"Yes," Bellamy says, breathlessly.

"We're here!" Thayer adds helpfully.

More silence.

"I assume I have you to thank for this?"

"Oh, um," Thayer splutters, unprepared for the question. "Well, it was a group idea really…"

"Coward," Nera mouths at her in response.

"I'll get you back for this, mark my words," Rogue growls through the phone. "When you're least expecting it is when I'll strike."

"Sounds like you're announcing the start of a prank war," Thayer quips.

Bellamy gets to her feet, taking the phone with her as she heads to her room.

"Babe, how could you think I would do that to you?"

I hear his quiet, ruminating answer as she walks away.

"I thought you were getting me back for the shit I pulled with Lyra," he confesses. "It's not like I wouldn't deserve it."

"So you thought I'd actually cheat on you?" she asks, disbelief coloring her words.

More silence follows.

"I wouldn't have let you leave me if you had," he finally answers.

"I told you, never…"

Rogue is still new to the concept of people loving him and actually sticking around. He's got some abandonment issues he's working through so I see how this prank could have triggered them.

"I'll get you all the flowers you want," he vows. "You won't ever need to get them from anyone else."

"I don't need any more flowers. I'm already yours forever."

"You're the only person I truly love, sweetheart," I hear him answer as her door closes. "I can't afford to lose you."

"*Rude*," Thayer mouths in the background. "I thought the psycho and I were friends. You think you know someone."

"She brings out the softest side to him, it's adorable to see," Nera says, pulling my attention away from Bellamy's bedroom and back to the living room where the three of us are still seated.

Thayer is now head bent and giggling as she types away on her phone.

"Why are you laughing?"

She looks up at me with a smile still on her lips.

"Rhys is giving me a play by play of Rogue's reaction. I'm laughing because he said he's proud of me for coming up with the prank and that it was hilarious, but also that he wouldn't be as forgiving as Rogue if I ever pulled that shit on him."

"Understandable," I answer. "Of our four guys, he's the only one who had to watch you date someone else."

She shudders, her hand tightening around her phone.

"Don't remind me."

Before I can say anything else, two ringtones erupt in the silence. I look down and see Phoenix's name flashing on my screen. Nera holds her phone up and shows me that Tristan is FaceTiming her as well.

With a grin, I swipe to accept the call. My husband's face comes on the screen and his black eyes soften when they find mine.

"Wild girl," he purrs.

***

Chapter Four

Nera

"We said no texting or calling, Tristan," I admonish him after answering his call.

"If everyone else can break the rules, then so can I," he quips. "Plus, what I really wanted to do was go over there and force you home with me, so you should be thanking me for all the restraint I'm showing, really."

I laugh and he sits up, getting closer to the camera.

"I don't like it when you laugh when I'm not there."

"Well, that really can't be helped, baby."

"It can. Hope you enjoyed this one night without me, you're not getting another one for a while."

"Define 'a while'."

"Ever."

"You're going to be so sick of me if we spend every waking moment together."

"First of all, I don't just want every waking moment, I want the sleeping ones too," he clarifies. "Secondly, I'll never be sick of you, my beautiful fiancée."

I smile and look down at the ring on the fourth finger of my left hand. Every morning, when I go to my bathroom and slip it on, there's still a moment of disbelief that this is all real.

Tristan blew into my life like a tornado. A stubborn one at that, one that refused to disappear, no matter how much I pushed. And unlike a real tornado that leaves nothing but a path of destruction in its wake, he came in and healed. He was a tornado in reverse, taking all the broken, mangled pieces of me strewn everywhere and putting them back together one by one until I was whole once more.

As much as I like to tease him, I don't want to spend time without him anymore than he does.

"Those moments already belong to you, baby," I tell him.

He groans, his head dropping back against the couch as he stares at me through half-lidded eyes.

"I can't get enough of you."

Next to me, I hear Sixtine whisper to Phoenix, "Do you think we actually traumatized my horse?"

"Traumatized?" he scoffs. "We gave him the best show of his entire life. I'm sure he went back to the stables and told all his horse friends what he was lucky enough to witness."

I laugh again. A grumble from Tristan pulls my attention back to him.

"Get a pen and paper," he orders.

I frown but do as he asks. There's a notebook in the miscellaneous box with a pen attached to its spine so I grab both.

"What am I doing with these?"

"If you're going to keep laughing when I'm not there, then I need you to write down every time you do and exactly what it was that made you laugh. That way I can read it later."

I roll my eyes even as a smile tugs at my lips. "Tristan—"

"I earned your laughter, baby. I don't want to miss a single giggle."

He turns my insides into a puddle of warmth with just a few words. The craziest part is he's never rehearsed in his declarations. He simply tells me what he feels as he feels it, and it's always the most romantic words I've ever heard.

"I love you."

The smug expression that stretches across his face shouldn't be as attractive as it is. "Good."

"Do you know what today is?" I ask him.

"No, w— what is it, Phoenix?" he cuts off, speaking to the man in question just off camera. "How should I know if it's possible for horses to be traumatized? I've never even ridden one before. Ask Rhys."

Six's head whips in my direction. She crawls over to sit next to me. "I heard you ask Tristan, Nix," she accuses. "So you *do* think it's possible we traumatized him?"

Phoenix pops up on screen, much to Tristan's annoyance.

"No. I don't want you to worry about it, wild girl."

"Oh, god. What have I done?" she laments.

"Look what I found," he answers, pointing his phone at the camera to show her. "It's a luxury spa retreat for horses. I'm booking him in for a week. A little trauma isn't anything a daily eucalyptus and lavender salt bath won't fix."

"I'm a terrible person," she continues.

"Two weeks. I'll throw in the massage therapy add-on too."

"I—"

"Fuck it, *a month*."

"Will you two get back on your own FaceTime?" Tristan grumbles, shoving Phoenix out of the frame. "I'm trying to talk to my fiancée here."

Phoenix appears once more, dark eyes flashing on Tristan.

"Not a problem. My *wife* and I will continue this conversation elsewhere."

"Don't get competitive with me," Tristan answers, jaw flexing in bad temper.

"Silver!" Rhys bellows, appearing behind the couch Tristan and Phoenix are sitting on.

Thayer comes to sit on my other side and I watch her face pop up on camera next to mine.

"Yes?"

"*He* gets to call Sixtine his wife," he says, pointing first at Phoenix and then at Tristan. "And *he* gets to call Nera his fiancée. Meanwhile, I can only call you my girlfriend. Don't you think that's fucked up?"

"Extremely fucked up," she acquiesces.

"Then let me do something about it."

"Not just yet," she answers, shaking her head. "I need to see if fame is going to change you first."

Rhys looks affronted. "Excuse me?"

"What if once you're a soccer star you get a really douchey haircut? Or start unironically wearing atrocious Louis Vuitton man purses? Either one of those might be a deal breaker, you know, and that's before I throw in the hordes of adoring groupies I'm going to have to fight through in order to get your attention."

Rhys looks down at Phoenix. "Is it me or does she seem more worried about the man purse than she does the groupies?"

"That's because I know I don't actually have to worry about the groupies. But the man purse?" she shudders. "That's a real lady boner killer."

"Fine, if I agree to no man purses, can I marry you already?"

"It's a good start to the negotiations. Check back in a few years."

"A few *years*, love?"

"Can I speak with my fiancé now, please?" I finally cut in and ask.

Rhys makes a disgusted noise. "No need to show off, Nera. You can have him."

Six, Thayer and I turn at the sound of a door opening and then Bellamy walks back into the room.

"Alright, I finally managed to calm him down."

"I take it you're never doing another prank again?" Thayer asks.

"I'll get back to you on that tomorrow. Depends how the makeup sex is," she finishes with a wink.

"Ewwww," Rhys calls through FaceTime. "Never conjure that image of Rogue thrusting in my mind ever again, Bellamy."

"That's my girl," Thayer says proudly, ignoring her boyfriend.

"Oops, sorry Rhys. Didn't know you were on the phone. I'm ready to get back to girl's night if you guys are."

"We are!" Six says, before turning back towards my phone. "I'll talk to you tomorrow, Nix."

"Talk to you tomorrow, wild girl. Love you to the stars and back."

"Love you to the moon and back." Once he's gone, she smacks a kiss on my cheek. "Sorry for taking over your FaceTime, Nerita."

Six joins Thayer and Bellamy in the kitchen as they pour the next round of drinks.

"I have to go as well, Tristan."

"What were you going to say before?" he asks. "What's today?"

I look at the time in the top left corner of the screen.

"As of twenty-one minutes ago, it's exactly eleven months until our wedding day."

Tristan's eyes gleam heatedly, his gaze burning an intense path across my face. "I'm counting down the days, baby."

"Me too."

"Okay," he says with a sigh. "I guess I'll let you get back to it. Have fun and remember – keep track of your laughs for me."

"Have fun with the boys. I'll see you tomorrow."

"I'll be waiting with breakfast. Love you so much."

"Love you too."

I hang up and put my phone away just as the girls come back to join me around the coffee table. They sit and Six hands me a fresh glass of champagne.

"Alright, we let ourselves get a little distracted by the boys," Bellamy starts.

"My fault," Thayer cuts in.

"But we're back on track for girl's night now. So I wanted to propose a toast of sorts," she says, holding up her glass. "It's going to be half toast, half speech, so bear with me."

We raise our glasses to match hers.

"A year ago, I was living in Chicago. I could count on one hand how many flights I'd been on and I'd never been out of the country. My life was a routine. Safe and comfortable. One that I probably would have been very content with, never knowing what else was out there. So I want to thank you, the three of you, for showing me exactly what I was going to miss out on. For opening my eyes to the world. For always having my back and supporting me. For the *best* year of my life so far." She smiles at Six and I. "I met Rogue, but I also met you two and that's meant just as much to me."

"B is the eloquent one so I'm not going to add much to what she's already said, except to echo that this has been the best, wildest, most fun year I've ever had. It's crazy to me that we've only known each other a year and not our entire lives because it feels like you've always been there at our sides," Thayer adds.

Tears sting the corners of my eyes. Up until a few months ago, I'd gone years without crying. Now it seems that I can't go a couple days without shedding a few tears, thankfully mostly of happiness. Looking over, I can see that Six is similarly affected.

"We should be thanking *you*. You taught me how to be brave—"

"And you taught me how to be vulnerable," I jump in.

"I don't think either of us realized anything was missing until we met you both. And then it was like the final pieces of a puzzle coming together. We fit perfectly because we were always meant to find each other and form a complete picture together. That's what I believe," Six says.

"Whatever we found with our boys, we found in each other just as much. Platonic love is real and it's powerful and it's what we have together. Nothing's ever going to change that and I'm so happy to have found it. I hope that when we have kids they'll know each other and hopefully feel that as well," I finish.

"Of course they will!" Bellamy says.

We bring our flutes together, the sound of clinking glass filling the room as we finally cheers.

"To our final sleep at The Pen," Thayer says.

"To our last night, but not *the* last night," Bellamy adds.

"To the four of us," I add.

"And to the rest of our lives. Together," Six says, looking each of us in the eye one after the other. "This is just the beginning."

***

A year after graduation

Chapter Five

Tristan

I'm in the kitchen taking a pan of salmon and potatoes out of the oven when the doorbell rings.

Frowning, I make my way to the door. I was in the middle of preparing a candlelit dinner for Nera and myself. We're certainly not expecting any guests tonight so I have no clue who it could be.

I open the door and groan loudly when I see who's standing on the other side.

"Oh, for fuck's sake. What do you want?"

"Hello to you too, *huevón*," Thiago answers, glaring at me.

Thiago da Silva is the head of the da Silva cartel, one of the largest criminal organizations in the United Kingdom and Latin America. He's a cold-blooded murderer and a violent, unfeeling psychopath.

Inconceivably—and very much to my chagrin— he also happens to be my brother-in-law.

He kidnapped my sister, Tess, forced her to marry him, and, most egregiously of all, somehow, some*way*, worked some kind of voodoo magic shit that made her fall head over heels in love with him.

When I told her she was definitely suffering from Stockholm Syndrome, she simply laughed and shrugged, patting my shoulder with a playful "absolutely" before walking off.

She's in too deep I fear, so I've had no choice but to grudgingly accept Thiago.

That being said, my brother-in-law and I's relationship resides somewhere comfortably between the North Pole and the Arctic Circle temperature-wise, so finding him on my stoop is surprising to say the least.

"What the hell are you doing here?" I ask. My voice takes on a hopeful tone when I add, "Has my sister finally come to her senses and left you?"

Thiago's fists clench and a dangerous gleam cuts through his eyes. "My wife made me promise to never shoot you, but put those words out into the universe again and I'll carve you up like a turkey on Thanksgiving day."

Crossing my arms nonchalantly over my chest, I lean against the doorframe and raise an unimpressed brow at him.

"First of all, given that you've shot her best friend and gotten Tess herself shot, I'm not surprised she made you promise that. Secondly, can you please cool it with the 'my wife' bit?" I click my tongue against my teeth in disgust. "That's my sister you're talking about. It's weird."

"Wife trumps sister."

"She's been my sister a lot longer than she's been married to you. And a lot more willingly, I might add."

He shrugs. "I did what had to be done."

Part of me can respect his approach to trapping my sister in their marriage, although there's a higher chance that I'll suddenly decide to shave my nipples off with a cheese grater than there is of me ever admitting that to him.

A year and a half ago, Nera and I broke up after I lied to her about who I was. My wife is the strongest, most stubborn, take-no-prisoners type of woman I know, and she made me *pay* for my betrayal.

She refused to see me for four months.

Four. Fucking. Months.

Four months during which every second felt like I was dying, like I was being withered down to dust then blown into oblivion by the wind.

Her family had forced her to bend to their will her entire life, so I refused to do the same thing to her, to be just another abuser in her story.

But, *fuck*.

Not a day went by where I didn't wish I was taking the Thiago approach and just forcing her to marry me and forgive me.

A babbling sound pulls me from my ruminations and draws my attention down to Thiago's feet where I finally take notice of the baby carrier.

My brother-in-law didn't come alone.

"Is that—" I start, my gaze flicking back up to his. Thiago's black expression smooths away in a heartbeat, and just like that, the violent killer recedes to the background, replaced by the proud father. "Is that my little nephew?" I coo, my voice rising two full octaves and reaching a pitch I'd categorically deny ever using if questioned, even under heavy torture.

I crouch and reach into the carrier, freeing Theo from the maze of straps wrapped around him and taking him into my arms.

As much as I wouldn't miss Thiago for a second if he disappeared from my life tomorrow, I know that's no longer in the cards because the bastard had the gall and the brilliance to immediately impregnate my sister, tying her—and thus me—to him for life.

Yet again, I can't help but respect his game.

I'm out here playing a clean game of checkers while Thiago is playing grandmaster-level chess.

"Hey, little man. Did you come to see your favorite uncle?"

Looking down into his tiny face, I can't help but wonder if he's going to turn out to be a bloodthirsty killer like his dad or a corporate genius like his mum.

God protect us all if he turns out to be a combination of both.

"He only has one," Thiago answers dryly.

I glare at him over my six-month-old nephew's head.

"What are you still doing here?" I question again, very much interested in the answer. "Theo can stay, but you can go back to mutilating and murdering random people. Or whatever it is you like to get up to in your spare time."

"Don't be ridiculous, Tristan. Mutilation and murder are my career, not my hobbies," he corrects pleasantly, watching me bounce his son against my chest with observant eyes. "Trying out new torture methods, however? There's a hobby."

I pause mid-bounce. "I'm sorry, are you making jokes now?"

"Apparently."

"Please stop."

Before I can add anything else, I hear the soft cadence of heels on marble and feel my wife approach from behind me.

A small hand finds my lower back and runs up my spine, settling comfortably between my shoulder blades as she snuggles up against my side. An addicted shiver shakes my body at having her dainty touch on me. All of sudden, I want to throw Theo at his father so I can push Nera up against the wall and slam my mouth down on hers.

"Can we not talk about torture and murder in front of the baby, please?" she asks.

Looking down at her with heated, yearning eyes, I whisper, "I want one."

If it were up to me, I'd have put ten babies in Nera by now, biological impossibilities be damned. But my wife is training for her second Olympic medal so I have to wait three more long years. It's only my unwavering support for her dreams that's keeping me from saying 'fuck it' and pumping her full of my babies.

But once that second gold is around her neck, it's over for her.

"Soon," she answers with a soft smile. Leaning forward, she kisses Thiago on each cheek, much to my displeasure. "Thiago, it's lovely to see you, come in."

She steps back, but I block his entrance. "Kissing my wife before you've even set foot in my home. What's next? Do you want to sit at my dining table? Help yourself to my robe and slippers too maybe?"

Nera scrunches her nose. "Are you comparing me to inanimate things?"

"No, I'm just saying he's too comfortable touching what belongs to me," I answer grumpily.

"Play nice," she admonishes me.

"What is he doing here anyway?" I ask. My eyes drop down her body for the first time since she joined us and my brows shoot up into my hairline. "And more importantly, what the hell are you wearing?"

It's a rhetorical question. I can see with my own two disbelieving eyes the black strappy dress she has on.

The very *tiny* black strappy dress.

"Tess and I are going out for a much needed, much deserved girl's dinner," she explains, grabbing her purse off the foyer console.

"But I was preparing dinner for us," I pout.

"And that's why Thiago is here," she counters. "You two can enjoy a nice boys' dinner together."

I could also *'enjoy'* a nice firing squad, but I similarly choose not to.

I turn towards him with an affronted look on my face, still holding his son against my chest. "You were okay with this?"

He gives me a deadpan look. "What do you think?" With a deep sigh, he adds, "Tess threatened to not speak to me for a weekend if I didn't say yes, so I didn't exactly have a choice."

Christ. There's no hope for any of us where our wives are concerned, and it seems that he's as whipped as the rest of us.

Looking back at my wife, I shake my head. "I'm not letting you go anywhere without me in that dress, Nera."

Thiago cuts in before she can answer. "I felt similarly about Tess's outfit," he grumbles. "But I have that covered."

He turns and waves at a couple of black cars parked on the street behind him. Six men in suits step out and nod at him.

Thiago faces us once more. "Tess has six of her own bodyguards tonight. These six are for Nera. They have orders to shoot to kill on sight if any man gets within breathing distance of our wives."

Turns out, I might have judged Thiago too quickly.

He seems like a good man after all.

Very good morals, even better judgment.

Excellent discernment.

All around great bloke.

"That's overki—" Nera starts.

"If we're forced to stay home while you two go out, then that's the condition, baby," I tell her. "Take it or leave it."

"Fine," she says with a pout.

"Now kiss me before you leave," I order.

"*Jesus*," Thiago mumbles, reaching for Theo. "Give me my son before he witnesses something that'll permanently stunt his frontal lobe development."

He takes him and walks into our house, heading back towards the kitchen.

"You got my sister pregnant within three months of marrying her," I call after him. "Don't pretend all you two do is crochet when you're together. And also, you're a *murderer*, I'm sorry to inform you but there's not much hope for my beloved nephew's frontal lobe with you around."

34

Turning back towards Nera, I find my wife's eyes and smile pointed in my direction.

"Come here you," I whisper, reaching for her hips and tugging her against me. "Be good tonight."

She wraps her arms around my neck and gets up on her toes. "I will. Enjoy your playdate," she adds with a grin. "You two are so similar. No, don't deny it, you're already bantering like an old married couple. Your enemies to friends arc is going to be *so* powerful."

"I hope you know that you're going to owe me for this. I'll be getting my payment from you later."

Nera blinks cutely up at me. "Do you promise?"

I cup her nape and yank her against me, claiming her mouth with mine. It's violent and ugly, just like the need and love I have for her. Marrying her only made it worse.

Ripping my lips off hers with difficulty, I say, "Get out of here before I change my mind."

Nera takes a step back, then twirls, giving me a three-sixty view of her dress. The bodyguards swarm protectively around her as she walks down our front steps and onto the sidewalk.

She looks over her shoulder and blows me a kiss. I catch it and press it up against the left side of my chest where my heart is. I miss her already and she's not even gone yet.

I close the door with difficulty and make my way into the kitchen where I find Theo back in his carrier and sound asleep, his father standing next to the table I'd set for Nera and I.

"How romantic," he says, his tone mocking.

I put out the flames of the taper candles with my fingers. The last thing I'm doing is having a candlelit dinner with Thiago.

"How would you know? You don't have a romantic bone in your body."

"I'm romantic."

I snort.

"I'm romantic," he assures me, louder now. "Call my wife, she'll tell you I'm romantic."

"Sure you are."

I don't know what it is that's so satisfying about needling him, but I can't help myself.

"Do it," he orders like I'm going to do anything he says.

"No, thank you."

Next thing I know, his phone is up to his ear and he's pacing the length of my kitchen.

"*Amor*," he starts, putting Tess on loudspeaker. "Your brother thinks I'm not romantic. Tell him I am."

My sister's melodic laugh comes through the phone.

"Are you two fighting?"

"No–"

"Yes."

Thiago glares at me. "Are you sure I can't shoot him?" he asks. "Please? A flesh wound, just for fun."

I don't even bat an eyelash. No way my sister is going to let her husband shoot her favorite brother.

"You made me a promise, Thiago…"

Her voice is tinged with disappointment and his eyes widen.

"I did," he assures her. "I'm fulfilling it. Enjoy your dinner, *amor*, I love you."

"Love you, baby. Kiss Theo for me."

Thiago hangs up and puts his phone away in his jacket pocket. He pulls out a chair and sits down, looking expectantly at me.

"What are you doing?" I ask.

"Sitting and enjoying your company."

I look around my kitchen for the hidden cameras that would explain this shift in behavior. Finding none, I ask, "Did you just have a stroke?"

"No."

"I think you might have. Your facial features are going to start drooping any minute now. I'm sorry to be blunt but I think my sister is with you only for your looks—it certainly can't be your personality keeping her around—so let me call an ambulance before that happens and irreversible damage is done."

"Sit down." I open my mouth to tell him to piss off when he adds, "*Please.*"

I blink at him. "Okay, now I know you've definitely had a stroke. I'll let the paramedics know the symptoms appear to be severe."

"I made my wife a promise."

There he goes again with the 'my wife' shit.

"Not to shoot me?"

"To spend time with you."

That's the last thing I expected him to say. "Huh?"

He sighs, settling back into his chair. "I don't care what we do or what we talk about. *Joder*, we can sit here in silence for all I care, so long as I spend three hours here with you before going home."

"Why?"

"Because a long time ago, I promised Tess that I'd get to know you and befriend you. Then she got shot and we had the baby and we got caught up in our own little bubble so it fell by the wayside, but I did make her that promise. And I keep the promises I make to my wife."

"Why did you promise that?"

"Because it'll make her happy." He says it like I just asked him if water is wet, like the answer could not be more evident. "I'd be willing to do things a thousand times more painful than hanging out with you if it made her smile."

I stare at him for a long time, at this notorious, ruthlessly callous and violent man who's sitting in my house and basically trying to date me just because it'll make my sister smile.

Walk him like a dog, sis.

In the year and a half since they've been together, we've never spent time alone, just him and I. We've always had the company of my friends or his to buffer us, mostly because I was uninterested in spending any more time with him than I needed to.

He'd forced my sister into this marriage and that's all I needed to know. I'd obviously seen many examples of his infatuation with her, from how he'd cared for her after she was shot to the birth of Theo, but I always thought it was obsession and not love. Doomed to burn hot for a while and then eventually fizzle out.

But seeing him now, sitting in my kitchen, his spine straight, his jaw set in a determined line, and his eyes flashing with intention, I realize that this is a man who would do anything to make my sister happy.

Maybe he's not a lost cause after all.

I grab the salmon from the island behind me, pull out a chair opposite Thiago, and sit down.

"Well, come on then. Let's eat. You're married to my sister so I know she's not feeding you. Or if she is, it's not edible."

"I have a chef," he says, coming to her immediate defense as he forks a piece of salmon. "She doesn't need to cook."

"Of course not."

"She's very talented at other thin—" He cuts off abruptly after taking his first bite. Then he groans, shoving a second forkful into his mouth. "*Puta madre*, are you sure you two are related?"

I laugh and reach over to clap him on the back.

Our wives were right to set up this impromptu 'playdate', as Nera called it. There's hope for me and my brother-in-law and I after all.

***

Two years after graduation

Chapter Six

Rhys

Cold water hits my bare back and rips me out of a particularly vivid dream I was having of Thayer running down a football pitch.

Some guys dream of their girlfriends naked, I dream of mine kicking a ball around, those long legs of hers pumping, her French braid swinging, a brilliant smile on her face. That easily beats the hottest pornos I've ever seen and I'm none too pleased to have been pulled out of it before I could watch her score.

"What the fuck?" I roar, whipping up into a seated position.

Next to me, Thayer is absolutely fucking drenched. Whatever water hit me, it was just cast off from what originally missed her. She sits up slowly beside me, rubbing the liquid from eyes and pushing her wet hair off her face.

"You alright, Silver?" I ask her, kissing her bare shoulder.

"Go back to sleep, Rhys," a cold voice drawls. "This is between me and your girlfriend."

My eyes lift to meet Rogue's. He's standing next to our bed, holding a now empty bucket by his side.

He and Bellamy are visiting from Chicago and have been staying with us for the past couple of weeks. Although after this Guantanamo-style wake up, he's getting booked on the first flight back to America, the wanker.

"You're fucking joking," I growl. "You're not still mad about the prank, are you? It's been *two years*," I point out.

"She made me think my girlfriend was cheating on me, she has to live with the consequences," he counters.

Thayer groans and lets herself fall back against her pillows.

"Oh my god, Rogue. I *have*. I took it on the chin when you put toothpaste in the filling of my Oreos, I didn't say *anything* when you signed me up for a porn addiction recovery program for fundamentalist Christians, and I smiled and waved when you played a video of me getting ready in the morning—zit cream still on and everything—on the big screen in the Arsenal stadium for tens of thousand of people to see, but this is getting ridiculous," she cries. "You're like an escalating serial killer. Any idea when you intend to stop this one-sided prank war?"

"When the memory of that phone call is burned out of my memory."

"So… never?"

He gives her a thin smile. "That's correct."

Thayer sits back up, pointing a long finger at him. "Then I have no choice but to engage. And you'll regret it, because I'll involve Bellamy."

Rogue crosses his arms over his chest, not threatened in the least. "If she's fair game, then so is Rhys. Think of all the groupies that'll be tickled pink at the chance to help me."

Thayer glares at him and jumps to stand on our bed, revealing her very skimpy, very wet, silk pajama set and sending my blood pressure skyrocketing in the process.

"Bellamy!" she calls. "I'm kicking your boyfriend out of my house."

Rogue turns towards the door just as Bellamy walks in. Taking advantage of the opening and his momentary distractedness, Thayer jumps on his back and wraps her forearms around his throat.

"What the—"

"Just kidding, Roguey. You can never get rid of me, no matter how much of a *dick* you continue to be. I'm your family now," she says, stuck on his back.

"Get off me, you animal," he growls, ripping at her forearms to try to release the hold she has on him. "You're soaking wet."

Bellamy starts laughing in the background, enjoying the play fighting happening between her boyfriend and best friend.

She's the only one.

"And whose fault is that?" Thayer singsongs.

"Get off him, Thayer," I snap.

Her head swings towards me, her expression startled. She immediately slides off Rogue, dropping down to the floor.

Of our friend group, I'm the jovial, good-humored one, so my severe tone surprises her.

"Ah, fuck." Rogue straightens, having taken one look at my face. He grabs Bellamy's hand and tugs her after him out the door.

"What is it?" I hear her ask.

"I give it less than two minutes before they're tearing each other's clothes off and I don't want to be there when that happens."

"Hey, I'll be getting you back for this!" Thayer calls after him, but he closes the door behind him without responding.

"No, you won't," I inform her. "This ends now."

"But—"

"I'll talk to Rogue. He won't prank you again."

Thayer reaches for me but I grab her wrist before she can touch me, holding her hand just off of my chest. Her eyes widen. She tries to retract her hand but I don't let her, instead using my hold to tug her closer to me.

"I don't like you touching him, Silver."

"I was messing around. I didn't want him thinking I was being serious about kicking him out given his abandonment issues. And you know he's just like another brother to me, even if it's one sided. The only thing he cares about is Bellamy, so you're being jealous for no reason."

Over the past couple of years, the girls and Tristan have integrated into our original trio like life before them never existed. Each of us had experienced loss or struggled with our parents in some way and that common thread had brought us closer together, creating an unbreakable bond. We'd found family in each other and I knew I could trust those seven people with my life.

But that didn't mean the protectiveness I felt over my girl ever went away with my friends.

If anything, my possessiveness grows stronger with every passing day because so do the stakes involved with potentially losing her. The more indispensable she becomes to my survival, the more the thought of not having her is crippling.

42

I join Thayer's other hand with her first at her lower back and use my hold to pin her against my chest.

"All I saw was your wet body against his. He felt exactly what I can feel right now – every single inch of you. Every single inch that belongs to *me*."

Thayer shifts and her hard nipples graze against my chest, making me shudder.

"That's right," she whispers seductively, pushing against my hold to get on her toes. I let her and she sucks my earlobe. Goosebumps erupt down my neck and chill me. "I belong to *you*. I don't need a reminder. There's no one else I think about or dream about."

"Dream?" I question.

She blushes prettily. "I was dreaming about you. You were beneath the covers and between my legs. It felt so real." Her lips twist in a disappointed moue. "He woke me up before you could finish. Or rather, before *I* could finish."

Well, well, well. Her dreams are decidedly more X-rated than mine. I love that we're as equally obsessed with each other, so much so that sleeping next to one another isn't enough, we have to fully inhabit the other's dreams as well.

Gripping her hair with my free hand, I use it to tug her head back, opening her throat up to me. She moans loudly when I run my tongue from the base of her neck, up her throat and over the underside of her jaw until I reach her lips.

I hover over her mouth for long seconds. She makes a discontented noise when I keep her from closing the distance.

"I'm here to make your dreams a reality."

"Best boyfriend ever," she says with a happy sigh, her eyes closed and a giddy smile stretching her lips.

I stare at her for a few seconds longer because I can never get enough, no matter how much I look. Only when it feels like I physically can't pull in a breath from how my love for her is suffocating me do I finally close the gap and kiss her.

It's sweet, at first, and then it's passionate and needy. I grab her shorts and push them off her hips, then I throw her on our bed. She shivers when her back hits the wet sheets, but I ignore it. I'll have her body hot enough to burn a hole through the mattress in about thirty seconds anyway.

"Spread your legs," I order.

Her gaze sparks, her eyes heating at the hungry tone she recognizes in my voice. She does as I ask and I step between them, my hands coming to rest on either one of her knees. They move to the sides of her thighs, softly caressing her as I drop my gaze down to her now wet folds.

A strangled groan leaves my lips as I stare at her perfect pussy.

Mine. Mine. Mine.

I brush my thumb down her slit and she whimpers.

"Mark my words," I growl, voice hoarse with lust. "I'm going to be the first to put a baby in here."

"Oh, god," she answers tremulously.

"'Oh, god', yes?" I question. "Think about it—little mini mes and yous running around, calling me Daddy."

She swallows and arches into my touch, her back bowing off the bed.

"Our very own little soccer prodigies," she mutters feverishly.

I bend over her body, my fingers continuing to stroke her clit. "We're going to have to agree to call it football. I won't have my children referring to it as 'soccer'."

"Convince me," she orders on a gasp.

A smirk pulls at my lips.

"My pleasure, Silver." I drop a quick kiss on her mouth and then get on my knees between her legs. I run my tongue from her entrance up and suction her clit into my mouth.

She shrieks when she feels my lips close around the sensitive peak. I smack the inside of her thigh punishingly then grin up at her from between her legs, my mouth hovering just above her folds.

"Quiet while Daddy eats his breakfast," I order.

Her mouth parts in a combination of shock and arousal and I dip back between her legs, eating her out until I put forth a winning argument by making her come to a screaming orgasm.

***

Four years after graduation

Chapter Seven

Rogue

Bellamy parks the car in front of Phoenix's house and turns towards me. She leans across the console, wraps her hand around my nape and kisses me.

"Have fun tonight, baby. I'd wish you good luck, but I know you're going to kick their asses."

"I'd be disappointed if you thought otherwise," I answer, kissing her even more forcefully.

She laughs. "Try not to make them lose too much money. We're hosting that viewing party for Rhys' game tomorrow and Phoenix is unbearable to be around when he's in a bad mood."

"No promises, sweetheart," I say with a grin.

Bell and I just moved back to London a couple of weeks ago and it's been nonstop parties, events, barbecues, and unnamed get-togethers with our friends since. I never had any doubts that we were making the right decision leaving Chicago, but the way we've been welcomed to London feels like coming home. We slotted back into the group like we never left.

One thing we're going to have to do though, is establish some boundaries. Because her friends seem to always be around and it's cutting into the time I have with Bellamy.

I won't lie and say that I haven't thought about taking Tristan's brother-in-law's approach. I haven't met the man, but I heard that he shot one of his sister's best friends.

Every time I think Bell and I are alone, one of her friends bursts through the door or calls or makes their presence known somehow, so it's no wonder that I dream about shooting them. Non-fatally of course, I'd never do that to my friends. And now that I have proof that someone can do it and their marriage can get past it, the idea gets more attractive by the day.

But I see how happy Bellamy is, how settled she is since moving here and that kills the thought every time. Her happiness is the only thing that matters to me, no matter.

Tonight, Phoenix organized a poker night for the boys, our first since I've been back. The girls decided to do a movie night at ours so they wouldn't be in the way.

On the one hand, poker night is for the boys.

On the other, not seeing Bell in her cute little pjs and her having fun without me was a non-starter. Within five minutes of being told the news, I'd bought cameras and had them set up around the house so I could check in on her from afar.

So what if I'm obsessed? Sue me.

My now fiancée is starting law school in a few months, she can defend me.

I'm looking forward to her getting me off in more ways than one, Lord knows I'll more than likely need criminal representation again at some point.

I glance down at the massive ring sparkling on her fourth finger and feel the familiar warmth of comfort that spreads behind my ribcage every time I see it.

She'd told me I could propose only once she graduated college and I'd counted down the days until I could.

Literally.

Short of carving each passing day in the wall of our house like a prisoner counting down the days until his release, I'd done everything else. My first thought when I woke up was that I was one day closer to making her mine. I had an app that sent me nightly reminders so I had something to look forward to the next morning. I even had my assistant remind me every time I flew into a rage because there was no surer way to immediately calm me down than to tell me I only had a certain number of days until I could get down on bended knee.

And I'd made sure that when I finally did, I had the biggest ring possible so no one ever doubted who she belonged to. I'd actually tried to make it even bigger, but the jeweler had respectfully told me that if I did, Bellamy might have a hard time lifting her arm.

I relented, although only because I knew she wouldn't want that. If it were up to me, I'd have hired an assistant whose full-time job it was to lift her arm for her if that's what it took.

She said an enthusiastic, heartfelt 'yes' when I proposed and now we're getting married in a few months.

It's a whole new set of days I'm counting down to.

There's a knock at my window and I turn to find Six waving at me.

I kiss Bell one more time, pressing my lips fiercely against hers, then reach for the handle.

"I'll see you tomorrow, sweetheart."

Her hand comes down on my forearm. "Wait," she says, eyeing me distrustfully. "You're being suspiciously chill."

"What do you mean?" I ask innocently.

"You typically throw a tantrum every time we're separated."

"I do not throw a tant—"

"And now you're just letting me drive off with a kiss and that's it." Her eyes narrow on me. "Cough it up, Royal. What did you do?"

So what if I didn't *tell her* about the cameras? Double sue me.

"If you make my wife wait outside your car for one more second, I'll shove the first roll of poker chips I find down your throat, Rogue," Phoenix snaps from the doorway.

"Phoenix!" Six exclaims.

"She doesn't have a jacket on and there's a breeze," he continues, unperturbed.

"You heard him, sweetheart. Be safe on the road, text me the second you're home."

"You're doing what Phoenix asked you to? Now I *know* you did something bad."

"Love you," I tell her as I exit the car.

"Nice to see you, Rogue," Six says, patting my arm. She knows that touching me beyond that, especially while her husband is watching, is a bad idea. I grunt in response and brush past her, coming to stand next to Phoenix at the top of their stoop.

"Hello, wanker," he calls distractedly, his eyes still pinned on his wife. She gets in the car and they drive off with a wave.

His body tightens the second they're out of eyesight, a feeling I understand all too well.

"Don't worry about it, mate. I'm keeping an eye on them."

"How?"

"I'll show you in a bit. Are the others here?"

Phoenix leads me down the hall and downstairs where their game room is located. "Tristan's downstairs. He made some sort of intricate gourmet snacks for poker night."

I roll my eyes as we emerge into the room. "Pompous asshole."

"I know. I wanted to give him shit for it, but annoyingly they're actually delicious as fuck."

"Dickhead," I say, making eye contact with the man in question.

"You're welcome to stick to the chips and salsa, Rogue," Tristan answers, casually flipping me off. "I wouldn't want your unrefined palate to go into shock when it comes into contact with something sophisticated."

"Given that every time I eat your food it's something ridiculous like deconstructed duck mousse or jellied dolphin nose, the fact that I'm still standing here, palate intact, is a small miracle."

"Weird. I seem to remember your name being the very first reservation when my newest restaurant opened," he points out, nonchalantly dapping me up.

"That had nothing to do with you," I argue with a sniff. "I want my wife's best friend to have a certain standard of living and unfortunately that means supporting you."

"Right."

"No other reason."

"Uh huh."

"It wasn't memorable."

"Of course not."

"Barely edible."

"Is that why you have another reservation in two weeks?"

Ignoring him, I grab a cracker topped with sauce, a piece of smoked trout, and a slice of cucumber and pop it into my mouth.

"This isn't the worst thing I've ever eaten," I say around the mouthful, grabbing another and shoving it into my mouth before I finish swallowing the first.

"I'm sorry, can you repeat that? I'd like to get it on tape," he says, holding his phone up to my face.

I shove him back. "Fuck off."

Before he can answer, the sound of a crash of rhinos tumbling down the stairs comes from behind me.

I turn to find that it's only Rhys making more noise than I thought was humanly possible for one man to make as he erupts into the room, fists held proudly up to the sky in celebration as he exclaims, "Congratulate me assholes, I'm going to be a father. My wife is pregnant!"

"You don't have a wife," Phoenix counters.

"Fuck you, Phoenix. Semantics. She's going to be my wife in a few months."

"But she isn't yet."

Rhys seems impervious to Phoenix's attempts to goad him. The large smile on his face remains as his arms spread wider.

"She may not be my wife yet, but she is pregnant. My child is growing in her belly as we speak, something you absolutely do not have yet."

"Thayer's pregnant?" I question.

He beams. "Yup. Three months and a day. We waited until we'd cleared that milestone to let you know."

"Congrats, mate," Tristan says, stepping up to him and clapping him on the back.

God, he's going to be insufferable. Not just because all he's going to talk about for the next six months is the fact that Thayer is pregnant, but because he'll have been the first of us to do so.

"The last thing the world needs is more of you," I point out.

"Why? I'm hot, funny, smart, loyal, and supremely talented. There's some emotional damage there, but my fiancée has mostly fixed me. Really, when you think about it, I'm perfect."

"Humble too," Phoenix points out dryly.

"World class athletes shouldn't be humble. It's unattractive and off brand."

A smile curves Phoenix's lips before he gives him a congratulatory handshake.

50

As intolerable as Rhys is going to be, he deserves this. He lost his parents suddenly and unexpectedly in a car crash when we were teenagers. That event ripped the world out from underneath him, taking the only family he had in one fell swoop. If anyone deserves to build their own family and to know happiness in that way, it's him.

I fold his hand in mine and our eyes meet.

"They'd be proud of you," I mutter, loud enough so that only he hears me. "I wish they were here to see this."

The line of his lips falters for a second before he composes himself. And then he's pulling me into a hug, one that's many years in the making.

"Thanks, brother."

After a moment, I pull away and clear my throat. "Do you know if it's a boy or a girl?"

"Dunno. Don't care. That baby ties Silver to me for life, the sex doesn't matter to me."

"Want to check in on the two of them?" I offer.

"How?" Phoenix responds, taking an interested step forward.

I take my phone out and pull up the surveillance app with ease. The different camera angles come up on screen and I tap the one for the kitchen. It goes full screen, revealing the girls spread out across the space. Nera and Bellamy are sitting at the counter, Six is digging around the fridge, and Thayer is leaning against the sink.

Tristan gives an impressed whistle over my shoulder.

"Are the cameras new?"

"Yup, as of yesterday," I answer proudly.

"Nice. What company did you use?"

"I'll send you their info. They might do a package deal discount if the rest of you are interested?"

"I'm in," Rhys says. "Definitely."

"Same," Tristan says. "Very annoyed I didn't think of this myself."

"Count me in for the package deal," Phoenix adds. "Although, I think — I *think* — we can afford it even without the discount. Haven't checked my accounts in a minute but unless my balance has dropped nine digits since then, I should be good."

"Speak for yourself. I'm about to be a dad, I need to start saving."

Tristan gives Rhys an unimpressed look. "You signed a five hundred million pound contract extension last year, and that's not even taking your endorsements into account."

"Yes, but what if I have a daughter? I want my princess to have whatever she wants, whenever she wants it."

"Fair enough," Phoenix acquiesces.

"And five hundred million plus isn't enough?" Tristan questions. "Good luck to the poor bloke who marries your hypothetical daughter. Better hope he's rich."

"He'd better be if he's coming within spitting distance of my daughter. Now zoom in," Rhys instructs me. "Can you see a bump? She's starting to have a little baby bump, it's so cute. I guess you can only really see it when she's naked." He straightens, coming suddenly to his senses. "Actually, what am I saying? Don't you dare fucking look. Avert your eyes, wankers."

Phoenix shoves him out of the way and pinches the screen with his fingers. "You think I give a shit about your fiancée? The only person I'm looking at is my wife." He zooms until Six's face takes up the entire screen. She's looking at something off camera, her eyes widening in surprise. "She's so pretty," he says dreamily.

"You fuckers get your own feed. This is mine." I slap Phoenix's hand off my screen.

I zoom out and hear Rhys whisper a muttered "shit" as I make eye contact with Bellamy.

And I do mean, *eye contact*.

Because my fiancée is standing right beneath the camera, staring straight into the lens, her fists poised sternly on her hips.

"Looks like you've been caught out," Tristan points out.

"No shit."

She points a finger up at me and starts talking. I turn on the volume so I can hear her.

"Rogue Royal, you are in deep shit. I know that you'll have gotten a state-of-the-art spy system so I'm willing to bet you can talk to me through this camera. Unmute yourself now."

A smile curves my lips. She knows me so well.

"Hello, sweetheart," I say. I see the girls react as my voice echoes through the kitchen.

"Don't you 'sweetheart' me. This is why you were so chill earlier. You were spying."

"I wasn't spying."

"What would you call this?"

"Not wanting to miss out on a single moment with you."

I see her spine soften a fraction, a smile fighting to loosen the straight line of her lips.

"I didn't have the volume on, I just wanted to be able to check in from time to time and make sure you were okay."

"Sorry to interrupt your domestic," Phoenix says, grabbing the phone from my hand. "But hi, wild girl." On screen, Six sits up straighter, a delighted smile taking over her face. She waves at the camera. "Miss you," he adds.

"Miss you too!"

"You should have told me, Rogue."

I yank the phone back from Phoenix. "I know. Don't take them down."

"Give me one good reason."

"I don't want to have to punish you when I come home. I'm not saying any more than that in front of an audience."

She flushes a pretty scarlet color and remains silent.

"You guys should actually go play poker now," Nera suggests.

"Hi, baby," Tristan says, pushing to the front so he can speak close to the phone.

"Hi, Tris," she calls back, making a heart sign with her hands.

"We're going, we're going," I answer her, before adding, "Oh, and Thayer?"

The woman in question was about to take a bite of ice cream when I call her name. Her spoon pauses halfway to her mouth and she looks up. "Yes?"

"Procreating with Rhys? You're a brave woman," I drawl. "Congratulations."

The other girls freeze. Three pairs of eyes slide slowly towards her.

"What is he talking about?" Bellamy questions.

"Are you..?" Sixtine asks.

"Is he— Are you fucking serious?" Nera jumps in.

"I hadn't gotten around to telling the girls yet," she explains sheepishly. "But yes. I'm pregnant. We're going to have a baby."

Shrieks of joy, happy and shrill enough to pierce the sound barrier, erupt before she's even finished her sentence.

Bellamy and Nera round the counter as Six jumps on Thayer, and the three of them embrace her in a massive group hug, laughing, crying, screaming, and placing hands on her stomach as the joy of the news cancels everything else out.

And the boys watch through the camera, silent and entirely focused, mesmerized by the sight of our girls celebrating.

I knew the cameras were a good idea.

***

Chapter Eight

Phoenix

Tristan walks into Rogue's game room where we're playing *Call of Duty*. He's rubbing his hands together and smirking, looking like the very definition of the cat who got the cream.

"What's that look for?" Rhys asks, glancing away from the screen for a second and getting himself killed by me in the process. "Twat," he says, glaring my way.

"Skill issue," I retort with a yawn.

"That look is *delight*," Tristan answers. "Delight that I get to tell you this in person and see your reactions live. Nera's pregnant. I'm going to be a dad."

"Fucker," Rhys accuses, sitting up. "How dare you steal my thunder!"

We only recently found out that Thayer is also pregnant. Their kids are going to be born a month apart.

Tristan's smile widens. I've never seen the wanker happier in my life.

"And get this," he says, drawing out the mystery. "*Twins.*"

"Motherfucker," Rhys growls.

"Quite literally, as it turns out," Rogue chirps. "You're having twins? As in two?"

"That is the general definition, yes."

"You just had to one up me," Rhys says, his lips twisting into what can only be described as a pout.

"Couldn't help myself." Tristan looks delighted, his entire face split with a huge smile.

"We've got to time this better in the next round," Rogue says thoughtfully.

"Next round?" I question.

"I assume they're not going to stop at one kid. Or in Tristan's case, two."

"Fuck no," Tristan answers with a grin. "I want an entire basketball team."

"Nera will probably have something to say about that," I point out.

"I can be convincing," he answers suggestively.

"Ew," Rhys adds.

"Before you idiots go impregnating your wives again without telling the rest of us, let's make a pact," Rogue says. "We time the next round of kids so they all come together."

"Why?" Rhys questions, his eyes narrowing.

Rogue shrugs. "It'll be fun."

"I'm fine with Phoenix and Tristan's kids being in my kids' year, but I'm not sure about yours, Royal. I don't want your progeny anywhere near my children. God forbid they let their eyes wander over to my precious offspring."

"Your kid should be so lucky to get my kid's attention."

"Over my dead fucking body will I ever let that happen."

Rogue's expression darkens into a lethal smirk. "Good luck keeping a Royal from what he or she wants."

Rhys stands, glaring down at his friend. "No need for luck, I'll just pop their eyes right out of their sockets if I see them stray."

Rogue jumps to his feet. "You—"

"Alright," Tristan interrupts, separating the two. "No use arguing over theoreticals, those kids aren't even here yet. And once they are, we're talking about an infinitesimal likelihood they'll ever like each other."

"My fiancée didn't like me and look at us now."

"Shut the fuck up, Rogue," Tristan answers with an irritated sigh. "All that being said, I love the idea of having kids at the same time. I'm in. Phoenix?"

I'd been quietly watching Rogue and Rhys bicker back and forth, amused by their sparring. All three pairs of eyes turn towards me.

"Sure," I say.

Unlike the rest of them, I'm in no rush to have children. If that's what Sixtine wants, I'll give them to her the second she asks for them, but only because it'll make her happy and that's my priority in life.

If it were up to me, it'd be just the two of us until the end of time. My wife consumes me and that's how I want it. My entire focus, attention, and love unwavering on her with no distractions.

Just her.

Making room for anyone else seems like an impossible task. I wasted so many years letting myself be blinded by misplaced anger and I need to make up for them. I'm still playing catch up, and will be for a long time, so that's what matters to me.

If we have children, I'll love them because they're a part of her, but the thought of sharing her right now makes me want to die.

I'm not ready for that yet, so I'm certainly not going to plan for a kid, but there's no use telling the lads that now.

Six and I are both starting the same law school as Bellamy in a couple of weeks. I'm excited for the beginning of this new journey with her, if not annoyed at the thought of her being exposed to hundreds of new people who'll be vying for her attention. If I could keep her locked up somewhere for only me to enjoy, I would.

I'd once threatened to make that a reality and, I have to say, the idea only grows more attractive with time.

Maybe I should tattoo my name on her again, this time somewhere more visible so it's clear on first glance at her that she's not available.

"He sounds as excited as ever," Rhys comments drolly.

My phone vibrates in my pocket. Pulling it out, I see it's a text from my wife.

Six: come upstairs.
Six: I need to show you something.
Phoenix: coming baby.
Six: :)

"I'll be back," I tell the guys before pausing. "Actually, I might not be."

"Go be with your wife, Phoenix, you're annoying as fuck when you go too long without her anyway," Rogue drawls without looking away from the screen.

"Moody git," Rhys mutters under his breath.

"Congrats, Tristan," I add. He gives me a grin and a nod before I head upstairs

In the kitchen, I find Nera, Thayer, and Bellamy chatting as they make a fresh batch of Aperol Spritzes.

"Should you two be drinking those?"

Nera beams at my acknowledgment that she's pregnant.

"Aw, are you being protective of us, Phoenix?" Thayer asks, reaching to ruffle my short hair. I duck before she can make contact.

"As if."

"No use denying it now," Nera adds. "You care about us, admit it."

"Pregnancy seems to have addled both of your brains," I drawl, walking away. I've only taken three steps when I curse under my breath, turn back towards the kitchen and pick up Nera's glass. I take a sip and set it back down. "Orange soda," I confirm.

"Of course it's orange soda." A slow grin stretches her lips. "But I think you might have just earned yourself a godfather title, Phoenix."

I give her a horrified look. "I'm walking away now."

"I'll let you pick which child you want!" she calls out after me.

I head towards the back of the house, instinctively knowing where I'll find my wild girl.

She's sitting where I expected to find her; in a chair in the backyard, wrapped in a blue shawl that makes her bright red hair shine even against the black of night. A glass is held in her hands as she looks up at the sky.

"Hi, baby," I whisper as I reach her side.

She turns towards me with the kind of smile on her face that I've only ever seen her give me. Warmth spreads through my chest at an alarming speed. When I die, I'll be donating my body to a research center so they can study the unique phenomenon that happens inside me when my wife looks at me.

It's the least I can do for science.

Six stands, giving me room to sit on her now empty chair. I grab her around the hips and pull her back down on my lap. She snuggles into me, pulling her legs up against her body as she lays on my chest and burrows her face in my neck.

The bothersome static that's always there in my head when she's not near me quiets and I welcome the inner peace that the silence brings.

"What did you want to show me?"

"*Regarde.*" She points at the sky, excitement clear in her voice. "Look how bright Sirius is tonight."

I look up at the sky.

At our star.

Well, it's not technically ours because the IAU won't let me buy it no matter my repeated attempts, but it's *ours* in every other way. It has been ever since we both looked at it from our respective countries when we were separated over Christmas, ever since I had it tattooed on me.

And tonight, it shines brighter than ever.

I often find my wife away from the group, staring up at it in awe and something else, something like longing. I know how much it means to her and I won't give up until I get the International Astronomical Union to sell it to me.

"You're right, it looks even closer than usual."

"I know," she answers happily. "I wanted you to see it."

I hum, kissing the top of her head. I hold her more tightly as I reach into my pocket and pull out an envelope.

"There's no better setting than this one to give you your present." I hold it out to her. "Happy anniversary, wild girl."

Six sits up, turning towards me and waking my cock in the process. "It's not our anniversary."

"It is. It's fourteen years to the day since you made me a flower crown."

"Nix," she says with a fond smile. "You can't make every day an anniversary."

"Why not?"

"Because I didn't get you anything!"

"You got me you. I don't want anything else."

"I feel the same way and yet you still get me presents."

"That's because I still have some groveling to do to make up for how I treated you."

She cups my cheek lovingly. "Nix…"

Her eyes tell me there's no need for me to keep apologizing, but she doesn't say the words.

She knows they won't do any good.

I was an asshole to her for *years*. If there was ever a time where I deserved her love, my behavior erased that. Every day I wake up knowing how lucky I am that she ever forgave me. Telling her and showing her how much she means to me is how I atone.

Six turns the envelope over and opens the lip, pulling out the certificate inside.

She gasps and her eyes fly back up to meet mine.

"You bought me a star?" she asks incredulously.

"A hundred stars," I correct.

Tipping her chin back up heavenward, I settle her against my chest once more and point at the sky.

"They're spread out across the galaxy. Some you can see, some you can't. They're minor constellations; I'm still working on the major ones but encountering some resistance at the IAU." I look down at her face, at the sheen of tears in her eyes. "Every time you look up at Sirius now, I want you to know he's being well looked after."

Six throws her arms around my neck and kisses me. Her lips move passionately over mine, her tongue dipping into my mouth. I let her take the lead, content to have my wife taking what she needs from me. My hands roam up and down the length of her back, keeping her pressed against me.

After a few minutes, she pulls back and looks up at me with heavy-lidded eyes.

"I'll take it you like the gift then?"

Her hands stay on the back of my neck, her nails raking up and down the smooth expanse of skin and sending a lethal shiver down my spine.

Her words are tender and warmhearted when she speaks. "Sometimes it feels like you know me better than I know myself, Nix."

"That's the benefit of having loved you for more than half my life, baby."

She smiles and I feel like I come out winning in the trade. Because I got her some measly stars but she just gave me the most beautiful sight in the world.

"*Merci, ça me touche énormément,*" she says in French. "Thank you for getting them for me."

"It's only the beginning, wild girl," I say, finding her lips once more. "When I'm done, the whole sky will belong to you."

***

Five years after graduation

Chapter Nine

Nera

A shrill cry pulls me from a deep slumber.

"I'll get him," Tristan says before I've even fully reached consciousness. He kisses my cheek, throws back the covers and skips out of the room just as his words finally hit my brain stem.

I've never seen someone so giddy to be woken up at three in the morning, literally sauntering out of our bed like he was just given jolly good news, but that's Tristan as a father for you.

Within a month of the twins being born, he'd been able to recognize their cries and know which baby needed us. Their crying sounds identical to me, but he tells me that the cadence of Kiza's screams is about an eighth of a second faster than Cato's.

I rolled my eyes at him when he first said it, but, amazingly, he hasn't gotten it wrong a single time since.

Correct yet again, he walks back in minutes later with a still crying Cato cradled in his arms.

Of the two, he's definitely the fussier baby. Kiza is quiet, so quiet that sometimes I'll assume she's sleeping only to look in her crib or carrier and see that she's simply examining the world around her like she understands it better than she possibly could at six months.

Tristan sets Cato down next to me then slips back under the covers and snuggles close.

"Hi, little love," I coo at my son.

He immediately quiets at the sound of my voice, his wide eyes finding mine in the darkness.

Tristan says he has my eyes; that we have the same shape, the same depthless intensity in our gazes. Looking into them now, I agree with one major difference. They're the same minus the hardened edges. Cato is unblemished and unhurt by the world, his stare is open and full of love and exuberance, and I intend to keep it that way forever.

It's true what they say about motherhood changing you, because the protectiveness I feel for my children is unmatched.

"He's obsessed with you."

I look up at Tristan to find him staring lovingly down at his son. When he feels my gaze on his cheek, he lifts his eyes to mine.

"He always stops crying when he sees you," he explains.

"A mama's boy in the making," I say fondly.

"He's your clone already. They both are. My genes didn't stand a chance, it's like they weren't even in the room when we made them." He smirks arrogantly. "You can confirm I was, if the question ever comes up."

I laugh quietly, careful not to make any noise as I watch Cato's eyes flutter shut. Tristan hums a soft lullaby to soothe him back to sleep.

He's not wrong. The twins both have dark, almond eyes and even darker hair. It's too early to say if they'll look like Tristan or not, but I think they will. I can't imagine that his genes, like the man himself, will let that one go without putting up a fight.

Tristan has never been one to give up.

"That just means we're going to have to try again," he adds with a cheeky grin. "How about baby number three?"

My mouth parts in shock. "Don't you think we have our hands full already?"

"We have two babies and four hands between the both of us. By my count, that leaves two available hands." His eyes light up. "We could even go for a second pair of twins."

I put my index over his lips in a quieting motion. "Hush. Don't put that out into the universe."

"Why not? If we keep having them two by two, that's half the work and twice the reward."

I snort. "Speak for yourself."

Tristan reaches for me, his fingers coming out to brush the hair away from my face. His hand moves down my arm to my waist and finally comes to rest on my hip. He curls me towards him until Cato is squeezed between us.

"If there was a way for me to carry the physical responsibilities, I would, baby." His hand moves to my stomach and his fingers dip beneath the hem of my shirt. He splays his palm against the bare skin of my tummy, his touch sizzling. "There's something about you pregnant, about seeing you carrying my child... It's indescribable. I want you visibly pregnant almost as much as I want the actual baby. I want to put you on display, to show you off so the whole world knows that you're mine in the most primal way a woman can belong to a man." His fingers brush against the lining of my shorts, teasing the sensitive skin there. "Whenever you're ready, I'll be ready."

I tilt my hips forward, searching for his errant fingers. He makes me lose all reason when he touches me like that. "Okay," I say breathily. "In the meantime, there's certainly no harm in practicing."

His smile turns downright devious. His hand clamps around my hip, his fingers digging into my flesh.

Cato mumbles softly, pulling Tristan's attention down to him.

"Son, I'm going to need to put you back in your crib so your mummy and I can do an undressed rehearsal of giving you another sibling." Tristan dips his head and kisses Cato's forehead, then scoops him into his arms. He's walking away with him when I hear him whisper. "No crying, don't be a cockblock for your daddy now."

I laugh as he disappears but don't hear the telltale sign of Cato starting to cry again. He must have listened to his father's request.

Tristan returns and closes the door softly behind him, his eyes pinned on me from the moment he's back in our bedroom. I sit up and hold my weight on my elbows as I watch him approach.

He grabs the collar of his shirt and pulls it off over his head slowly, his gaze finding me again the second he's free. His eyes stay on mine as he pushes his briefs down his legs and steps out of them. Then he straightens to his full, towering height, unashamed and certainly proud of his nakedness as he closes the remaining distance between us.

"Wife," he whispers, his voice laden with lust as he crawls onto the bed and over to me.

I reach for him, wrapping my arms around his neck and pulling him close. "Husband."

"Have I told you I love you recently?" he asks, burying his face in my neck and pressing hot kisses against the underside of my jaw, my throat, and down to my collarbone.

"Not today," I pant, threading my fingers through his hair.

He makes a disappointed noise as he pushes my shirt up my chest, revealing my breasts.

"I've been remiss." I cry out when his mouth closes around my taut nipple. His fingers slide beneath the band of my shorts and dip between my folds until they find my entrance. "Can you ever forgive me?"

I giggle and nod.

"I love you," he whispers reverently.

His lips find mine and swallow the moan that rips from my throat when he pushes two fingers inside me. I feel his body shudder against mine, overcome by the sensations of feeling my pussy.

"Do you know my favorite thing to call you these days?" he whispers against the shell of my ear, his fingers moving deftly in and out of me.

I shake my head and he bites my earlobe.

"Guess," he orders.

"Nera?"

"No."

"Baby?" I ask breathlessly, my eyes squeezed shut.

"No."

His fingers drive inside me with determined, possessive thrusts until I feel like I'm losing my mind.

"Wife?"

"Always. But no."

"I don't know," I pant, quickly approaching my release. "Tell me."

Tristan's heated breaths hit the side of my face as he stares down at me, taking in the way my features are screwed in pleasure. My fingers dig into his shoulders as I hold on for dear life.

And then he lowers his face until his lips brush against mine and our breaths merge into one.

"Mother of my children," he reveals.

Oh, *fuck*.

"You're all I talk about at the restaurants. I used to say "my wife" or "Nera", but now I find myself saying "the mother of my kids". "She's the mother of my kids", "wait until you meet the mother of my kids"," he lists. "I can't help myself. The more I say it, the more I want to say it. The more kids I want to put inside you so that when people inevitably follow up with asking how many children we have, I can say the most exorbitant number imaginable and it'll be true."

I come with a shocked cry, almost blinded by the wave of pleasure that crashes through me at his heated, possessive words.

"You like that, baby?" Tristan questions with a smirk.

He shoves off my shorts and spreads my legs, positioning himself between them. Then, with his eyes on mine and his hands on my hip and splayed beside my head, he drives inside me with one thrust to the hilt, not giving me any time to adjust.

My back arches off the bed at the impossible stretch but his hand cuffs my throat to keep me pinned to the mattress.

"That's a good little wife," he purrs. "Your cunt is so wet for me, baby. You're clenching me so tightly, it's a wonder I didn't come the moment I slid inside you."

His thrusts are savage and unrelenting. He pounds into me until stars explode behind my eyes and I come with a full-throated scream that rips at my vocal cords. My muscles clamp down around Tristan's cock and then he's coming moments after me, roaring my name loudly, his seed shooting into my sore pussy.

Tristan slumps over me, trapping my body with his. His weight is reassuring, his heartbeat comforting against my own as he holds me. My arms come around him and I drag my nails up and down his back in a gentle caress, just the way I know he likes it. He rumbles appreciatively, pressing a kiss to the area right behind my ear.

"Go to sleep, baby."

He seems to be forgetting something.

"Are you going to stay like that?" I tease.

Tristan shifts slightly so that his still hard cock twitches inside me.

"Mhmm," he mumbles, already half asleep. "I'm keeping every single drop of my cum inside you. I take my "practices" seriously, I learned that from your best friend's husband."

I frown. "You mean, Rh–"

His hand clamps over my mouth, but his head stays next to mine, his lips pressed hotly against my ear.

"Don't say another man's name when I'm inside you." He nips my lobe again. "In fact don't say it at all."

I giggle and Tristan's arms tighten around me.

"Goodnight," he mutters.

"You're really going to stay…inside me?"

"Yes."

I wiggle under him. "I don't think I can sleep like this."

His hands move under my hips and then he's lifting me and rolling us both until he's on his back. I come to rest on his chest, with his cock still firmly inside me and his arms now wrapped tightly around my lower back.

"How about now?"

I set my head down, slotting my face into the curve of his throat and snuggling in close until I can hear his heartbeat.

"Perfect," I say with a happy sigh.

***

Six years after graduation

Chapter Ten

Bellamy

I stare at my husband across the breakfast table. Rogue is dressed in a white button-down shirt and slacks, the picture of corporate excellence even though it's the weekend. Even though the civilized exterior masks an unhinged interior.

It's one I've loved since I was eighteen years old, one that I can't seem to get enough of. You'd think almost seven years into our relationship and just over a year into our marriage that the obsession would have somewhat cool.

Well, I'm thrilled to report that it has not. I'm as bewitched by him as I have been since that first day.

And now I have some news to share with him. News that I think he'll be happy to hear and yet I'm nervous nonetheless.

I wring my hands in my lap, anxious.

Should I tell him now? Is this the right moment?

I'd thought about telling him last night when he'd taken me out for dinner to celebrate my graduation from law school. The words had been on the tip of my tongue all evening, but it hadn't felt like the right moment. Last night was about the two of us and I'd wanted to keep it that way.

After dinner, he'd taken me to a nighttime roller-skating disco where I'd watched him struggle to take even one step on wheels and had laughed so hard I'd cried. Then we'd gotten ice cream and walked hand in hand along the Thames.

It was perfect.

Staring at him now as he brings his cup of coffee to his lips, his gaze steadfast on the newspaper in his hand, I feel the very familiar rush of love I get every time I look at him.

I'm so excited for this next chapter of our lives.

For bringing more of him into the world.

"You're staring, sweetheart," he notes, smirking into his cup without lifting his eyes from the paper.

Just bite the bullet, B.

"I have something to tell you."

He sets his mug and paper down and looks at me, his gaze intense.

I wish he was closer. We're sitting at the smaller of our dining tables, but it still feels like an ocean separates us.

Not for the first time since we've been together, I wonder if we're telepathically connected, because no sooner do I have that thought does he get up and come to stand next to me, his hand finding the back of my neck in a possessive and comforting gesture.

"Tell me."

He coaxes the words from me with his gentle tone, his fingers caressing the sensitive skin at my nape.

A smile blooms across my face and I meet his gaze. "I'm pregnant."

Rogue's hand stills on my neck. Weirdly, I feel it tighten, as if inexplicable tension stiffens every muscle and joint in his palm and fingers.

His expression, which had been so open and adoring on me seconds before, shutters, his features turning impassive. It's as if a stranger takes over my husband's body as he wraps himself in aloofness, his gaze a million miles away.

I'm familiar with this version of Rogue, with this chosen defense mechanism of his. I'm just surprised to see him pull on it now. Not only because he hasn't reacted this way in years, but because I've just given him good news.

Right?

"Oh, that's great," he says, bending down to kiss me. "I'm really happy."

I'm frozen in shock.

My body is wooden as his response lands. His smile is genuine, as are his words, but they lack depth and feeling. There's a reservedness that I don't understand. His eyes are haunted and won't meet mine. I dip my head to search for his gaze, but he looks away.

"Rogue—"

"I, uh," he starts, interrupting me. "I forgot I have an errand to run. I'll be back."

He kisses the top of my head.

"Rogue, wait—"

But he's already gone, walking from the kitchen and out of our house without a backwards glance.

I stare helplessly at the door, completely at a loss as to what just happened.

I didn't see it going this way. At all. I thought the timing was perfect, with me having just finished school. I thought he was going to be thrilled.

He's the one who's been talking about having kids for over a year now. His reaction makes no sense to me and frankly, it scares me. I don't want to have a baby if he doesn't want it as much as me, if he's not in this as wholeheartedly as I am.

There's a bothersome throbbing at my temples that announces an oncoming headache. It's probably from holding in the tears that demand to be set free. But I won't cry, I won't let myself freak out until we've actually spoken. Maybe this is how all men react to pregnancy news?

I'm not sure, but I can be patient. I always have been with him. My friends like to joke that I built him with my bare hands.

It's not Rogue's fault.

He was never taught how to feel and process his emotions, only how to suppress them or project them onto others via explosive anger.

But that was before.

He's changed over the past six years.

***

The longer he's gone, the more the initial worry turns into concern, which morphs into fear, which grows into alarm and agitation.

When I can't take one more second of this torture, I group call the girls.

"So what happened?" Nera asks.

I can hear Tristan speaking in the background, followed by Cato and Kiza's answering giggles.

My stomach lurches listening to it, wondering if I'll have that.

I never thought that I might not until a couple hours ago.

"There's not much more than what I put in my text. I told him I was pregnant and he freaked out and ran away."

"What do you mean, "ran away"?" Six asks.

"Just that. He left the house and he's been gone for over two hours now. I tried calling him, but he hasn't picked up."

I'm chewing on the skin around the nail of my thumb. I've been going at it since he left, so much so that I've gnawed the skin down to the quick.

The girls are silent on the other end of the line.

Great.

I move on to my other thumb and go about mutilating that digit next.

"Oh, my god. Someone say something," I beg.

"I'm sure, it's fine!" Six says sunnily. "Just some jitters."

"Six is right," Nera adds. "He'll be thrilled, he just needs a moment to himself."

"You don't run out of your house if you're thrilled."

"Thayer!" Six exclaims.

"I'm sorry," Thayer says, her voice kind. "I just don't want to sugarcoat anything. B, had you guys talked about kids?"

"Yeah, we had. At length. Actually, he's the one who brought it up initially, which is why this doesn't make any sense. At all. I don't understand, I thought he'd be over the moon—" A noise interrupts me mid-sentence. "Shit, that's the front door. He's home. I have to go."

"Tell him to get his act together or so help me God—"

"Okay, okay, I will. Bye," I say, rushing them off the phone.

Rogue walks straight back into the living room where I've been pacing for the last hour. Dark energy swirls around him as he comes to a stop halfway into the room, his inscrutable, intense green eyes pinning me in place.

His chest moves with every deep breath he takes. For a long moment, neither of us says anything. We simply stare at each other, taking stock of the volatile emotions swirling around us.

I don't understand any of it. I don't understand why I can feel a distance that wasn't there a few hours ago.

He shakes his head slowly and then lifts his gaze back to mine, the skin around his eyes creased with regret.

"I'm sorry."

The apology is clear in his tone, his voice thick with obvious misery. It pulls at me, beckoning me to go to him. I close the distance between us and wrap him up in a hug. He drags me into him, holding me tightly against his chest like he never wants to let go.

I breathe a small sigh of relief. He had me worried for a second.

I'm just happy he's home.

"Where were you?"

His voice is muffled against my neck when he answers. "I went for a walk on the banks of the river."

I release him and push against his chest. He tries to hold onto me, but I step out of his embrace and put space between us.

He reaches for me but his arms fall limply to his sides when I move away.

I turn to face him once more and find him looking as tormented as when he first walked in.

"What happened to you, Rogue? Why did you leave? Did you…" My words catch on the mass stuck in my throat. I can barely get the words out. "Do you not want this baby?"

He works his jaw back and forth as he seems to mull his answer over. The silence draws out for an unbearably torturous amount of time.

Oh, god.

Anything other than an immediate 'yes' from him is horrible. It isn't enough.

There are no words to describe the emotion that claws at my insides. It feels like grief and disappointment bundled into one, like someone just plunged a dagger right through my heart.

A long-held tear escapes and slips down my cheek. I look to the side and whisk it briskly away with my index before he can see it.

"Well, the good news is it's not too late. We can get it taken care of," I say, my voice emotionless.

"Bell."

My name rips from his lips hoarsely, heavy with feeling. He calls to me to meet his gaze, but I can't.

I can't.

"I'll make an appointment with a doctor and it'll be like it never happened."

"Bellamy."

I can't bear to think about it. The thought alone flays me alive—I can't imagine actually going through with it.

But it's what I have to do.

It's better this way.

Better than having a baby with someone who isn't a hundred percent on this journey with me.

"*Bellamy.*"

Rogue's stern voice cuts through my spiraling thoughts like a knife. The strict authoritativeness of his tone forces me to finally look at him.

He walks up to me, a massive thunderstorm raging in his eyes as he approaches. There's everything in his gaze; love, fear, anger, possessiveness.

It's all there, and it's all aimed at me.

Rogue stops mere inches from me. His eyes drop slowly down to my stomach.

He reaches out with a tentative yet tender hand and presses his palm just below my navel. Electricity zaps through me the moment he touches me, sending a shiver up the length of my spine.

"I want this baby," he confesses, his eyes lifting back up to mine. "I *desperately* want this baby. More than you could ever know."

More tears pool in my eyes, except this time there's no hiding them. They crest past my eyelids and fall down my cheeks.

I shake my head and wipe the tears away with both hands. "Then why are you acting like this?"

His throat works as he swallows with difficulty. I've never seen him like this, never seen him so unsure of himself.

"Talk to me," I coax gently.

"What if…" His voice trails off. When he speaks again, it's so low, barely a murmur, and I can hardly make out the words that slip past his lips. "What if I'm not a good dad?"

Shock makes me internally recoil. What is he talking about?

"Why wouldn't you be?"

His gaze remains fixed steadfastly on the place where his hand caresses my stomach. He speaks the words like he's saying them to himself, like they've been playing on a loop in his mind for hours, tormenting and torturing him freely.

"You met my father…He was a narcissist. An abuser. A murderer. He hurt me. He hurt *you*. I have to believe he wasn't always evil, that my mother saw something good in him at some point. What if I turn out to be just like him?" His voice breaks and I watch a single tear fall down his face. I've never seen my husband cry before. His next words come out in a terrified whisper. "What if I turn out to be the monster in my kid's story?"

"Oh, baby," I cry out with a sob. I throw my arms around him and crush him to me. All too quickly I understand exactly why he reacted the way he did. "No. Never. You could never be."

"You can't know that."

"Yes, I can." I palm his face in my hands. "Of course I can. You're going to be the best father in the world, I don't have a doubt about that. Not a single one."

"I can't bear it, the thought that I could one day hurt them."

"Rogue, I love you," I say, pressing my lips to his. "I love you so much. You won't hurt this baby, or any others we have. Erase those thoughts from your mind right now, because it's not possible and I know that for a fact."

"How?"

The dejection and agony in his gaze is excruciating to watch. There's nothing I wouldn't do to take it all away.

My hand covers his where it still rests on my stomach and I squeeze it gently.

"I know because I can see that the doubt and fear are eating you alive. The fact that you're even asking yourself this, that you're worrying you might one day be anything like him is evidence enough that you will *never* be," I declare fiercely. "You're a protector, you always have been. No one is going to love their children more than you because it's your instinct—your very nature—to protect. Believe me, *trust* me, when I tell you that you have nothing to worry about. Our children will be happy and healthy and they'll be *loved*. I guarantee it."

"Bell…"

Little by little, I can see that darkness receding from his gaze. I'm talking him off a ledge he should never have been on to begin with, and with it comes an unfathomable amount of relief. That he would ever doubt himself like this is intolerable to me.

"You're going to give them the childhood you always deserved. I wouldn't be having this baby with you, I wouldn't be over the moon excited about it if I wasn't a thousand percent sure that you're going to be an even better father than you are a husband, and you're already the very best husband there is. Okay, baby? There's nothing for you to worry about."

He crushes his mouth against mine. His lips suffocate my soft whimper as he kisses me like this is both the first and last time he ever will. Our lips mingle with the saltiness of both our tears as we devour each other.

"I'm not the best husband. I'm so sorry I walked out like that," he pants, ripping his mouth from mine. "I'm so fucking sorry. That you would ever think I wouldn't want this baby…I fucked up. Badly. That couldn't be further from the truth."

"You scared me," I admit, holding on to him. "It broke my heart thinking you didn't want a family with me."

"I'll make it up to you," he vows. "I've wanted this for so long. Far longer than I think you know. If you'd asked me, I would never have said that I'd have a reaction other than elation when you told me you were pregnant. And I was. I *am*. But the moment you said those words, it's like my worst fears hit me in the face and started suffocating me. I realized that with my greatest wish coming true also came the possibility that I could turn it into a nightmare. I freaked out and I'm so sorry. You deserve someone who isn't going to ruin your happy moments."

"I deserve *you*," I argue, clutching his face. "No more, no less than you. My happiness is inextricably linked with yours. We do this next part together, just like we've done everything else that's come before."

He nods, swallowing thickly.

"Pinky promise?" he asks, extending a pinky my way.

Relief shakes a laugh out of me. I wrap my own pinky around his and look up into his eyes.

"Pinky promise."

Releasing me, he reaches for something in his back pocket. "When I was out, I walked by a children's store. There was something in the window, I don't know why, it just stopped me in my tracks." He shows me an adorable little stuffed pink bunny the size of his palm. "I don't know if we're having a daughter, but this'll be hers." His voice catches. "Her first present from her dad."

I take the bunny and hold it preciously in my hands. There's a little collar around its neck with a blank space.

"I'll get her name stitched there when she's born," he explains.

I squeeze the bunny against my chest, overcome by this gift for her before she's even here.

"I love it." Reaching up, I cup his face, dragging my thumb gently across his cheek. "And you dared to think for one second that you wouldn't be a good father," I muse. "You're already taking care of our little girl and she might not even be here for a while."

***

Chapter Eleven

Sixtine

"Are you sure you don't want to sit or something?" I ask Bellamy.

"No, I'm fine! Where would I sit anyway?" she answers, gesturing at the crowd around us.

I laugh. "Okay, fair enough."

The four of us are at an underground club, pressed against the ring as we wait for Phoenix's fight to start. Tristan, Rhys, and Rogue are off somewhere getting us drinks.

My husband is a law school graduate, just like I am, and he splits his professional time between Sinclair Royal, the law firm we started with Bellamy, and Blackdown, my father's weapons company, and yet he still finds the time to fight.

No, he *makes* the time.

It's a way to relieve stress for him, to clear his mind and wipe the slate clean after a hectic day.

He also says it's some of his best thinking time. It's hard for me to argue with him when his most brilliant ideas seem to come after he's stepped out of the ring.

Being a supportive wife, I come to each and every single one of his fights, even though I can hardly bear to watch them. I usually have to look at them through the hands I have clamped over my eyes, flinching any time his opponents throw a punch or a kick.

I'm lucky though, because Nix is good.

He's great even.

Actually, he's the best.

I'm not just saying that because I'm biased.

Even when he's physically outweighed in a matchup, he seems to find a reserve of strength and will to beat the living daylights out of the other guy.

When I asked him once how he does it, he told me it's because he refuses to lose when I'm watching. So I come to every game to make sure he never does.

He did ban me from ever being a ring girl again though, so I watch dutifully from the sidelines, cheering him on as loudly as I can.

"Plus," Bellamy adds with a conspiratorial grin, absentmindedly rubbing her belly. "You now need that chair just as much as I do."

I place a hand on my own stomach. "Do you think he's going to be excited when I tell him?"

"Are you kidding?" Nera chimes in. "I'm legitimately afraid that I'm never going to see you again once he finds out. That man is going to lock you up in your house until the baby comes."

I laugh because it very much is a possibility with Phoenix. But something else niggles at me.

Unlike his friends, Nix hasn't been pushing me to have kids. He says he's happy with it being just the two of us. I don't want him to be disappointed that that's about to change.

The crowd moves and a man trips backwards, jostling Bellamy in the process. I grab her by the arms, stabilizing her, and am about to yell at the man when he suddenly lifts right off her.

"Touch my wife again and this face will be the last thing you see before you die," Rogue seethes, appearing as if from nowhere.

"I-I'm sorry," the man stutters in response. "It wasn't my fault–"

Rogue shoves him off like he weighs nothing and turns towards Bellamy without giving the man a second thought.

She gives him a small pout.

"I really don't think it was his fault specifically. He stumbled into me."

His hand comes to rest possessively on her belly as he pulls her into him.

"I can threaten the whole crowd with the same punishment if you prefer," he offers sweetly.

"Okay, *no*."

He presses his lips to her temple. "Speaking of which, how are you doing with the crowd? Is your anxiety okay? Any shortness of breath or racing heart rate?"

Bellamy suffered from panic attacks when I first met her in Switzerland. They've mostly abated since, but Rogue always keeps a watchful eye on her in situations that could cause her stress, looking out for signs that one might be brewing.

Ever since she got pregnant, he's been even more overprotective.

"Nothing," she replies with a smile. "I'm totally fine, don't worry about me."

"Worrying about you is my default setting, sweetheart."

"Well, reboot your factory settings then."

He chuckles warmly and presses his chest against her back, wrapping his arms around her and holding her snuggly.

The lights dim suddenly and the crowd goes wild.

Moments later, Phoenix's opponent, a guy named Blade — I've already judged him to be a douchebag based on his name alone — skips down the walkway towards the ring.

I don't spare him a second glance.

He's not who I'm here for.

My head turns towards the other end and I watch as my husband emerges. Where his opponent chose to wear a robe, bedazzled shorts with his name on them, and over the top gaudy gloves, Phoenix comes out wearing a pair of simple black shorts, matching gloves, and nothing else.

His only accessory is the ink covering his body. It wraps around the dips and valleys of his muscles, blanketing his entire chest and a large part of his arms.

There were twenty-seven tattoos dedicated to me when we graduated from RCA.

He's up to forty-six now.

He never tells me when he's going to get one done. They just appear and I discover them when we're naked in bed or making love in the shower.

I'll trace each new tattoo with my finger and tell him I love it, because I do.

I think it's one of his favorite things, watching me come across a new tattoo. He always stares obsessively at my face, taking in the delight that etches itself into my features.

There's no memory too small for him to immortalize on his body. He has a plumeria flower on his hip simply because he had a bouquet of them delivered to my office on our first day and I stuck one behind my ear and walked around with it in my hair all day. He slipped out of a meeting and I saw the fresh ink that night when he fucked me on the dining room table.

He's slipped out of many more meetings since that day.

My mouth waters as I watch him approach. He doesn't even spare a glance for his opponent.

No, he stares at me instead.

"If you weren't already pregnant, that look alone would get the job done," Thayer whispers to me with a laugh.

I blush and smile sweetly at my husband. He exhales deeply, his chest settling with ease like seeing me alone brings him peace.

"Is that your girl, Sinclair?"

Phoenix's jaw tightens. His gaze drags slowly over to his opponent.

"Quit while you're ahead, Blade," he suggests, his tone managing to remain even.

In a move that shows years of boxing have dulled Blade's cognitive abilities down to that of a primitive cave person's, he slinks over to where I'm standing and shrugs his robe off, dropping it insolently on the mat in front of me.

"A souvenir to remember me by, darling," he swaggers arrogantly.

I throw him a disgusted look.

Nera emits a world-weary sigh, shaking her head pityingly. "We're about to witness a murder."

Blade crouches so his face is level with mine. His forearms rest on the ropes as he leans towards me.

Rhys puts a protective hand on my shoulder, glowering at the man in front of me, his stare daring him to come closer and see what happens.

But I know what this is.

It's an intimidation tactic. Nothing more than a psychological trick from Blade to mess with Phoenix's head before their fight.

This isn't about me.

Phoenix watches the exchange silently, his entire body so tense it looks like it's going to snap.

But he doesn't intervene.

He knows I'm well protected and that nothing's going to happen to me.

Blade continues. "Make sure to close your eyes, darling. I don't want you to watch when I KO your boyfriend."

I take a step forward, pressing against the ropes. I hear Phoenix hiss in warning, a sound that lets me know I have ten seconds to wrap this up before he does intervene.

"Enjoy your last few seconds of consciousness, *Blade.*" My gaze lifts to Phoenix and I give him a conspiratorial smile. "I hope you like bedtime stories because my husband is about to read you one."

Out of the corner of my eye, I see Blade flinch. His gaze pings back and forth between us, taking in the way I look at Phoenix and the way he stares intensely, unflinchingly back.

He turns away, his steps markedly more uncertain than when he first swaggered over to me.

"Well," Bellamy says, clapping her hands. "The good news is this is going to be a quick one, which means we can get food after. I'm hungry."

"You're hungry?" Rogue asks, alarmed. "What do you want? I'll get it for you now."

She places a hand on his chest. "Chill, babe. I can wait."

"But you don't have to. Tell me what you want. Noodles? Tacos? Fries? A Burger? What?"

"Seriously, I don't—"

"Chicken wings?"

"*Christ.* Just pick something, B, you've set him off now. You know he won't stop until he brings you food," Thayer says with a sigh.

"Um… it's random but," Bellamy says, "I'm kind of craving strawberries and nutella."

"Strawberries and nutella? Done," Rogue answers, pulling his phone out of his pocket and typing as he starts to walk away. "Tristan."

82

"I'll look after her, mate," Tristan answers without needing additional prompting.

The girls and I are laughing at Rogue's over the top protectiveness when the sound of a first punch pulls our attention back to the ring. We watch as Phoenix unleashes a flurry of merciless hits on his opponent.

Blade takes a dazed step back, his eyes going unfocused. Instead of finishing him, Phoenix backs away.

"Don't make it this easy for me," he taunts. "Fight back a little."

Blade pushes off the ropes and goes for a jab hook combo that Phoenix easily weaves away from. Blade comes back with four more punches, every single one missing their target. He throws a desperate kick, but Phoenix puts up a shin to stop him.

The secondhand embarrassment I get watching Blade punch at the wind is almost crippling. For my own sanity, I can't watch a second more of this.

I cup my hands around my mouth so my words are heard above the crowd. "Phoenix!"

"Yeah, baby?" he answers immediately, keeping his eyes on Blade as he moves around the ring.

"Stop toying with him and wrap it up, please. I have something to tell you."

Blade's eyes bulge out of his head at the easy conversation between Phoenix and I, as if he isn't mid-fight but rather we're talking while one of us is doing a household chore like taking out the trash.

In a way, that's exactly what Phoenix is doing.

"Okay, wild girl. You got it," my husband answers.

Then he takes two steps forward and lands a left hook, quickly followed up by a devastating uppercut, to Blade's jaw.

His head snaps backwards and then he crumples to the ground, out cold.

The crowd explodes in cheers, hands slapping against the mat as people start chanting Phoenix's name.

"Like I said," Nera comments dryly, "A murder."

"That whole sequence of events cracks the top five of the funniest things I've ever witnessed," Thayer says, laughing so hard tears bead in the corners of her eyes. Rhys, standing beside her with his arm draped over her shoulder, is laughing equally hard.

Phoenix walks over to my side of the ring, bends and snatches Blade's discarded robe off of the ground.

He goes back over to his fallen opponent, snaps the robe up so it's laying flat in the air, and drops it over Blade's unconscious body until it covers him like a blanket.

"Nighty night, asshole," he throws over his shoulder as he walks away.

And then he's back in front of me, crouching so we're more or less eye level.

"Hi," he says, not even slightly out of breath.

I smile. "Hi."

"What did you want to tell me?"

Our friends, the crowd and the noise all recede into the background until it's just the two of us staring into each other's eyes.

I go straight to the point.

"What if I told you that you're going to be a father?"

Phoenix freezes, every muscle in his body locking in place as my words hit him. His mouth parts in shock.

And then he weaves his upper body past the ropes and reaches into the crowd for me, easily lifting me up and into the ring like I weigh nothing. He sets me down in front of him, his hands remaining on my arms.

Surprised eyes find mine. "Are you saying you're pregnant?"

"Yes," I answer with a laugh. "That's exactly what I'm saying."

His gaze drops to my stomach, a look of wonder playing out in his eyes. For long seconds, he doesn't say anything. I can't gauge his reaction at all.

I'm about to ask him if he's happy, but the words die in my throat when he does the last thing I expect him to.

He falls to his knees.

His hands grab my flowy shirt and he shoves it up to just under my bra, baring my stomach to him and everyone else watching us.

"Phoenix!" I exclaim, covering his hands with mine.

He ignores me, his face coming towards my stomach instead. And then he presses a soft, long kiss on my belly, right above my navel.

"Hi, baby," he whispers in awe, speaking directly to my tummy.

I watch, speechless and throat constricted with emotion, as he splays his palm on my skin and caresses it gently.

84

"I'm your Daddy."

Phoenix looks up at me from his knees and the expression on his face is so raw, so open, it brings immediate tears to my eyes.

"We made a baby, wild girl," he says, wonderment filling every word.

I choke on a sob. "We did."

He looks back at my belly, quietly stroking my skin with his thumbs in awe. He says his next words almost to himself. "I wish Astor was here to see this."

I run my hands through his hair. "I think he is. He's looking down at us and smiling right now, I'm sure of it." My nails rake down his neck. "So you're happy?"

He nods, looking back up at me. "I'm happy if you're happy. I want what you want. I could have happily lived the rest of my life with it being just you and me. I didn't need anything more. But now we have our very own little star and it's my job to protect her."

Warmth heats my insides and floods my chest.

"Why are you saying 'her'? You don't know that it's a girl."

He kisses my tummy again. "Yes, I do. She's already daddy's little girl."

Phoenix jumps to his feet, grabs my face with both hands and kisses me passionately. I'm laughing against his lips at the intensity, at the pure joy coming off him.

He rips his mouth off mine, wraps an arm around my shoulders, pulling me close, and turns towards the crowd.

"My wife is pregnant!" he announces happily.

I hear a loud cheer and when I face away from Phoenix, I see dozens of strangers jumping up and down, celebrating our joy, and I see the faces of my friends pressed up against the ropes, screaming for us with abandon.

My heart is so full.

***

Chapter Twelve

Rhys

I jump up and down in the tunnel, loosening my legs and releasing the lingering tension from my body.

"You ready for this, Mackley?"

"Yes, Coach," I answer, shaking out my calf.

"Good. I'm going to need some second half heroics from you."

We're down one-nil against Chelsea, playing on their home turf and being absolutely lambasted by their fans in the process.

That's par for the course when two London-based teams play each other and it always fuels my competitiveness.

But I have to admit, being down going into the half absolutely fucking sucked.

Thayer usually comes to all my games if they're in the city, but this morning she told me she was busy, that she'd try to make it, and that I should go on ahead without her.

Her evasiveness has been on my mind since. I haven't played my best football because my mind has been elsewhere, and as the team's playmaker and star attacking midfielder, when I have an off day, so does everyone else.

I need to get my head in the game and leave my personal feelings to the side.

"I always deliver," I tell my coach confidently.

He walks away with a stiff nod.

"Come on, Mackley," a familiar voice calls from beside me. "It's about time you showed you're more than just a pretty face."

"About time? Remind me, Everett, who leads the team in goals?"

Seymour Everett is a recent addition to the team. A center forward, he was a late transfer from Man U and is a former enemy now turned friend.

He steps up to me and flicks the back of my neck like the annoying gnat he is. "And how many of those did I assist on?"

"I'm sorry, did I say 'team'?" I say, grinning. "I meant league. I lead the *league* in goals."

We jog out side by side onto the field to the roaring applause of the crowd. There are a number of stars on our team but, like me, Everett has his own dedicated fandom.

Unlike me, the man is as single as they come and dedicated to introducing himself to every one of his groupies.

We come to a stop in front of our team's bench and kick our legs up to do one final stretch.

"Then what do you say we put our collective brilliance to good use and shut these Chelsea fans up once and for all?"

"I'd like nothing more," I say, squirting water from a bottle into my mouth.

The crowd roars behind me but I ignore it, used to tuning out the noise and focusing on the work at hand. Everett's eyes lift and slide to the left, looking at the giant screen above our heads.

A smile takes shape and grows slowly on his lips until it splits his entire face.

"You're going to want to see this, Mackley," he says.

"What is it?"

He tips his chin up towards the massive screen. "Look for yourself."

I turn and look first at the crowd, not understanding why they're going crazy. Then my gaze trails over to the big screen and my heart does a double somersault.

The camera is zoomed in on Thayer in the WAGS section.

All of a sudden, the oxygen being pulled into my lungs feels clearer, fresher somehow. Like smog is being aired out of them, leaving room only for crisp, breathable air.

She came after all.

And she looks as breathtakingly beautiful as ever, her silver hair shining in the sunlight. I can see exactly why the cameraman loves her.

Pride burns, deep and languid in my veins, at seeing her on the big screen, knowing thousands will look at her and know she's mine.

She's standing and jumping around as she holds our two-year-old daughter Hayes on her hip and dances with her. Hayes is giggling and throwing her arms up to wave at the screen her mum points out to her.

And then Thayer makes eye contact with the camera, reaches for the hem of her jersey and starts to inch it upwards.

My blood pressure plummets and my temper rises just thinking about her baring her stomach to the eighty thousand people in attendance, but when she lifts it, she reveals another shirt underneath.

Thayer points enthusiastically at her stomach, at the same time swaying energetically to the beat of the music. My gaze drops to read the words printed in white ink on black fabric.

"*BABY ON BOARD!*"

My heart stutters in my chest, missing a beat or ten or a hundred.

Holy shit.

"Oi oi!" cheers Everett from behind me.

Thayer and Hayes both point at my daughter's shirt next, revealing that it says, "*BIG SISTER*".

And then Thayer turns her back to the camera and points at my last name where it's printed on her back, doing away with any confusion about whose baby this might be.

It's *our* last name.

She looks over her shoulder at the camera with a brilliant smile on her face. I don't know if she can see my reaction, but based on the look in her eye, I'd bet there's another camera pointed at me, broadcasting my shock and delight back at her in 4k.

I'm running for the stands before she's even turned around.

"Mackley! Halftime is almost over. The game's about to start!" I hear my coach roar after me.

"Sorry, Coach, there's something more important I have to do."

I jump over the partition with ease, clearing a line of crouching photographers who all have their lenses aimed at me. I'd bet a lot of money one of those images will make it onto the front page of the Daily Mail tomorrow morning.

I'm taking the stairs two, then three at a time as I race for the WAGS's section.

I can see Thayer's face in the distance, getting closer with each step, her smile growing wider as she watches me approach.

"Excuse me. *Excuse* me. *Move*," I growl, pushing clamoring fans out of my way as I go down a row towards Thayer. "Move the fuck out of my way."

Finally, I'm free, and with five more steps I'm reaching my wife and daughter.

"Daddy!" Hayes screams, throwing herself out her mum's arms and into mine.

"Hi, darling," I say, throwing a quick glance down at her before reverting my attention back to my wife. I curl a hand around her waist and drag her to me. "Is the t-shirt real? Are you actually pregnant, love?"

"Yes!" she says, laughing and cupping my cheek. Mirth shines brightly in her eyes. "I'm sorry, I didn't think you'd jump into the crowd to come to us. I wanted to surprise you, not distract you."

I set Hayes down, keeping her safely between my legs, and grab Thayer's face.

"As if I could stay away once I knew," I whisper. "We're having another baby?"

"Yes!"

"Holy fuck. I love you." I smash my lips against hers in a bruising kiss. I only dimly hear the crowd erupt once more like they're watching their favorite Lifetime movie couple kiss. "I love you so fucking much."

Thayer laughs, an open-throated peel of laughter that sends delight rushing down my spine.

"I love you too. Now go back down there and win this match. We can't lose the day I tell you we're having a baby. Oh, and fuck Chelsea."

"You're unbelievable, you know that?" I tell her, pressing another furtive kiss to her lips. "Fucking love you. Going to go win it for you now."

And I do.

Forty-five minutes and two goals later, the Chelsea fans have been successfully quieted, and we come out victorious.

Me in more ways than one.

***

Chapter Thirteen

Thayer

"Where is Daddy?" Hayes questions as I place an order at a small coffee shop near the pitch.

We just left the stadium. It was a thrilling match, not just because of the come from behind victory, but because of Rhys's reaction to my pregnancy news. I'd expected him to be over the moon but I hadn't expected him to abandon the game and come bounding into the stands towards us.

In retrospect, I really should have known.

Rhys is the best father there is. The moment Hayes was born, he morphed into the kind of super dad I would have liked to have growing up. He takes her with him everywhere — to daycare in the mornings, to the supermarkets during the weekends, to baby swim class in the evenings, to his practices when he can.

He's counting down the days until she's old enough to be enrolled in soccer classes so he can coach them.

They rarely spend time apart so it comes as no surprise to me that Hayes isn't happy to leave the stadium without him.

"Daddy has to do a post-match debrief with the team and then he has press obligations so he won't be home for a few more hours."

"I'll see him for dinner?"

I grab my coffee from the pickup area. "No, Hay, but he'll come give you a kiss in your room when he's home."

Predictably, her face screws up and she starts howling her heartbreak. I bounce her on my hip to soothe her, with little success. She wants her dad and anything less than his reappearance won't do.

"Thayer?"

I turn towards the voice that calls my name with a hint of disbelief in his tone, and come to an abrupt halt, my mind short circuiting for a second.

My reaction is so sudden that it startles Hayes into stopping her crying. She blinks with tears gathered on her lashes and looks from me to the man who spoke my name.

"Carter?"

Running into my ex-boyfriend in the middle of a busy London coffee shop when the last time I saw him was six and a half years ago in Switzerland and we met, dated, and I knew him in *Chicago*, is shocking to say the least. My brain can't reconcile the fact that he's here, in front of me.

"Hi, fancy running into you here," he says, adding, "It's good to see you."

He looks the same, except he's settled into his features with age. He smiles at me and I'm relieved to find it seems genuine. We didn't exactly leave things on the best terms.

"Hi. What are you doing here?"

My question comes out somewhere between dubious and accusatory, but he pays no mind to my tone.

"Work," he replies. "I'm a video game developer. There's the largest gaming competition in the world happening in London this weekend so I'm here with my company."

"Oh, that's great."

I'm still reeling from the shock of seeing him and not sure what else to say.

His gaze slides down. "Is this your daughter?"

That pulls me out of my momentary fog. I look at Hayes who's still firmly on my hip, clutching a stuffed animal to her chest.

"Yes, this is Hayes. Hayes, this is Carter, he's a... he's a friend of Mommy's."

"Hello, Hayes," he says, giving her a small wave.

My daughter sticks her tongue out at him and turns away, burying her face in my shoulder instead.

Her father would be proud.

Carter straightens, an easy grin playing on his lips as he looks back at me. "I heard you married him. Well, she looks just like him."

He doesn't say Rhys's name.

He doesn't need to.

When I broke up with him, he accused me of leaving him for Rhys. He'd met him briefly when he visited me in Switzerland and had picked up on the connection between us.

I broke up with Carter because the relationship was over, not because of Rhys, but... men and their egos.

Time really does dull all wounds because I'm pleased to hear that Carter's voice doesn't hold any of the heat it did back then.

"Does he make you happy?" he asks.

The answer to that is an obvious one.

***

Later, once Hayes is in bed, I'm on the phone with Bellamy and debriefing her on seeing Carter again after all this time.

"Did he look the same?"

"Yeah, just... older."

"Don't we all," she says with a groan. I watch her reposition herself with difficulty on her couch. "I want this baby out."

"Only a couple more months and he'll be here," I say reassuringly.

"I may not get up from this couch until he does."

I laugh, settling in at the counter of our kitchen island.

At her last appointment, Bellamy's doctor congratulated her on the fact that she was expecting a son, one who was apparently in the ninety-ninth percentile for weight and size.

Rogue told me the incinerating look she turned his way was powerful enough to reach back three generations into his family tree.

92

"Anyway, that's not important. If I remember correctly, the last time you saw him in person, it didn't exactly go that well. What was it like seeing Carter? Did he behave?"

"What was it like seeing *who*?"

Because I've never been lucky a day in my life, Rhys decides now is the most judicious time to come home. His voice is cold and clipped as he strolls into the kitchen.

Bellamy's eyes widen at his sinister tone.

"*Oops.* Fuck. Sorry, Thayer, I'll leave you to deal with that. Glad it's not me, *bye.*"

"Cheers," I reply with heavy sarcasm before hanging up.

I turn towards my husband. He's standing on the other side of the island, a large bouquet of blood red roses dangling from his hand and an expression like thunder darkening his features. He drills holes into the side of my face with his glare.

My skin sizzles with excitement. There's a toxic little part of me that loves seeing my man get jealous. Only because he has no reason — and never will have *any* reason — to doubt me.

"Hi, baby."

"Tell me the Carter she mentioned is someone new you just met and not who I think it is, love," he replies, cutting straight to the point.

I swallow thickly. My lips part to answer him but no words come out so I close it.

Next thing I know, the flowers land on the counter with an angry *thwack*. Rhys storms towards me, his fists clenched tightly at his sides.

I jump down from my chair just as he reaches me. His hand comes up to grab my throat and he drags me against him with a snarl.

"You met up with your ex?" he asks, his voice dangerously calm. The twitching muscle in his jaw tells me he's anything but.

"No." I place a soothing hand on his chest. "I ran into him by chance after your match. He's in London for work, he's a game developer now."

"I don't give a fuck," he seethes through clenched teeth. "So you said hello and went on your way?"

This is the part he's really not going to like.

"We both had coffees in hand so we sat down for a few minutes and talked." His eyes burn with jealousy. His hand tightens around my throat so I clarify, "As friends only."

Rhys laughs humorlessly. Cold fury pours off him in waves. I haven't seen him this angry in years.

"Do you want me to go to jail, love?" he says, his thumb rubbing warning circles over my pulse point.

"No."

"Then what are you doing?" he demands, giving my neck a warning squeeze. My lips part but he doesn't let me answer. "Did you think I'd be anything other than absolutely fucking *livid* that you sat down for a cozy little catch up with your ex-boyfriend? The ex I had to *watch* you be with when you were already mine?"

I cup his wrist with one hand and reach for his face with the other, stroking his cheek fondly as I stare into his eyes.

"You're right, it sounds terrible," I admit. "But do you want to know what we talked about?"

"No," he snaps, releasing me and taking a step back. "I don't."

I fist the fabric of his shirt and yank it firmly to keep him from walking away. Grabbing his face with both hands, I force him to look back at me.

"*You.*" His eyes lift up to mine, narrowing suspiciously on me. "We talked about you. About our family. I showed him pictures of us together. Of Hayes as a newborn." I place a hand on my stomach. "I told him about our second little one."

Rhys sucks in an angry breath. His hand covers mine protectively and he steps forward, crowding me against the counter. "Did you let him touch your belly?" he demands territorially.

"Of course not," I say, genuinely offended. "I would never."

He grunts, his chest settling. "Good."

"He asked me if you make me happy."

Rhys's jaw snaps shut. "I'm going to kill him."

"*No.*"

"Was he hoping you'd say no so he could step in and take you away from me. Is that it?" Rhys fists my hair and forces my head back to look up at him. "I won't stand by and watch like I did last time, Silver. I won't give you a choice. You already made yours seven years ago, and choosing me was a lifetime vow. If he comes anywhere near you again, I'll deal with him like I did Devlin, except this time I'll handle the problem *permanently.*"

94

The jealous rage that flies off my husband is something to behold. He's incandescent with it, his grip on me brutal and possessive.

I keep stroking his cheek to calm him down.

"Baby, he told me he's seeing someone and he's happy. He's going to propose to her. I promise you this was genuinely like old friends catching up, nothing more."

He squeezes my sides, pressing me up against his chest. "So what was your answer?"

"The truth, obviously," I answer. "That I'm one of the lucky ones because I got to marry the love of my life. That you've given me everything I've ever wanted and made every dream of mine come true. That I've never been happier in my whole life."

Rhys makes a noise of quiet satisfaction and drops his face into the crook of my neck, pressing a hot kiss against my throat. "Good girl."

I laugh. "I thought you'd think so."

"Did he kiss you on the cheek when he left? Or touch you in any way?"

"Nope. He actually said he's seen us in the tabloids enough to know you don't play about me and to keep his distance."

"Smart man." He kisses a path up to my ear. "To an extent, because he let you slip through his fingers." He brushes his lips against mine, heating my blood. "And for that, I thank him."

I wrap my arms around his neck.

"Am I out of the doghouse?" I ask, looking up at him from beneath my lashes.

He groans, his palm trailing down my back to grab a handful of my ass. "You were never in it, love," he says, pressing me against his hard cock and squeezing my cheek. "He was going to be dog *food*, but you were going to stay mine regardless."

"I wouldn't want to be anyone else's."

"Good answer," he purrs. He takes a step back, releasing me. His gaze rakes slowly down my body before coming back up to meet mine. "Now get naked."

The corner of my lips lifts even as I reach for the strap of my nightie and slowly pull it off my shoulder.

"Straight to business, huh?"

The satin dress falls to the floor in a pool of fabric and Rhys's gaze turns downright ravenous.

"Daddy's hungry," he says, the husky timber of his voice sending a shiver coursing through my entire body.

His newfound obsession with being called Daddy in the bedroom does something to me. If you'd asked me when we first started dating if that was something I'd be into, I would have said no. But these days, that's all it takes to get me going.

"And you need to be reminded of who you belong to."

I reach behind me and undo my bra, letting it join my nightie on the ground. My panties come off next and then I'm standing completely naked in front of Rhys.

His blue eyes are completely black and liquid pools of lust. He takes a step back, grabs a chair from our kitchen table and sits, settling comfortably on it with his legs spread.

"Come here, love," he orders, undoing the button of his jeans and slowly dragging the zipper down.

He reaches into his briefs and palms his cock, closing his fist around his thick length and stroking it as he watches me approach with animalistic eyes.

I come to stand between his legs. He reaches for my pussy, runs his fingers through my wet slit, and immediately plunges two in to the hilt. A gasp leaves my lips and my knees buckle. I grab onto his shoulders to keep from falling.

He's so tall that even with him sitting and me standing between his legs, I barely have to look up to meet his gaze. There's something so unbelievably dirty about the fact that he's fully clothed while I'm standing before him completely naked.

"Whose pussy is this?"

"Yours."

His other hand goes to my stomach.

"Whose baby is this?"

"Yours."

The sounds of his fingers thrusting into my pussy echo lewdly around us, wet and crude and so erotic they make me clench my thighs around his hand.

"Who's going to fuck you?"

"You," I pant.

He presses his thumb against my clit and rubs it with fevered intention.

"Oh, fuck."

"And who am I?" he demands.

His fingers curl inside me, finding and tickling that sensitive spot. The desire that had been building and coiling inside me reaches a boiling point.

"My husband," I say and then I tumble over the edge and come with a loud scream.

Rhys clamps his hand over my mouth as I shatter around his fingers and slump forward against his chest.

"Shh, love. Don't wake up our daughter."

"Speaking of which," I pant, trying to gather myself. "She wants you to give her a kiss goodnight."

"I will," he mutters against my hair, pulling his fingers from me. "As soon as I'm done kissing her mother. Now sit on my cock."

"Rhys," I moan helplessly, my legs still shaking from the orgasm he pulled out of me.

"Do it yourself, love. Show me how much you want it."

Still breathing heavily, I reach between us and grab his cock, positioning it so it's flat between my legs. And then I tilt my hips, up then down, and start rubbing my wet pussy against it, teasing him.

His head falls backwards on a strangled groan, his throat opening to me, and I dive in to take it. My lips close around his skin and I suck it into my mouth.

He grabs my ass, his greedy hands palming a cheek each. He uses his hold to guide me up and down his length with progressively faster strokes.

I place a hand on his chest to stop him. His eyes open, dazed and completely overrun by lust, and he stares into my soul.

Without a word, I grab his cock and place it at my entrance. Once it's in position against me, I press gently, lowering myself slowly down his entire length. Fire blazes in his eyes as he watches me, his gaze never leaving mine until our pelvises are flush against each other.

I close my arms around his neck and start to ride him. My hips move up and down in steady, deep strokes as I move off until only the tip remains and back down until he's fully seated inside me.

He sits up and wraps his large arms around me, one of them staying over my ass while the other closes around my back and holds me to him.

"Feel my cock," he grunts, his voice unrecognizable. "The only cock that's ever been inside you. And there's a reason for it." His hand dips between my cheeks and finds my back hole. I draw in a breath when his finger swirls around the ring of muscles and then he pushes it into my ass. "Because you belong to me. You always have." He moans, the sound low in his throat. "You always will."

I mewl at the double penetration and bury my face in his neck, keeping my rhythm the same. His finger starts moving in and out of me in tandem with my hips and I pant loudly.

He turns his face into mine, breathing his next words heatedly against my ear. A shiver rattles through me, shaking my entire body.

"It's about time I took this ass, don't you think?"

He pushes a second finger in next to the first and I freeze, the bite of pain stiffening my muscles. My breaths are raw and ragged, ripping from my throat and falling against his as he forces my ass to open around his fingers.

"I'll take your silence as a yes," he says and I can hear the darkly pleased smile in his voice. He gives a sharp slap on my ass. "Stand up and turn around."

I do as he says, completely under his control like a marionette with its puppeteer. When my back is turned to him, he grabs my hips and pulls me snuggly between his legs. Then he places one hand on each of my cheeks and parts them, exposing my most delicate place to him.

He leans forward and spits on my asshole, making me almost come at the obscenity of the act. He rubs it in with his thumb, dipping into the tight passage to lubricate it.

"Sit this pretty little ass back on my cock, Silver," he orders. "You're in charge. You control this."

With a shuddering breath, I place both palms on his thighs and push my ass back. I feel him place the head of his cock against my asshole and I pause, apprehension suddenly tensing my body.

One of his hands leaves my ass and he runs a soothing palm up my spine until he cups the back of my neck.

"Push down on me now, love. I promise this'll feel good."

His thumb rubs comforting circles on my pulse point from behind and I feel my heart rate start to level out.

With a final exhaled breath, I do as he says and push back against his cock. My mouth drops open the moment I feel his head start to breach my muscles. It's thick and throbbing and insistent as it searches for entry.

Rhys's hand comes back down to my ass and he parts my cheeks wide, exposing me to him. Even without turning around, I can feel his gaze laser focused on where his cock is pressing into me, the first inch of his head disappearing into my tight hole.

The stretch is unbelievable, the passage impossibly tight. If the groans and grunts coming from my husband are anything to go by, it feels the same for them.

Finally, the head pops through, providing some much-needed relief and bringing with it a new bite of deep pleasure.

"Good girl," he praises, his voice sounding borderline manic. "That's a very good girl." His hands grip my hips and then he's guiding me to push down on his length. I yelp as two more inches make their way inside me. "Come on, love. I want more. You can take all of me."

The feeling of his cock parting my walls and burying itself deep inside my ass is indescribable. It's dark and deviant and delicious all wrapped in one.

My hands on his thighs and his on my hips set the pace for his invasion until he's completely and irrevocably buried nine inches inside me.

"There you go," he praises. "Fuck, Silver, that feels so good."

I fall back against his chest with a tortured moan and he holds me, his mouth finding my ear once more. "Your ass feels just as nice as your pussy. Just as hot, just as tight as this," he growls, his fingers finding my entrance and driving in. I scream and buck off his chest, only managing to bury his cock deeper inside me. His arm wraps around the front of my shoulders and he pins me back against him. "All your holes belong to me now."

And then he tilts his hips back and thrusts forward, spearing me with his cock.

I whimper loudly.

"Seven years I've thought about taking your ass. And now it's mine."

He drives into me over and over again until my body is limp against his and he's doing whatever he wants to me. I'm so delirious, I can't do anything but listen and feel my climax building.

"I'm going to fuck it every single chance I get," he grunts. "You're lucky I'm taking it easy on you tonight." His thrusts are so brutal that my teeth clash together every time he bottoms inside me. "Because if you *ever* see your ex again, I'll punish fuck your ass so hard you won't be able to sit for another coffee catch up with him without feeling me nine inches deep in your asshole."

"Rhys!" I scream when his fingers pull out of my pussy and slap my clit.

"You're going to come, love. You're going to come with my cock deep in your ass and my fingers torturing your clit and when you're done, you're going to be a good little wife and you're going to apologize to me."

"For w-what?"

He wraps a hand around my throat and squeezes, then spanks my clit continuously with the other.

He bites my lobe sharply, grazing my ear with his teeth when he rasps, "For making me jealous."

My climax builds from zero and then hits me like a category five hurricane. I come so loudly that I fear I wake up the entire neighborhood.

Rhys curses and dips his head. His teeth dig into my flesh and he bites my shoulder as he comes. His hips jerk as he shoots his cum deep into my ass.

He holds me like I'm the most precious thing in the world as we both catch our breaths. He lifts my hips gently and pulls out of me. I whimper and he lays me back down on his lip. I turn so that I'm snuggled into him and wrap my arms around his neck.

"I'm sorry," I say, kissing his throat.

I can feel his cum leaking out of me and onto his lap. We're making a mess, but I don't care.

Neither does he.

A possessive rumble rolls up his chest as his arms tighten around me.

"You're forgiven."

***

Chapter Fourteen

Phoenix

"Come on, Sixtine, *push*," the doctor urges.

Six sits forward and screams, making the kind of noise I'm never going to forget. The pain and agony that echo freely in her screams tear at my insides.

She slumps back down against the bed, spent. Her beautiful red hair is plastered to her face. Sweat covers her forehead and trails down her pale cheeks.

"I'm trying, Nix, I'm trying…" she moans, her face fracturing.

"You're doing a great job, baby," I reassure her, stroking her face, her hair, her shoulders, anything to give her a bit of relief. "You're doing so good. We're almost there. It'll be over soon."

Seeing her struggling, in such obvious pain after almost eighteen hours of labor is excruciating.

If I could turn back the time and not get her pregnant, I would.

Nothing is worth putting her through this.

What should be the happiest day of our lives has quickly devolved into a nightmare. The baby is refusing to be born and Six's small body can't seem to push. It's tearing her from the inside out and all I can do is stand by and watch uselessly, as purposeless as an elephant in a minefield.

"Is her blood pressure okay?" I ask the doctor. "Is it stable? What about her heart rate?"

Eight weeks before her due date, Six was diagnosed with a complication of pregnancy called preeclampsia. It's a condition in which her blood pressure spirals randomly out of control.

It needs to be monitored carefully. I know it can lead to very severe consequences if not treated properly and I'm not about to let any of those happen to my wife.

"Phoenix," she answers kindly but firmly. "Sixtine is in good hands. I need to focus on getting your baby out right now. Relax and let me do my job."

I turn back towards my wife. She looks so small in her hospital bed, her eyes so open and innocent.

We're never doing this again.

I'm not putting her through another round of this torture.

One baby is enough.

"I'm so sorry, baby," I say, kissing her forehead. "I'm sorry you're in pain. But can you push for me now? Please?"

"I c-can't," she says, her face screwing up and tears coming down her cheeks.

Internally, I vow that I'll never do anything to make her cry ever again.

I palm her hand in mine and grab her elbow, sitting her up once more. "Yes, you can, baby. You've got this. You're the strongest woman I know." Her eyes find mine and lock in. "Come on, push."

She screams, ripping me to shreds once more. Why I ever thought this was a good idea is beyond me.

Her entire body contracts as she gives it her all and pushes once more.

From behind me, I hear the doctor whisper something to the nurses. One of them runs out. And then the doctor lifts her head and looks at Six.

"Okay, Sixtine. The baby is breech. Unfortunately, that means we're done here. We're going to take you in for a c-section, okay?"

"Wait, what?" I ask, my voice rising an octave.

"Phoenix," the doctor warns, grabbing my elbow and pulling me to the side. It's only because she's a doctor and we need her that I don't turn violent at her having taken me from my wife's bedside. "I understand this isn't an easy time for you. It's confusing and it's scary because you don't understand what's happening, but imagine what it must be like for *her*. I know you want to lose your cool, but you need to be strong for her. You need to put on a brave face so she knows it's going to be okay. Can you do that?"

My head's a mess and my heart rate isn't any better, but I work to pull myself together.

For her. Always for her.

"Of course," I say, throwing a glance back at Six who's resting against her pillows, her eyes closed. "I'll do whatever it takes to keep her safe."

The doctor squeezes my upper arm. "Good man. We're going to get everything ready and we'll roll her up in a few minutes."

I stop her before she can walk away.

"I'm going with her. I'm not leaving her alone in there." My voice brooks no disagreements, no arguments.

She smiles. "Of course you are."

The doctor leaves and I turn back towards Six. She's crying silently, so tired the tears just slip from her eyes without a change in her expression.

"I couldn't do it," she whispers quietly, her voice breaking. "Why couldn't I do it?"

I get in the bed beside her, wrapping an arm around her shoulders and pulling her against me.

"No, baby," I comfort her. "That's not what happened. You created such a great home in your belly that the baby just doesn't want to come out, that's all. I get it; I wouldn't want to leave either. We just have to show the baby the world out here is going to be even more amazing than the one you built in there."

Six lifts her head and looks up at me. Tears pearl on her lashes. "You think so?"

"I know so."

The nurse walks back in and smiles at us. "We're ready for you now."

I hold Six's hand as she's rolled into the operating theater and stay steadfastly by her head as they anesthetize her and set up the caesarean.

"Alright, Six, we're getting started now," the doctor calls. "Are you ready to be a mum?"

"Yes," she answers breathlessly, turning her head to look at me.

I hum at her soothingly, continuing to hold her hand and stroke her forehead as they get to work. The repetitive beeping of the machinery around me lulls me into a false sense of security. I'm comforted by the fact that Six's vital signs are stable.

"You're doing so well," I repeat for what feels like the thousandth time.

"So are you."

I chuckle softly. "Me? What am I doing?"

Six squeezes my hand. "Calming me down. Making me feel safe."

"I'm glad you feel that way, wild girl." I lean over and kiss her forehead.

Her skin is clammy and pale, a far cry from the usual healthy flush that lives in her cheeks.

Taking the doctor's words to heart, I don't let my anxiety spin me into a downward spiral.

What do I know about childbirth? This must be part of the process.

"You're going to be such a great dad," she whispers. "Do you still think it's a girl?"

We've purposefully held back from finding out the sex of the baby, preferring to discover it when he or she was born. From the jump though, I've thought it was a girl.

Nodding, I ask, "And you still think it's a boy?"

"Yes," she smiles.

"I look forward to being right."

She rolls her eyes, the first sign I've had in hours of my feisty Six. Something like relief bursts to life and nestles its way comfortably into my chest.

"And we both know how much you love being right."

I laugh, cupping her cheek. "It's one of the few simple pleasures I get in life."

"Almost there," the doctor calls over to us. "Then we can settle this for you," she adds with a smile in her voice.

Six and I grin at each other. Doctor Miller obviously already knows the gender of the baby, but she's been great at keeping the secret to herself.

104

The smile slides gradually off Six's face, wiping mine off in the process. It's a progressive transformation, but her face slowly shutters and she turns gray. Then her lips go blue.

At that very same moment, the sound of wailing pierces the air.

"Congratulations!" Dr. Miller calls. "You're officially parents to a…"

I don't hear the rest of her sentence because Six's eyes roll back into her head, then close.

The hand that holds mine goes limp.

And then several machines — the very same that had comforted me only moments earlier — start howling an atrocious alarm that freezes the blood cold in my veins.

"Sixtine?" I call, remembering not to panic. I nudge her face with my hand but it turns to the side with no resistance. A cavernous, bottomless black pit opens up in my stomach. "Six?"

Don't panic. I've been told not to panic.

"*Six!*"

Behind me, I hear the doctor curse quietly, followed by, "She's hemorrhaging. Get another bag hooked up, asap!"

"What's going on?" I ask, eyes wild. I start to stand but a nurse forces me back down by my shoulder.

"Sit down," he orders. "Believe me, you don't want to see your wife opened up like this."

I shove his hands off. "What's going on?" I repeat. "Why is she unconscious?"

The machines blare around us, a cacophony of terrifying sounds announcing the end of the world.

It's a symphony I'm never, ever going to forget.

I don't look at Six, opened up as she is on the table. No, I look at Doctor Miller and my heart hits the ground and shatters.

Because the usually cool, unperturbable doctor I've come to know over the past seven months is standing, her face ashen and twisted, her hands working furiously as panic inscribes itself on her features.

"She's bleeding out," she answers simply.

Like they're words she's used to saying.

Like they're not words that rip the world out from under my feet and kill me with the ease of a bullet.

"I'm going to try and save her life," she adds grimly.

"Save her... Save her *life?*" I say dumbly. I'm confused, uncomprehending in the face of a worst-case scenario I never even considered possible. "What do you mean?" I shout, turning back towards my wife. "What do you mean 'save her life'?"

She's out cold and it's not like when she's sleeping. I would know, I watch her sometimes.

Often.

Most nights.

No, she looks... I can't even think the words.

I grab her face and try to shake her into consciousness.

"Wake up, Six. *Wake up.*" She jerks in my arms, but it's from the way I'm shaking her, not her own movements. "Please wake up. Please, please, *please* wake up, baby."

My voice is crazed.

Demented.

Unrecognizable to my own ears as I scream over and over and over again.

"Please, wild girl, you have to wake up. This isn't funny anymore. Wake up for me. *PLEASE.*"

"Get him out of here!" Doctor Miller shouts.

Hands come to my shoulders. I don't know who they belong to, but I shake them off.

"Get off me!" I snarl, my voice twisted ugly by raw fear.

I reach for Six again but the hands come back on me, more insistent this time.

They're trying to keep Six from me.

To take her away from me.

"*Get the fuck off me,*" I roar. "Don't fucking touch me."

I turn around and punch blindly at whoever is trying to get between me and my wife. My sanity is gone, all rational thought absent. All that's left is the animal, primal part of my brain that seeks to protect my wife.

"Baby..." I call, my voice thick with unshed tears. "Please, baby." I cup her face and find the skin cold and slick. "Please wake up. I need you..." A sob breaks free from my lips. "I need you."

I'm tackled to the floor by someone.

The only thing I can think of is that I feel the exact moment my hands leave Sixtine's face and I wonder if that's the last time I'm ever going to touch her.

It can't be.

It can't be.

"Let me go!" I scream, wrestling on the floor with my attacker.

I'm writhing against him when I see the blood. It stops me cold. Ice slithers into my veins, hardening my body to stone.

Blood is dripping off the other end of the table. It falls in thick, continuous drops and splatters to the floor. It's everywhere.

There's already a massive puddle.

And seeing it is like being eviscerated myself.

I fight against the hold with that much more vigor, determined to get back to Six. She needs me. She's bleeding.

She's dy–

No.

No, she's not.

She can't.

More hands come to restrain me on the floor until it's me against four people and even I can't win that fight.

It's the most important one in my life, and I lose.

I'm hauled out of the theater against my will, my body dragged across the floor by nameless, faceless hands. I fight and grapple and swing every inch of the way, screaming my fury and my fear to no avail.

No one listens to my demands.

No one understands that I won't live if she doesn't.

Somewhere deep inside, I know that they're trying to save her life, but I can't reconcile my brain to that knowledge. Not when I've been forcibly separated from her.

I'm thrown out into the hallway without a second glance. Scrambling to my feet, I reach blindly for and successfully grab a hold of someone's arm.

Who, I don't know, but it doesn't matter.

"Please," I beg. "Please save my wife. Please save her."

The kindly nurse takes pity on me, his face softening a fraction when he sees the frantic desperation in mine.

"That's what we're working on."

"You have to save her."

I claw at his arm, my nails digging into his skin and coming up with blood as I clutch desperately at him. "Let me see her," I plead. "I need to be with her. I need to be with my wife."

He grabs my wrist and gently removes one hand, then the other. I let him, the fight suddenly draining out of me.

"You need to wait here and let the doctor try and save your wife's life. You'll do more harm than good if you go back in there."

He turns on his heels and walks back into the theater, shutting the door behind him and leaving me hanging on one word.

Try.

"*Let the doctors* try *and save your wife's life.*"

Like it's not a certainty that they will.

Like they're even considering an outcome in which they don't.

I stumble backwards blindly, numbly, weakly, my back hitting a wall and my legs giving out until I slide all the way down to the floor.

I bring my knees up to my chest and bury my head in my forearms, dooming myself to despondency and the bleakness of my thoughts.

The world tilts on its axis and I find myself dizzy beyond belief, experiencing severe motion sickness just sitting on the floor.

My stomach roils. Nausea grabs me by the throat, threatening to introduce my breakfast to the hospital floor.

My mind is already lost but I feel it slip further and further away until it feels completely beyond reach.

I can't do this.

I can't imagine a world without Six, let alone consider living in it for even a second.

I'm assaulted by every horrible thought and I—

A hand wraps around my forearm.

It's strong and squeezes my flesh reassuringly, in a completely different way than how I was grabbed before. It's a much-needed anchor back to Earth, back to reality and the present moment from where I've been spinning out of control.

I lift my head and my eyes collide with Tristan's.

He's crouched in front of me, his left hand still gripping me. His face is as serious as I've ever seen it, his expression steady as he stares back at me.

"I—"

My voice comes out as nothing more than a croak. I find that words are impossible, that I can't seem to remember how to even form them.

He doesn't press me, doesn't urge me to do anything until I can get my tongue working again. He simply lends his quiet support when I need it most.

"I can't live without her, mate," I finally manage to get out, my voice cracking loudly mid-sentence.

He shakes his head slowly, the first time he's moved since I laid eyes on him. His hand squeezes my arm again and it pulls me slowly from the brink.

"You won't have to. The best doctors in the world work here and they're taking care of her right now. She's going to make it."

Rogue and Rhys are a few steps from us, just off to the side so that I don't see them right away. They stare silently at me, at the devastation that's so clearly pouring off of me, at the way I've been driven to the ground by my grief.

They've never seen me like this.

Not even when Astor died.

Behind them, I see the girls, all with tears in their eyes. Bellamy has her four-month-old son, Rhodes, strapped in a baby Bjorn to her chest. Thayer just recently left this hospital herself, having given birth to baby Ivy only five weeks ago. Her hand covers her mouth in shock as she watches me. And Nera is outright crying, tears streaming down her face as she holds her heavily pregnant belly and stares at me silently.

We did manage to get all of our wives pregnant at the same time and now I might lose mine forever.

Rogue takes one look at the mess that I am and grabs the nearest doctor he can get his hands on. He fists his shirt and shoves him up against the wall.

"Do you make the decisions around here?" he asks.

"N-no."

He shoves him away. The doctor stumbles a few steps, dropping down to a knee before turning back to look at my friend.

"Bring me whoever does," Rogue tells him with dispassionate cool.

Minutes later, an erudite looking Black man walks into the hallway and goes up to Rogue, the first doctor hot on his heels.

"You wanted to see me?"

Rogue tips his chin in my direction. "Save her life," he orders. He turns his face back towards the man in charge. "Save her life and I'll buy this hospital a whole new wing. An emergency room. A research center.

All of the above. Whatever you want, I don't give a fuck. If she lives, you'll have it."

Rhys steps up next to him, until both their backs are turned away from me. Still, I hear him say, "I'll throw in unlimited visits until the end of time from myself and two other Arsenal stars. Think of it as your personal Make A Wish program on standby."

The doctor splutters. "That's not how it wor—"

Rogue takes a step forward, shutting him up. "Let me make this crystal fucking clear for you since I can see you're in the mood to argue and we frankly don't have time for a pissing contest, one that I would inevitably win anyway. If your best surgeon isn't already in the operating theater saving my friend's life, I need him or her to be in the next two minutes. Same with the best anesthesiologist. Same with the nurses. That's what we're asking for."

The doctor swallows, then nods. "I'll see what I can do."

He's on his phone before he's even left the hall, and then he's gone.

Rogue and Rhys turn around. When they find me staring at them, they give me an almost imperceptible nod. Together they walk over to where I'm seated and take their places on the floor to either side of me, their backs similarly pressed up against the wall.

Rhys's arm comes over my shoulders and he presses me into him once, firmly, before releasing me.

No further words are exchanged between us.

Time drags on and we wait.

It's agonizing.

The worst pain I've ever known as I try not to let my mind roam to potentially walking out of here without my wife.

As I try not to let my mind roam to the last time I was in a hospital, when I almost lost Six after an allergic reaction to peanuts.

As I try not to let my mind roam to the time before that, when I walked into a similar hospital wing with a twin brother and walked out without one.

***

Chapter Fifteen

Sixtine

Slowly, I blink my eyes open.

It's more difficult than I expected, like I'm fighting my way through molasses just to lift my eyelids, but eventually I get them opened.

I appear to be laying on my back, outside somewhere. The ground is soft and damp beneath me. Above me, I see a thick line of treetops.

The sun peeks out through the leaves, illuminating the ground with beautiful rays of light. A quiet, peaceful sort of calm sweeps over me.

Where am I?

Where's Phoenix?

Last thing I remember, I was in the hospital, about to give birth to our baby.

Placing a hand on my stomach, I'm surprised to find that it's flat. There's a soreness in my belly and body that I can't explain, but other than that I'm not outwardly pregnant.

I sit up with a groan, massaging the muscles in my neck. My gaze moves from the tops of the trees down to inspect the forest around me.

With one look I realize where I am. I know these woods. I know them like the back of my hand.

Looking around me, I find what I expected to — I'm lying at the base of the treehouse my dad had designed and built for me when I was a child.

I'm home.

I'm home and I'm more confused than ever because I know I shouldn't be here. I'm supposed to be in the hospital.

Is this some kind of fever dream?

A rustling sound sends a scared shiver down my spine, raising the hairs on the back of my neck in the process. I jump to my feet and turn with my fists held up, ready to take on whoever is trying to sneak up on me.

I realize I look ridiculous, but I won't be caught unawares. My husband taught me better than that.

A figure emerges from behind the trees and my gaze collides with the trespasser's.

My arms fall back to my sides in shock.

A soft, disbelieving whimper leaves my lips and I cover my mouth to muffle it. Tears immediately pool in my eyes, blurring my vision until I can't see him anymore. I blink them away hastily, not wanting to lose sight of him, and kind eyes meet mine once more.

"Hi, ladybug."

My shoulders slump forward when he speaks, my body overcome with emotion. I drop my face in my hands and sob tears of grief and joy combined.

He waits patiently as I wipe the tears off my cheeks with the palms of my hand, blinking a few times to make sure he's still there.

That it's really him.

His name leaves my lips almost like a prayer.

"Astor."

He's standing less than ten meters from me, as real to me as anyone has ever felt. But I know he's not.

He can't be.

Part of my tears are because I grew up, but he didn't. I stand before him as a twenty-four-year-old adult, but he looks back at me as the same ten year old boy I last saw.

The same boy I knew. The same brilliant blond hair, the same easy grin.

This is the second time I've seen him since he died. The first was in a dream, when I was eighteen. He came to me and spoke only briefly, yet I cherish that memory more than I do almost any other.

But this isn't a dream, I know that.

It doesn't feel like it did last time.

It feels real and that's instantly more sobering, because if I'm not dreaming him, then how are we here together?

"It's good to see you," he says, flashing me his signature crooked grin.

"It's good to see you too," I answer, more tears streaming down my face. "I can't believe you're here."

"You're telling me."

He says it like I shouldn't be.

I look around me once more. This place looks like home, but it doesn't feel right. It's too quiet, the air too still, the colors around us almost muted.

"What are you doing here, ladybug?"

I look back at him, shaking my head gently. "I'm not sure," I admit. "But this doesn't feel like a dream." Piecing together where I was before I woke up here, I ask the next obvious question. "Am I dead?"

I'm holding my breath for his answer, but then he ruffles his hair. He always used to do that when he was thinking through how to answer a complicated question. Seeing him do the same now sends a nostalgic pang to my stomach.

This may not actually be real, but it's real to me in every way that matters.

"It isn't a dream," he confirms. "And you're not dead. But you're not amongst the living either."

I blow out the breath I was holding. So, I was right. This isn't a dream, this is my very own purgatory.

It all comes back to me, suddenly.

Pushing, the c-section, feeling so beyond weak.

Slipping into a deep sleep, oblivion beckoning to me with bewitching fingers.

Giving in and letting it take me.

The anesthesia explains why I'm having this hallucination. If I'm not dead, then the doctors must be working to save my life as we speak.

Surprisingly, I don't freak out at the news that I'm dying. That same calm from earlier washes over me.

"I think I understand why I'm here, but why are you?" I ask. "How come I can see you and talk to you?"

He stares at me, his eyes lingering on mine.

"I'm here to take you to the next place, if you're ready."

The next place.

In a way, I realize my brain is recreating a modified version of what happened fifteen years ago — ride my bicycle into the street with Astor or fall behind and eventually find my way back to Phoenix.

Follow Astor into the next place and die or go back to Phoenix and live.

I start to cry again, a fresh wave of tears making its way down my face.

"Why are you crying?" he asks gently.

"I want to stay with you," I say. My voice drops to a pained, raspy whisper with my next words. I wish I could take his hand and bring him back with me. "But I can't."

It's an impossible thing to say and my tears are somewhat of guilt, because I need to get back to my husband. As much as I want to see Astor, Phoenix is the one that I can't leave behind.

Astor's smile broadens and brightens like I've just given him the best news he's ever received.

"You've made the right decision, ladybug." I didn't realize it was mine alone to make. "It isn't your time. He needs you."

He doesn't need to specify who he's talking about. We both know who he means. Despair claws at that thundering organ in my chest because I need Phoenix as much as he needs me.

"It's not the first time you've said that."

He closes the distance between us until he's standing so close I could reach out and touch him. "My death almost killed him," he tells me. "But yours would put him in his own grave and nail the coffin shut. He can't survive without you. He's barely hanging on right now." He pauses, his eyes closing and a frown pulling at his brow like he's seeing something in his mind that he doesn't like. When they reopen, he says, "You need to get back, I don't want to have to see him here next."

It yanks at my own sanity to hear that Phoenix isn't doing well. I know that I stabilize him, that I bring quiet to the madness inside him.

Hearing that he's going off the deep end while I'm hovering between life and death is awful.

As much as I know I need to go back, I can't bring myself to end this just yet. Whatever connection exists between us that brings Astor to me when I need him most, it's rare and I want to make best use of the time I do have with him.

"And my niece wants to meet you."

My eyes fly to his. I find them shining with tears. Happy tears that he's shedding for me, for our family.

I bring my palms together and up to my lips. "Niece?"

He smiles that brilliant smile of his. "Yeah, my niece. Phoenix is going to spoil her rotten. You did good, Six."

I make a sound that's half-laugh, half-cry but entirely delighted. So Phoenix was right.

We have a daughter.

"She's okay?" I ask. "She's healthy?"

"She's perfectly healthy. But she needs her mum, don't you think?"

I nod, clamping my hands over my mouth as if they can physically restrain all the emotion from pouring out of me.

We have a daughter.

Fifteen years ago, the three of us would run through these very same woods, laughing and screaming and playing and fighting and loving each other, and today, Phoenix and I brought a daughter into the world.

Today, I saw Astor again.

Now I know that this was fate. That she was always meant to be born today and in this way so that her uncle could make sure I made my way back to her.

"Time to go, ladybug," he informs me. "But I can't take you back this way. This journey you have to make all by yourself."

My breath falters in my lungs.

He extends a hand towards me.

I stare at it, at his small hand that's only about half the size of mine, letting his words sink in.

He says them with a finality that tells me he doesn't expect to see me again. I realize with a sick feeling of dread in my stomach that he gives me his hand like it's goodbye.

I slip my fingers through his, surprised by the contact, surprised by how strongly his ten-year-old hand grips mine in return. He squeezes it in a way that carries all the emotion in the world.

"Where will you go?"

"Back to the next place." He smiles. "I only came here for you, ladybug. This isn't where I belong."

"Is it... is it okay for you there?"

"It's paradise." His smile broadens. "I told you, you don't need to worry about me. I'm at peace."

We stare at each other for a long, quiet moment.

"Thank you for meeting me here," I tell him. "You saved me."

He shakes his head, those dimples flashing once more. "You saved yourself."

Time comes to a standstill, the only movement the leaves as they fall from the trees and flutter slowly down to the ground around us.

Finally, I whisper the truth. "I'm not ready to say goodbye."

He understands that I don't just mean right now.

He tilts his head to the side and grins. "It's not goodbye, bug. I'll always be here for you if you need me." He squeezes my hand once more. "But you don't. Not anymore."

I feel something pull at me, something telling me to give in.

But I can't release his hand.

I can't be the one to let go.

"Give Phoenix a hug from me. Tell him I miss him. Tell him—" His words catch in his throat, emotion working its way into his voice. "Tell him I'm proud of who he grew up to be."

Those words break me. It's unfair that I should see Astor again when Phoenix hasn't. I know he also needs his brother.

But there's a reason it's me. The thing with Phoenix is, given the choice, he would always choose me over everyone else, even his brother.

"I will," I promise.

The pulling gets more insistent.

I blink, my eyelids getting heavy again.

They open with difficulty and close easily.

"Don't fight it," Astor tells me.

I open them one final time, for one last look at my friend.

"You'll keep an eye on us?" I ask.

It's a selfish request.

But he smiles. Again.

Always.

My eyes close and I let his hand go.

Right before I drift off, I hear my guardian angel answer, "What do you think I've been doing these past fifteen years?"

***

When my eyes open again, I'm back where I expected to be. I see white walls and a TV in the corner, the hallmarks of any good hospital room. There's the same soreness in my stomach except when I look down, I see my bump.

And I see Phoenix bent over my body, his head resting on my thigh, his hand clutching mine in a death grip as he sleeps. He looks tortured, his expression tormented.

I'm *back*.

Gently, I reach for him with my free hand and run my nails through his buzzed hair like I always do.

Except the second I touch him, he jolts awake.

Troubled, agonized eyes immediately find mine. Shock seems to freeze him in place, his voice turning disbelieving.

"Six?"

"Hi, baby," I murmur, my voice hoarse from lack of use.

The sound that rips from deep in Phoenix's chest is unlike anything I've ever heard. It's reminiscent of the sound an animal makes when it's in excruciating pain.

He rises to his feet and clutches my face in his hands.

"Wild girl," he whispers, his voice cracking. I grip his forearms, lending him support. He's shaking beneath my palms. "Six...You came back to me."

Try as he might, he can't seem to get any words out. Tears shine in his eyes as he pushes the hair from my face, as he stares at me like he can't quite believe I'm awake.

"I'm okay, Nix. I'm okay."

He shakes his head, the movement making tears fall down his cheeks.

"You don't understand…," he whimpers. "I can't lose you. I can't."

"You won't," I vow, squeezing his arms. "I'm right here. I'm okay, I promise I'm okay."

"You're my whole world, Six. My entire world. You're it for me. Don't ever try dying again. You can't ever do that to me again. I went mad with grief for those hours I thought I lost you."

"I'm so sorry."

"*Don't* apologize. I'm the one who's sorry," he replies vehemently. "We're not doing this again. If you want any more children, we'll adopt, but I'm not getting you pregnant again."

His tone makes it clear that he's not leaving this one up to discussion. The decision has been made and it's done.

That's okay with me. I'm not in a rush to put myself through this terrifying ordeal again, plus I'm an only child myself.

If, down the road, we want another child, I'm certainly open to adopting.

But that's a topic for a later day.

For now, we have a brand new baby to focus on.

"How is our daughter?" I ask. My gaze roams around the room until it lands on a crib just off to the side of the foot of my bed. Inside, there's a small bundle that sleeps quietly.

Phoenix stiffens. He doesn't look over at her.

I know my husband, I know him like I know every inch of myself. And I know what his reaction means.

"Phoenix. You've held our daughter, right?"

His jaw sets, his shoulders turning rigid. I understand that what he just lived through was traumatic, but he needs to prioritize the baby over me right now.

Gently, I move my hand to cover his where it's still on my cheek. "Baby," I say. "Go get our daughter. That's our little girl."

"I couldn't… Not when I didn't know if you'd be okay. Not when I didn't know if she'd cost me you."

"I understand, but now she needs her daddy."

He hesitates for a moment, then presses a long, closed-mouth kiss to my lips. He pulls away and turns, going over to her crib. When he picks her up, she almost completely disappears in his arms.

"She's so small," he notes, wonder tinging his voice. "I don't know if I'm holding her correctly." His eyes lift back up to mine, softened by affection. "She's as beautiful as her mother."

Phoenix walks back to my side and gently places her in my arms. He stays braced above us as I stare down into her little face, looking at her perfect nose and tiny mouth. At the strawberry blonde tuft of hair crowning her head. At her ten fingers and their minuscule nails.

"Hi…" I say, my voice catching. We had already picked out names, but none of them feel right anymore.

I caress her cheek softly with the tips of my fingers. I know her name. I know it in my soul.

"Hi, Astra."

A soft noise tumbles from Phoenix's lips. When I look up at him, emotion shines brightly in his eyes as his gaze moves from me to her.

"Astra," he whispers, his voice thick with unspoken feeling. "I love it."

It's only fitting that our daughter would be named after the other most important person in our lives. Wherever he is, I hope her uncle is smiling as he watches over us.

"Do you know what else it means?" I ask him.

He nods, bending towards me.

"Star," he breathes, his lips finding mine. "It means star. Our very own little star." He kisses her forehead next. "It's perfect."

***

Later, Phoenix will ask me how I knew it was a girl. I'll say that Astor told me and I'll tell him everything else he said. He'll go quiet before pulling me in for an emotional hug.

Later, he'll show me texts my dad sent him.

Callum: A little girl. Congratulations. You know what mine means to me.

Callum: Looking forward to her future husband putting you through even one tenth of the shit you pulled with me. I know I'm going to enjoy the show.

Later, the crew will burst into my hospital room, crowd around my bed, fuss over me, and coo over Astra.

Rogue will lean in and whisper with a teasing smile, "Almost dying. A little dramatic of you, don't you think?"

I'll shove him off with a playful smile and he'll kiss the top of my head, whispering that he's happy I'm okay.

Rhys will hug me with one arm and warn Bellamy to keep Rhodes away from Ivy with the other. She'll point out that he's only four months old and he'll say that it's never too early to start distrusting a Royal.

Nera will cry when she sees me and a doctor will appear thirty seconds later and wrap a blood pressure cuff around her arm. She'll be confused and Tristan will say that all this emotion can't be good for her or their baby and he wants to make sure they're both safe and healthy.

Later, my husband will take me and my daughter home. We'll spend our first night on either side of her crib watching her sleep and commenting on every perfect little piece of her. In that one night, the trauma of Astra's birth will be quickly forgotten and we'll be deliriously happy.

But that's later.

For now, I bask in the fact that I saw Astor. That I made it back to Phoenix.

That I *lived*.

***

Seven years after graduation

Chapter Sixteen

Nera

"How's the firm going?" I ask. "Congratulations on your one-year anniversary, by the way."

Six beams at Bellamy who raises her glass of orange juice in cheers, then turns back to me. "It's going really well! B is handling all criminal cases, I'm focused on family law, and Phoenix is taking on corporate litigation."

"Does he spend a lot of time at the firm?"

She hums thoughtfully in response. "I'd say thirty to forty percent. He spends most of his time with my dad at Blackdown but he uses his background in law to…" She pauses to think about her words. "To ensure Blackdown remains on the right side of the law in its shadier operations. I don't really know much more than that. Neither Phoenix nor my dad will let me get involved."

"Who'd have thought those two would ever call a truce in their Cold War for long enough to form an alliance against you?" Thayer drawls.

"Right?" She laughs. "But I don't mind. I'm glad they're bonding — for a while there, every family brunch felt like a knife might be thrown across the table in either direction, so I'll take this progress." She leans forward and grabs a piece of pineapple off her plate, popping it into her mouth. "Plus, I'm not interested in the company. I love the work I'm doing with families and making sure kids grow up in safe homes."

"I've always said it, but you're a real saint," Bellamy says, absentmindedly rubbing her belly. "Meanwhile, I'm over here defending rapists and murderers."

Six smiles at her. "Someone's gotta do it. Everyone deserves fair representation."

"I'm surprised Rogue is okay with it though. Seems his protectiveness would kick into overdrive," I point out.

She gives me a look that makes me laugh.

"You have no idea. Especially now that I'm pregnant again, he's never been worse. He wants me to come work at CKI after the baby is born."

Bellamy just announced her pregnancy to us a week ago, which is why I'm holding this celebratory girl's brunch in her honor. Tristan is upstairs with our kids, distracting them and keeping them from running downstairs and interrupting us.

The twins are two-and-a-half and have embraced the terrible twos with gusto, and Suki is six months and hasn't been the easiest baby by any means, so it's no small feat that he's managed to keep them quiet and upstairs somewhere by himself.

"How do you feel about that?"

"I don't know. Maybe down the road, but definitely not right now. I like that our professional lives are separate, that we each have our own thing. I'm also afraid that his possessiveness will be suffocating if I work there. You know how he can be."

Thayer snorts. "Oh, yes we sure do."

Bellamy drops her head back against the couch. "That being said, maybe it'd be a good thing. He's so busy these days, we barely see each other."

She pulls at a loose thread on her jumper and I can tell something is troubling her.

"Is something wrong?"

She sighs. "No, we just had a little disagreement last night. He didn't come home until really late and missed the dinner I'd cooked for him, so I was a petty bitch and left without saying bye this morning. It wasn't a big deal honestly, it's not like it was a special occasion, I was just cranky.

You guys know how these pregnancy hormones can be. And now that I've been fed this delicious brunch—thank you by the way, Nera—"

"Thank Tristan, I didn't make any of this. Obviously or you'd all be on your knees clutching the various toilet bowls of my home."

She laughs. "Well, regardless, the hangry bitch in me has been fed so I have access to my rational brain again and now I regret not saying bye. But it's nothing, I'm just being dramatic. I'll see him in a couple of hours. Ignore me, my emotions are all out of whack."

Six leans over and squeezes her hand. "Back to the question of you working for CKI or not, for what it's worth, I'll support whatever decision you choose. You could also split your time like Nix does if you want."

"Thank you," Bellamy answers, gratitude echoing in her voice. "I really appreciate that. I do know that would mean a heavier burden on you though."

"I don't mind. Astra is the sweetest little baby and we're not trying for another, so I can take it on. And I was actually going to talk to you and suggest we add a nursery slash playroom to the office. We could have care workers that we'd make available to all employees during work hours. I think that would be nice for working parents. And that way, I can bring Astra and see her when I want."

Bellamy sits forward, her entire face lighting up. "I think that's an amazing idea! You really were meant to work in family law, Six."

Footsteps coming down the stairs draw our attention to the door, and then Tristan appears and strolls casually in.

"Sorry to interrupt ladies, just need to get Suki's pacifier."

I don't think anyone hears what he says. We're all too focused on the fact that he struts in shirtless. He holds Suki with one hand against his bare chest as he goes in search of her forgotten paci.

She's so tiny that she barely covers up one of his tattooed pecs, making him look even larger than he already is. His muscles ripple beneath her body, the sinewy perfection of his abs making me drool. Every part of his chest is defined like it was chiseled by hand using fine tools.

He seems completely unaware of the effect he's having on me, my friends, and my lady parts.

His gray sweatpants are slung dangerously low on his hips, revealing the deep V of his muscles. The physical need I have to lick a path down those lines and straight to the promise land makes my blood throb in my veins.

"Ah, there it is," he says, finding it on a bookshelf. "Sorry, she just projectile vomited all over me so I'm between shirts at the moment."

He holds our daughter with such ease against his strong body. There's something about it that sends a bolt of lust straight to my pussy.

I didn't think Tristan could get any more attractive than in his professor era. That really felt like the hotness equivalent of the peak of Mount Everest—the limit had been reached and you simply couldn't go any higher. And yet it's being *easily* blown out of the water by him as a father.

When he's met with resounding silence once again, he turns around with a questioning expression on his features. He takes one look at my face and hisses in a breath.

"Watch it, Nera." His voice is heavy with intent and deep in tenor, his words more of a promise than a threat. "Or else."

I clear my throat of the needy moan that's itching to break free. "Or else what?"

He walks up to me and cups my chin with his free hand, tilting it upwards. "I'm not going to say it in front of your friends, baby." He pulls down my lip slowly, his thumb abrading the skin. His hungry eyes linger on my mouth, his voice turning husky with arousal. "But you know."

He walks out without a backwards glance, but I see him adjust himself in his trousers as he leaves. An anticipatory shiver shoots from the bottom of my spine and up to the base of my neck.

Behind me, Thayer whistles wolfishly.

I turn towards her, face flaming bright red. "What?"

She looks to either side of her, first at Six who's smiling knowingly, then at Bellamy, who's making every effort to hide her laugh, and finally back to me.

"I want to be the first to officially congratulate you on your next pregnancy, Nerita. I'm thinking baby number four will be with us exactly nine months from this afternoon. With this one, we might actually be able to time it down to the minute we leave your house."

I gasp and clamp a palm over her mouth. "You shut your mouth right now. Don't you dare say that within earshot of him, what if he actually hears you?" I release her, then add, "My vagina is screaming just thinking about it."

"Girl, and my mouth was watering just looking at him. *For you*," she quickly adds when I glare at her. "For you, of course." She grins. "You should have him walk around the house shirtless more often, that was the best part of brunch."

"You have one at home, just look at him."

She shrugs. "I sure do, but it's always fun inspecting other available merchandise. And, let me tell you, Tristan is a luxury good."

"I'm going to kick you out of my house if you keep mentally ogling my husband." I wave my hand energetically in her face and she laughs. "Forget you saw that!"

The doorbell rings. The girls throw me a questioning look that I give right back to them because I'm not expecting anyone.

I pull up the door cam app on my phone. Tristan had it installed the moment we brought the twins home. Having kids has made him even more protective than before.

I smile when I see who's at the door and set my phone back down on my lap.

"Bellamy, do you mind getting that for me, please?"

"No problem," she answers, getting up and heading towards the hallway.

"You're making the pregnant lady get the door?" Thayer asks, incredulous.

A deep voice followed by a delighted squeal answer her question for me.

A knowing look crosses Thayer's face. "Ah."

The muffled voices continue for a couple of minutes while Thayer, Six and I talk, and then Bellamy joins us back in the living room. She's clutching a bouquet of flowers to her chest and holding a paper bag in her hand.

There's a dreamy expression on her face that only one man knows how to put there.

"If I didn't already know who was just at the door, your face would say it all," Six tells her.

"It was Rogue," she answers with a lovestruck sigh that would frankly be disgusting if I didn't feel the exact same way about my own husband.

"Let me guess," Thayer says. "He came to tell you to never leave without saying goodbye again?"

"He came to apologize." She sits back down on the couch, placing the flowers on the coffee table. She takes a box out of the paper bag and sets it on her lap. "When we went to Paris for our honeymoon, he took me to this amazing patisserie where I tried a cake called *Le Merveilleux*."

"Yum, those are the best!" Six says.

"The best. I'm obsessed with them. I think I ate one every day we were there," she says with a laugh. "Apparently, when Rogue woke up this morning and saw I'd left, he knew I was upset." She opens the lid on the box and turns it to face us so we can look at its contents. "So he flew to Paris and got some in every flavor to show me he was sorry. He just got back. Who wants one?"

"Stop," I say.

"I'll have one," Thayer answers, reaching into the box.

"And *then* yes, he told me I'm never allowed to leave without saying goodbye again," Bellamy adds.

Thayer speaks around a mouthful of cake.

"Oh, my gosh, these are delicious."

Six moans as she bites into hers. "Brings back all sorts of memories."

I take a bite of one myself, relishing in the taste of cream, meringue, and chocolate. "Delicious. And I'm glad that's settled, B. I know you were feeling anxious about it."

"Mhmm."

We eat in silence for a few minutes before Bellamy speaks again. "But anyway, to go back to what we were discussing before he interrupted us—I see why you and Tristan are popping out kids at the rate some would pop drugs in a nightclub."

I narrow my eyes at Thayer who opens her mouth, silently warning her not to talk about how hot Tristan is again.

My friends have possessive husbands, and so do I, but I'm also a jealous wife. I can't stand the thought of anyone looking at him, much less talking or, god forbid, touching him. I don't know how Thayer puts up with her husband being in the spotlight and the subject of mass adoration at the hands of women everywhere. I couldn't do it.

I'm lucky that his obsession with me doesn't seem to be cooling with age. If anything, the more time we spend together, the more he wants from me.

"Believe it or not, they're not being popped out fast enough. If it were up to him, I'd be pregnant again right now."

***

A month later, I'm in my bathroom getting ready for the day when nausea hits me out of nowhere and takes me out at the knees. I'm clutching my stomach and diving for the toilet in the same second, getting the lid up right in the nick of time.

I throw up the breakfast Tristan just made me, watching the contents of my stomach hit the bowl with some measure of detachment.

Unfortunately, this doesn't seem to be the type of bout of nausea where you puke and immediately feel better, which is *so* inconvenient. I have things to do today.

Tristan and I are working on opening his tenth restaurant. It's a big project, one I'm leading from a design and interior decoration standpoint, and today I'm meant to share my mood boards with him.

I've spent *months* working on them. Digging through thousands of images and curating every single one I used until the board was perfect and fully captured the vibe I was going for — moody, sexy, and elegant.

His concept is an upscale Japanese restaurant. It's been his passion project since we spent three amazing weeks in Japan for our honeymoon. Every dish is inspired by memories we made there.

He recently cooked the whole menu for me and every bite brought tears to my eyes.

It's his best work to date.

This is his most important launch and I want to make him proud, especially because it means so much to the both of us. He's always so supportive of everything I do, whether professionally or otherwise, and I want to give the same back to him. I'm hoping the nausea will pass quickly and I can pull myself together so I don't disappoint him.

Another wave hits me and I bend over the bowl, vomiting once more. I'm so weak, I can barely hold myself up. I drape my body over the edge of the toilet for support. Proximity to the bowl is paramount right now.

A hand comes down on my back and then Tristan appears beside me, bringing warmth and relief with him.

It's as if he has a built-in homing beacon that alerts him when I'm in distress. No matter how far away he is, whether on another floor of the house or in another country altogether, he always seems to sense when I need him by my side. He never fails to drop everything at once and come to me.

He tucks my hair first behind my ear and then over my shoulders, keeping it out of my face as he comforts me. His presence instantly calms me, far more effective than any medication could ever be.

"It's alright, baby," he soothes, rubbing tender circles all over my back. I whimper weakly. "It's okay, shh. It's normal to have setbacks during your recovery." He presses a soft, lingering kiss to my temple. "We'll get back on track together. I don't want you spiraling over this, it's all part of the process. Progress, not perfection."

I shake my head but the movement makes me retch again. Tristan massages my back, his fingers digging gloriously into my shoulders.

He thinks that I did this to myself.

When we first met, my eating disorder was out of control. In fact, it actually controlled my life. Tristan played a major part in helping me get better. Seeing myself through his eyes taught me self-love.

It took a while, but slowly, I healed.

It's been years since I've made myself throw up, but I can see why he'd mistake one thing for the other. He would find me in very similar positions back when I was struggling with my mental health.

I used to think that I would feel empty forever. I didn't realize a person could come along one day and categorically refuse to be sidelined, instead stubbornly pushing past every obstacle I put up until he'd brought down every wall I'd built and filled that emptiness entirely with love.

A small part of me still feels like I don't deserve to be loved by someone like Tristan. He's too good and he loves me *so* much. He's devoted in a way that borders on idolatry. I can't quite believe I've ever done anything to merit that kind of happiness. My secret and most irrational fear is that one day he'll realize he doesn't love me and I'll lose him.

"I didn't purge," I tell him, fighting another powerful wave of nausea. "That's not...ugh, that's not why I'm throwing up."

I can't see his face, but I can hear the confusion in his voice. "Then why?" Alarm raises the pitch of his words and I feel his hand tighten on my back. "Was it the breakfast I made you?"

"I'm pregnant." I vomit again, except I've already emptied myself of my stomach contents so all that remains now is bile. I wipe my mouth with the back of my hand. "Surprise. It's morning sickness."

I steal a glance at his face and snort loudly.

"I knew you'd be grinning from ear to ear when I told you," I groan, my eyes closing to ward off the dizziness. "I swear to god, every time you look at me, you get me pregnant."

"If only it were that easy," he mutters moodily. Then, "Kidding, baby, making them with you's the best part."

Tristan goes to the vanity, opens up a drawer and takes out a face towel. He runs a stream of water, testing the temperature with his finger, then wets the towel and comes back to me.

"Don't make me laugh right now," I say as he sits behind me with his legs spread to either side of me. "I'm sick and trying very hard to be mad at you."

He chuckles warmly and reaches for me. Wrapping an arm around the front of my shoulders, he pulls me back against his chest and brings the towel to my forehead. He presses it to my skin, moving it every so often, and kisses my temple.

"Of course, baby. Work on being mad at me while I take care of you," he murmurs, kissing me again. "You can yell at me when you're better."

"The presentation today—"

I start, but he won't hear it. His voice is firm when he interrupts me.

"The presentation can wait. This is more important. *Far* more important." I rest against him with my eyes closed while he caresses my cheek.

Closing both arms around my chest, he squeezes me to him and sways us back and forth delightedly, peppering my entire face with kisses. "I'm so happy," he whispers warmly against my ear.

I smile because I am too. As much as I'm ribbing him for it, as inconvenient as the morning sickness is, I'm thrilled. I could never be anything other than thrilled that our love is bringing more children into the world. Even if I wasn't, Tristan's obvious joy is infectious.

"Four kids by the age of twenty-five," I muse. "People are going to think you're trying to break some kind of record with me."

He presses his mouth to the shell of my ear and whispers darkly, "Maybe I am."

"Okay, but I haven't worn non-maternity clothes in like, four years. Surely after this one, we're done?"

He hums, running his fingers through my hair and caressing my head softly. "We'll see."

"You're impossible," I answer with a smile I try to hide from him.

"What's impossible is the urge I have to buy you the most outrageously expensive thing I can find. Do you want a new house? A plane? An island?"

"For now, some Pedialyte and crackers will do."

"I can have those delivered in the next fifteen minutes," he says, pulling his phone out of his pocket and typing away with one hand while the other still holds me. When he's done, he turns his face back towards mine and whispers in my ear, "But if you don't pick from one of the options I gave you, I'll just have to buy you all three."

Another violent wave of nausea hits me and I sit up, dry heaving into the bowl. Tristan rubs my back comfortingly the entire time. When I'm done, I lie back down against his chest. He brings the towel up to my forehead once more.

"A house," I say, my eyes closing once more as I snuggle into him. "A new home for our family, please. And make sure it's big enough to house all these babies you keep putting inside me."

"Ten bedrooms, then? You got it."

"Absolutely *not*."

We stay seated on our bathroom floor for a while. The last thing I hear before I fall asleep is the sound of his laughter floating up to my ears. It brings a smile to my face as I drift off.

***

Eight years after graduation

Chapter Seventeen

Rogue

The doctor walks into the room with a bright smile on her face. I'm talking before she can even say hello.

"Doc, tell us the good news."

"Rogue," Bellamy reprimands, putting a calming hand on my arm. "Let her at least sit down before you start pestering her."

Doctor Miller starts laughing. "You only need to be patient a few minutes longer, Rogue. I can't tell you the gender of your baby from the doorway."

"Fine," I grumble.

"Hi, Rhodes," she says, waving her fingers at my son.

He's sitting on my knee, playing with some cotton pads I stole from one of her cabinets and ripping them apart for fun.

"Hi," he answers shyly, burying his face in the handful of cotton in his hands.

We're sitting in the new wing of the hospital that we donated after the doctors saved Sixtine's life. To say they've since rolled out the red carpet for us would be the understatement of the century. For the birth of our second son, Riot — who we left at home with Rhys and Thayer

— Bellamy was given a room they had built and reserved specifically for heads of states and royal families.

We're now expecting our third child and I've been anxiously waiting to find out the baby's gender. Bellamy wanted it to be a surprise given I've been very vocal about my wish that we have a girl this time. She was afraid I'd be disappointed if it turned out to be a boy.

Now six months into her pregnancy, I've finally worn her down and she's agreed to find out the gender together.

"Tell me it's a girl, Doc," I beg, bouncing Rhodes on my knee when he starts to fuss.

"Rogue. Remember we said we wouldn't be disappointed if it was another boy."

"I never said such a thing," I protest.

"Rogue," she repeats through clenched teeth.

"This is a non-issue anyway because it's going to be a girl. Right, doc?"

"Give me a few more minutes."

Doctor Miller is settled at the monitor. She rolls up Bellamy's shirt to just beneath her bra, revealing the pregnant belly I can't get enough of. I reach out and rub it, groaning when my fingers make contact with her skin.

Topping the list of things that feel like they should be illegal, but aren't, is having a rock hard cock in a hospital.

Bellamy usually only needs to blink in my direction for that to happen, but her pregnant belly is something else. There won't be any going down for my cock until she can do something about it. I glance up at her.

"None of that now. That look is exactly what got us in this situation," Bellamy says with a small smile.

"It's your fault, sweetheart. If you weren't so goddamn beautiful, maybe I could keep my hands to myself."

Doctor Miller grins to herself and squirts gel onto Bellamy's stomach.

"Rhodes, are you excited to be a big brother again?" she asks.

"The real question is are you excited to have a little sister?" I correct, leaning over to look at my son's face. "What do you think?"

I've been working on this question with him for weeks, so he's well trained when he looks into my eyes and answers, "Little sister!"

Fuck, being a dad is fun.

"Rogue!" Bellamy says, aghast. "I'm going to K—I—L—L you for that."

I smirk. "How are you going to continue threatening me when he's old enough to know how to spell?"

"By then I'll have evolved from threats to committing the actual act itself if you continue corrupting our son this way."

Doctor Miller chokes out a laugh.

"Don't worry Doc, this is our version of foreplay."

My cock twitches, agreeing with my statement.

She nods, looking dutifully at the monitor and avoiding eye contact as she moves the wand over Bellamy's stomach.

"Are you ready to find out?"

I reach over and grab Bellamy's hand, squeezing it in my own. My thumb rubs intimate circles over the skin on the back of her hand.

"We are," she says.

"Rhodes?"

"I am!"

"Alright, it's a… drumroll, please…" she says, drawing out the torture of not knowing. "*Boy!*"

Hope pops in my chest like a balloon and dies a quick death. I make a disgusted sound, followed by a groan.

"Fuck off."

"Rogue!"

"What? I'm happy," I answer, not managing much excitement in my tone.

And I am happy to have another son. Being a father to my boys has been the best part of the last few years. But ever since that day when I first learned Bellamy was pregnant, I've wanted a daughter.

That little bunny I brought home taunts me from the mantle of our newest baby room. It's desperate for a home and I'm desperate to give it one, but I'll have to move it out of this one like I have the last two.

"Dads are usually so excited to have sons," Doctor Miller points out. "This is new."

"I already have two of those. I want a daughter." I pause, then add with a pout, "Rhys has two."

Bellamy groans. "Is that what this is about? You want what Rhys has?"

"I'm just saying it's not fair. I just want *one*. Three sons is insane, what are we going to do with them?"

"Love them?"

"Well that's a given, Bell, but me and my sperm are also going to have a long conversation about why the boys keep winning the race to the egg. It feels sexist and I don't like it."

"Oh, my god."

"I'm being serious."

"I've been with you for nine years, baby. I know you are."

I look over at the baby moving around on the monitor and feel the familiar rush of warmth I experienced when looking at my first two boys. We're going to have an unruly household with that much testosterone under one roof.

"And now I'm going to have to share and compete for your attention with yet another boy. My time with my wife has been cut by three fourths because of my sons? This sucks."

"Daddy not happy," Rhodes points out.

"No, Daddy is not happy. But Daddy is going to *get* happy otherwise he'll find his time cut down to zero," Bellamy says with a sweetly threatening smile.

"You wouldn't," I say, horrified.

"For my sons? I would."

I drop my head in my hands. "See, it's already starting." I groan again and look over at the doctor. "Is it too early to schedule a c-section so we can get him out and get back to trying for a girl?"

"Doctor, ignore him."

"Sweetheart, I—"

The words die on my lips when I see the look she gives me.

Very simply, Bellamy taught me how to love. The emotion was foreign and held very little value to me before she came into my life. My friends may love their wives, but I'm dependent on mine. Our souls are tied together in such a way that if the fates ever tried to cut the string and take her from me, I'd follow her head first into the afterlife.

So when I say that I'm controlled by the slightest passing emotion on her face, I mean it.

I stand and set Rhodes down on my chair, leaving him to wage war on a fresh batch of cotton balls, and go to my wife. I stroke her hair

136

quietly for a moment, staring into the hazel eyes that first bewitched me nine years ago.

"Is the baby healthy, Doc?" I ask without turning towards her.

"Perfectly healthy. Ten fingers, ten toes. He's going to be as adorable as the first two."

"Good," I whisper, speaking to Bellamy now. I bend forward and press a soft kiss to her lips. "That's all that matters to me."

"I don't want you to be disappointed."

"I'm not," I promise. "I'm having another baby with you. That's what makes me happy. I'll love this little boy like I love the others." I straighten, squeezing her hand. "But fuck, good luck to the world. Three Royal boys? They're going to terrorize everybody."

She laughs. "The teenage years will be painful," she admits. "But we'll get through it." She reaches a hand out to our son. "Rhodes, baby. You're going to have another brother."

His face screws up in a grimace. "Yuck."

Bellamy glowers at me.

I give her the charming grin I only pull out on the special occasions when I need her to forgive me for something stupid I've done. This is one of those such occasions.

"Don't worry, sweetheart, I'll unteach him that."

***

Nine years after graduation

Chapter Eighteen

Tristan

I'm crouching and strapping my youngest son, Juno, into his carrier when an angry voice sounds from behind me.

"*You.*"

I straighten and turn to face my wife. She's coming slowly down the stairs, her eyes narrowed on me. She's wearing a flowery, full-length sundress that emphasizes her curves and reveals her breasts in a square neckline. She looks completely edible and I have to resist the visceral urge I have to cancel our trip to the park and just take her back upstairs instead.

If Thayer wasn't already here, getting Hayes ready in our living room, and if we weren't meeting the others directly there, I would be doing just that.

I hold up my hands playfully but can't keep the grin off my face at her thunderous expression. She's so fucking cute.

"What have I done, baby?"

"Don't play the innocent act with me, Tristan." Her finger comes up to point at me. "You know exactly what you've done."

"I don't, but tell me," I say, reaching for her and pulling her against my body. "I'll apologize so fast, baby. You'll see," I whisper, giving her a crooked grin.

"I'm pregnant. *Again.*" She takes in my stunned expression and holds her palm up between us, her fingers spread. "That's five babies, Tristan. *Five.*"

My hands tighten on her until I know my grip is borderline bruising. She flushes when she looks up and sees the shamelessly possessive look on my face.

"I take that back," I purr. "That's not something I can apologize for unfortunately."

My hand closes around the front of her throat and my lips find hers. I kiss her, my tongue forcing its way into her mouth as I moan my pleasure proudly. She fists the fabric of my shirt and pulls me closer. Even when she's annoyed with me, she can't get enough. Just like I can't.

I pull away only long enough to whisper, "I finally got my basketball team" and then my lips are back on hers, even hungrier than before.

She pushes firmly against my chest, ripping her mouth from mine.

"This is the last one, Tristan."

"Mhmm."

"I'm serious, otherwise I'm putting a complete and total embargo on my vagina."

The laugh that erupts from her at the horrified look on my face eases the previous tension in the air.

"You can't do that."

"I can and I will if you don't keep your super sperm away from me."

"What are you guys talking about?" Thayer asks, walking in holding Hayes's hand. Rhys is bringing Ivy to the park straight from her swim class.

Nera turns towards her. "I'm pregnant."

"Holy shit, *again?*" Thayer throws an offended look my way. "Keep your hands off your wife for like five minutes, Tristan. I'm literally begging you at this point."

"I gave her over a year off after Juno. Compromise," I reply happily. Thayer hugs Nera tightly and congratulates her.

"Then we're going to *compromise* on this baby being the last one," Nera answers.

"I can be okay with that." I pull her close once more. "Are you still happy about it?"

She softens, letting me hug her against me. "Always."

I smile. "Me too."

140

There's a small part of me that experiences something akin to grief that this part of our life is over.

I'm not ashamed to admit that part of the reason I keep getting Nera pregnant is that I know the more babies we have, the harder it would be for her to ever leave me should she one day feel the ill-advised and futile urge to try.

The fact that I constantly search for new ways to tie her to me is because of how often she tried to run away from me—from *us*—when we first started dating. Call it protective instincts or preventative measures, I don't care. The reality is there's nothing I won't do to make sure she stays where she belongs; by my side for the rest of my life.

It would also be much easier to stop at five children if they weren't all so fucking *cute*. Even now, as I look down at Cato, Kiza and Suki who are pulling a slinky toy between the three of them, and at Juno who's asleep in his carrier, the animal part of my brain is screaming "more!".

"Mummy's having another baby?" Kiza asks, wise beyond her years.

I crouch and grab my daughter, beaming up at Nera. "Yes, she is, darling."

"Where?" Suki asks, inquisitive as always.

"Where what?"

"Where's baby?"

Nera gets down on her knees next to me. She places her hand on her bare stomach.

"In Mummy's tummy."

Suki's eyes widen even though she's too young to understand any of this. "Woah."

All three of the children minus a sleeping Juno crowd around their mother. I wrap the four of them in a big hug, making the kids squeal delightedly.

"'Woah' indeed," I say, as happy as I've ever been.

***

Kiza and Hayes walk hand in hand just ahead of us as we approach the park where we're meeting the rest of our friends.

"Stop at the crosswalk," Nera calls out to them.

141

They listen, stopping well short of the road. Their heads come together and they start to whisper gossip back and forth as they wait for us. They started kindergarten this year and every time I come home and ask Kiza how her day was, she mentions someone new. It's getting hard to keep track of all her friends, but I'm pleased to report she hasn't mentioned any boys' names more than once yet.

As we come up to them, Cato is holding his mum's hand, Suki is in Thayer's arms, and I'm pushing Juno's stroller. We cross the road and enter the park, walking towards the main field where we said we'd meet the others.

"There they are," Thayer says. She looks down at Suki and points at something in the distance. "Do you see your Uncle Rhys?"

Suki's face lights up excitedly as they approach. "Ivy! Astra!" she screams, spotting her best friends.

"What am I, chopped liver?" Rhys answers with an offended pout.

Thayer sets Suki down and then she's running as fast as her short little legs can take her towards her friends.

"You're a lower priority to them," Thayer says, walking up to her husband. She places a hand on his chest and gets up on her tiptoes to kiss him. "But not to me."

A purr rumbles in his chest like a big cat's. "I better not be, love."

"Tristan!"

I turn towards the sound of the voice and find Rogue coming towards me. He was further out into the field and seemingly attempting to fly a kite with Rhodes, but he comes in when he spots me. He's almost running towards me but is doing his best to keep his pace as nonchalant as possible.

"Did you hear the news?" he asks when he's level with me. "We did it. We're having a girl," he says boastfully.

Bellamy is five months pregnant but I didn't know she was having her gender scan this week. A rare but brilliant smile splits his face. This may be the happiest I've ever seen him.

"Congrats, mate," I say. "Since we're sharing happy news, Nera's pregnant again."

The smile wipes off his face and he throws me a glare before walking off, cursing under his breath the entire way to his wife. I turn towards mine and find her dark eyes on me, a smile curling her lips after listening to that exchange. I wrap my arms around her and pull her into my chest.

"Thank fuck you're pregnant again. I can't have as many kids as Rogue, that smug asshole would never shut the fuck up about it."

She snuggles into me, laughing openly.

My proudest achievement in life isn't cutting off my father and going out on my own, it's not the restaurants, it's not even my children.

No, it's the fact that I make Nera laugh.

Constantly.

For years, my wife struggled silently with crippling but high-functioning depression. It would have been hard for most to spot that she was unhappy, but it was there. Right beneath the surface and quietly killing her.

Watching her laugh her way through our relationship together has been the most rewarding part of the last ten years. I make her happy and that in turn fuels my own happiness more than anything else ever has.

We rarely spend the night apart because I hate it — I'm sure a therapist would diagnose me with PTSD stemming from the four months we were broken up — but if we have to, I use a recording of her laugh as my alarm so I can wake to the sound of her voice.

"They could keep going and have as many as us," she points out unhelpfully.

My face drops.

"They better not. *Bellamy*!" I shout.

"Oh my god, Tristan, don't call her ov—"

"Yes?" Bellamy asks, walking up to us.

"Are you going to have more kids after this one?" I ask.

Nera elbows me in the ribs and I wince.

"What?"

"Aren't you forgetting something?" is her pointed reply.

"Oh, yes, congratulations," I say. "Very happy for you and all that. Are you going to have another kid after this one?"

"God, no," she answers, horrified. "He wanted a daughter and he's getting one. We're done after she's born."

I smirk, looking down at my wife and pulling her closer into my side. "Nice."

Bellamy watches the exchange with a small smile on her lips. "Any reason you're asking?"

"Not a reasonable one, I'm afraid," Nera answers for me. There's a smile on her lips when she continues. "My oaf of a husband wants to make sure he'll have more children than yours so he can rub it in his face until the end of time. Something for us all to look forward to."

Bellamy laughs, then looks at Nera. "*More* children though? Is there something you want to tell me?"

I squeeze Nera in my arms, pick her up and twirl her around. "We're expecting!" I crow happily.

"Our *last* baby. We agreed," she calls out mid-twirl.

"She threatened me with the unthinkable," I clarify.

"Don't worry, no one would think you'd agree to this decision willingly without some threats being involved," Six says, joining us. "We all know if it was up to you, you'd be a family of twenty." She reaches for my wife and pulls her from my arms and into her own. "Congrats, Nerita."

"Yes, congrats Ner Bear!" Bellamy adds, joining the hug.

***

We're all sitting on the tablecloths our wives brought and laid on the grass to form a wide eating and play area. The kids mill around us boisterously as we pick at the food spread and chat amongst ourselves.

Our wives are sitting off to one side. Bellamy is feeding her youngest son, River, on her lap. Riot is sitting between Six's legs, playing with her hair, while Juno sleeps in Nera's arms and Suki bounces on Thayer's knee, laughing giddily.

As usual, Rogue and Rhys are arguing. Phoenix and I watch on, happy not to be involved.

"Keep your son away from my daughter," Rhys warns.

"Please," Rogue scoffs. "He's a Royal. He's going to have the pick of who he wants. Why do you think he'd settle for *your* genes?"

Rhys snorts. "Because people love me?"

"Debatable."

"I won the World Cup this year. I brought it home. My name is going to go down in English history. Who's going to even remember you when you're gone?"

"Only every single person who made enough money to attend said World Cup or build those stadiums thanks to me."

Rhys yawns widely. "Boring."

"I think you're projecting."

At that exact moment, the four of us watch as Rhodes crosses the blanket, marching determinedly on short, unsteady legs towards where Cato and Ivy are looking at a coloring book. Without pausing, he pushes Ivy down to the ground.

She lands on her butt and looks up at him with eyes wide with shock.

Her lip trembles heartbreakingly and then she starts bawling, fat tears streaming down her cherubic face.

Rhys tries to dive for Rhodes but Rogue holds him back, keeping him forcefully seated on the blankets.

"Rhodes!" Bellamy yells, admonishing her son. She hands River to Nera and stalks over to him. "Why did you push Ivy?"

Thayer goes to her daughter and hugs her. Thankfully she seems okay. I think Ivy's tears are more due to surprise than they are pain.

Rhodes glares at his mother, looking far too much like his father.

"Why did you push Ivy?" Bellamy repeats.

He points at Cato, refusing to look at him.

"She was playing with Cato," he argues, his lower lip jutting out angrily.

"And what's wrong with that?"

He crosses his arms and glares at the older boy. "She's not allowed."

"Why not?"

He stomps his foot. "She can only play with *me*."

I disguise my laugh behind a cough.

Thayer shakes her head and throws an incredulous look our way. "Rogue, how is your *three-year-old* already showing signs of jealousy?"

Bellamy sighs, answering for him.

"He's his father's son, apparently." She turns towards Rhodes and grabs his shoulders. "You need to apologize to Ivy, Rhodes. It's not okay to push people like that." She leans closer, whispering her next words in his ear so softly that I only just manage to catch them. "If you like Ivy, you have to be nice to her. Otherwise, she won't like you back."

She releases him and tips her chin at him to go to her. We all watch as Rhodes seemingly walks in the opposite direction, away from Ivy.

Once he reaches the edge of the tablecloths, he bends and picks a yellow flower from the ground. He turns and goes up to Ivy who's still clutched against her mother's chest.

"Sorry," he mumbles, extending the flower towards her.

Ivy blinks, her wide eyes growing wider. And then her tiny hand reaches out and closes around the stem, taking the flower from Rhodes. She looks at it like it's her most prized possession and then smiles shyly up at Rhodes.

"Thanks. Let's play."

She jumps out of her mum's lap, grabs Rhodes's hand, and then they run off.

"Like I said," Rhys drawls from behind me, shaking Rogue off him. "Keep your son away from my daughter."

Rogue shrugs. "If he's decided he wants her, I fear it's over for her."

"I'll make sure it's over for *him*."

They continue bickering, because if death and taxes are the two certainties in life, then the third is that those two can always be counted upon to argue their way through a social gathering.

Phoenix, meanwhile, is paying them no mind. He's too busy with his daughter.

Astra is sitting balanced on his forearms, which he has crossed over his chest. Her legs are to either side of his torso, kicking happily. The expression on her face is laser focused, her tongue peeking out of her mouth in concentration as she does his makeup.

Suki, Ivy, and Astra each received a children's first makeup palette for Christmas, something they'd been requesting for months. It's a cheap, plastic set that features some truly horrific eyeshadow colors such as fuchsia, electric blue and toxic waste green.

Every single one of those colors are making their way onto her dad's eyelids and even his cheeks, creating a vivid canvas that would make Jackson Pollock proud. Flowery barrettes adorn his short hair in places so precarious they're in open defiance of all the laws of physics, and gaudy clip-on emerald earrings hang from each earlobe.

To say he looks both completely ridiculous and perennially unbothered is an understatement. He sits there serenely, his eyes closed as he lets his daughter paint his face every color of the rainbow, only speaking to ask if he looks pretty.

"Very pretty, Daddy," she answers.

"Good."

It's interesting to watch Phoenix with Astra and see how contrasting our relationships with our kids are. With four kids already here and a fifth on the way, my time has to be split equally between them.

Phoenix, on the other hand, is entirely, blindly, and unreservedly devoted to his daughter.

I fear for the man who'll eventually try and take her away from him. He might have to break into their home or something, because Phoenix is unlikely to ever let anyone near her.

"Are you doing Daddy's makeup?" Six asks, coming to sit by them. Phoenix's hand searches for her, coming around to rest possessively on her ass as she settles into a cross-legged position at his side.

"Yes," Astra answers, still so focused she's hardly blinking. She grabs an eggplant-colored tube from her case. "Gloss. Mummy show Daddy how to do the lips."

Lazily, Phoenix peels open an eyelid, his stare tracking Sixtine's mouth as she pouts her lips in demonstration of how to prepare for the application of lipstick.

His gaze darkens, his voice turning husky.

"Mummy has the prettiest lips," he rasps.

I turn away before I witness something that'll ruin our friendship. My gaze moves slowly over the other smaller groups that have broken off around our area — Rhys and Cato kicking a football back and forth, Rogue showing Kiza and Hayes how to blow bubbles, Bellamy and Nera sitting with Juno, River, and Riot as the youngest kids sleep, and Thayer playing tag with Rhodes, Ivy and Suki.

I watch them all and take a moment to truly bask in how lucky I am to have built such an amazing found family around me.

***

After a chaotic dinner and an even more chaotic bath time with the kids, I settle in the armchair of my study and call my sister.

"Hey, Tessticles."

She sighs, the kind of groan only a sister dealing with her annoying little brother can make.

"I know you're looking for a reaction, so I won't give you one."

"Disappointed to hear it."

"You know I have trained killers a mere phone call away who are just begging to do what I ask, right?"

I scoff. "You can't kill me, I'm your brother."

"Nice try, but that excuse is running a little thin."

I sit up, deciding on a different tactic. "I'm a father. Soon to be of five beautiful children," I add proudly.

She sucks in a surprised breath.

"Nera's pregnant?"

Tess can't see me, but we can both hear the smile in my words when I answer. "She is."

"Oh, Tristan. Congratulations, that's amazing. I'm so happy for you!"

"I only found out today. I wanted to tell you right away."

"How is she feeling?"

"Good so far. She hasn't had morning sickness like she did with Juno so that's good news. Let's hope it continues that way." I laugh, then add, "Other than that, she's told me pretty firmly that we're done after this one."

"I mean, fair enough. She's a saint for making it to five when she already has to deal with having you at home."

"I'll have you know that my wife loves me."

"Well, someone has to."

I laugh, enjoying the good-natured ribbing that flows between us every time we talk.

"Can you tell her I'll call her tomorrow? I need to take her out to celebrate."

"Will do."

"I'm really so excited for you both. A final little Noble baby," she says with a happy sigh.

"Matsuoka," I correct.

"Oh yes, sorry. Exhausted Mum brain — Rafe was sick last night so we were up with him."

"Is he okay?"

"Yeah, just a little stomach bug. He's thrilled that he gets to chow down as many saltine crackers as he wants." She yawns. "The Noble name really went extinct with our generation, huh?"

148

I hum in acknowledgment. Companionable silence stretches between us as we both retreat into our thoughts.

Neither one of us has seen our father in years. Once my mum moved out, he moved on pretty quickly. He never reached back out to her or us, much to our delight. Last we heard, he'd left England for the south of France and had settled in Nice with his twenty-two-year-old girlfriend.

When we married, it was the easiest decision in the world to take Nera's last name. I didn't give a fuck about tradition and I also didn't want her or our future children to carry a name stained by abuse.

"Ah well," I say with a shrug. "Pretty shit last name when you think about it."

"Lots of baggage," she agrees. "We're well rid of it."

"Speaking of baggage, is your husband still behaving?"

Tess laughs. "Don't pretend you two don't like each other these days. He told me just this week that you weren't his least favorite brother-in-law. That's high praise coming from him."

My lips part in shock.

Why am I... *offended* to hear this?

How dare he have someone he despises more than me?

"Devastating news. Clearly, I've been slacking. I need to step up my game."

"Mhmm," she hums, placating me.

"How is everything else?"

"Good. Theo is going to be ten in a couple months, can you believe it?"

I bring a palm to my chest, right over my heart. "Fuck, that just made me feel ancient."

"Tell me about it."

"Pretty soon, you're going to have a teenager on your hands."

"I fear we might already be there. He asked if he could get a tattoo this week."

"Shit."

"Thiago said yes."

I laugh boisterously, imagining my sister categorically refusing the request while my heavily tattooed brother-in-law agreed, likely seeing it as a bonding opportunity with his son.

"So he's getting a tattoo?"

"No, Tristan, my nine-year-old son is not getting a tattoo. But you can't imagine the conversation Thiago and I had and what I had to do to get him to change his mind."

"Gross. Nor do I want to hear about it, Tess."

I can almost hear her roll her eyes at me. "He started getting tattoos when he was thirteen so he doesn't understand what the big deal is. That's as late as I could get him to agree to. I have three years to come up with convincing arguments before my little boy comes home inked up."

Thiago getting tattooed so young is unimaginable to me, but we come from two very different worlds. I doubt Tess will allow her son to get inked before he's an adult, but if anyone can get her to change her mind, it's Thiago.

"Anyway, we had to promise Theo something out of this world as a present to get him to stop sulking, which is why I'm glad you called. Do you think your friend who plays for Arsenal would be open to a meet-and-greet with him?"

"Rhys? Yeah, of course. Let me know the details and I'll help get it set up."

She claps her hands happily on the other end of the phone. "Oh, that's amazing. Thank you so much. Tell Rhys that Thiago says he'll owe him a favor for his help. You know those can come in handy."

***

Ten years after graduation

Chapter Nineteen

Sixtine

Turning away from my desk, I blow out a breath and stand. Anticipation tickles my spine with cold fingers so I roll my shoulders to try and shake it out of me. I anxiously smooth down the front of my black Valentino dress and make my way to the bay of windows. Crossing my arms, I stare down at the city below from the twentieth floor of our office building.

Over the years, Sinclair Royal has grown into the largest firm in the U.K and one of the largest in the world. In addition to handling all external legal affairs for massive Fortune 500 companies such as Blackdown and CKI, our thousand employees represent over two hundred other clients.

Our success is due in part to the range of services and types of cases we take on, but also because of how much of a shark my husband is. The word "lose" isn't one that's ever factored into his vocabulary.

There isn't a part of the world where we can't provide legal assistance — and other not-so-legal services depending on what's needed — if reached out to.

Bellamy, Phoenix and I built it all together and I'm endlessly proud of that.

But now, it's time for me to face my husband.

I gather my hair and drop it down the slope of my back, then roll my shoulders once more for confidence. With a final glance out of the window, I turn on my heels and walk out of my office.

Our offices are equal in size and situated on opposite corners of the floor. We used to share a wall, but Phoenix would burst in every day and have his way with me, regardless of any meetings he or I needed to attend.

We got absolutely nothing done and eventually made the executive — and very hard — decision to add some physical distance between us, if only so we could actually get some work done. I'd originally suggested that one of us move down to the nineteenth, but he wouldn't have it. This was as much separation as he would allow.

I make my way across the floor, waving distractedly at some people along the way, but not stopping for conversation. My thoughts are elsewhere. The sooner Phoenix and I resolve what happened earlier this afternoon, the better.

When I get to his office, I blow out a final breath for good luck, knock once, and walk right in without waiting for an answer.

He already knows it's me.

I have no doubt he's been expecting me.

My heart hammers in my chest and echoes loudly in my ears. Its thundering beat is absolutely deafening.

Anticipation pounds in my bloodstream.

What mood am I going to find him in?

I expect him to be at his desk, but he's not.

He's standing behind it, facing the large bay windows and looking down at the magnificent view of London. It's the very same view I'd just been admiring, except where I felt awe, he stares at it like he owns the entire city.

I wonder if he too is thinking about our accomplishments. We've always been connected in that way, able to almost sense each other's thoughts. Secrets are impossible between us and I'm thankful for it.

His hands are jammed into his pockets and his suit follows the lines of his body closely.

Hugo Boss.

Black. Expensive. Tailored.

An arrow of lust pierces my lower belly, leaving a throbbing ache in its place.

It's criminal to be this attractive.

He turns his head degrees to the side when he hears the door open. His eyes slant over his shoulder and connect slowly with mine.

They're pitch black.

Moody. Angry.

He licks his lips slowly.

Hungry.

"Close the door behind you."

My heart jolts into my throat, excitement burning like gasoline in my veins at the way he issues orders, and I swallow thickly.

The door shuts behind me with a soft click.

"Lock it."

I'm shaking with exhilarated nerves at his tone of voice. It promises retribution.

He doesn't immediately turn around, so I walk deeper into the room until I'm standing in front of his desk.

The silence stretches. Taut, suffocating, tension pulls thickly between us and grabs me by the throat.

Finally, he turns to face me.

His dark gaze rakes roughly down my body and slowly back up. I can't stifle the shiver that courses down my spine in response to his intense scrutiny.

It doesn't go unnoticed by him, his eyes flaring in arousal.

"Nix, I…"

He doesn't interrupt me but my voice trails off nonetheless. I can't think with his stare pinned on me this way. His eyes are all consuming. A mix of anger and something else, something much more primitive and dangerous, swirls in his black irises.

Possessiveness.

No, *ownership.*

"Go on."

His voice is rough like gravel and it courses over my skin as menacingly as a hand wrapping around the back of my neck and squeezing.

"Have you calmed down yet?"

He lifts his chin slightly, his jaw twitching as he stares back at me. His unbroken stare makes my hands clammy. The intensity in his gaze is potent enough to start a wildfire with only his eyes as an accelerant.

"Does it look like I have?"

The sound of his words spat out through clenched teeth answers the question for me.

Earlier, we had a meeting with a prospective new client. Phoenix and I like to take those meetings together if we think there's a chance for full scope representation, inclusive of both corporate and familial assets.

Edward Chambers is a married, devoted father of three young children, and the head of a large oil and gas company based in London. As a client, he stood to bring us millions in annual revenue if we landed him, so we'd been excited and well prepared for the meeting.

We held it in our largest conference room, with Phoenix and I sitting on one side of the table while he sat on the other.

The meeting had gone well, so well in fact that we'd discussed not wasting any time and moving directly to the contract stage.

Phoenix had walked out to get the necessary paperwork and I'd headed over to the smaller table along the far wall of the room where we'd laid out some refreshments and pastries, continuing to speak animatedly to Edward as I did so.

I was pouring him a cup of coffee he'd asked for when I felt a hand come down on my hip and move slowly around to my lower back. Shock rooted me to the spot when I looked up, startled, and found Edward leaning over me. I hadn't heard or felt him move to follow me.

He grinned luridly down at me, and when our eyes met his lips touched my ear and he whispered, "Is extra sugar available?"

Disgust roiled in my stomach, followed quickly by fear crawling down my spine. Based on the boldness of his touch and the ease of his smile, I could tell he expected me to be included as a signing gift in our contract, regardless of whether I was personally inclined to it or not. The audacity of his actions shocked me.

When I turned around to tell him to take his hands off me and fuck off, my gaze slammed into my husband's.

Phoenix stood frozen in the doorway, one hand fisting the handle of the door, knuckles turning white, the other clutching a manila folder at his side, his expression caught somewhere between confusion and disbelief.

My immediate reaction was relief. Phoenix wouldn't let anything happen to me, I was safe.

Then his eyes dragged slowly down to where Chambers's hand still touched me and I watched the light in them shutter in real time. His pupils expanded, his irises turning as deadly black as a shark's.

When his gaze flicked back up to mine, all the humanity had gone from his eyes. Murder etched itself on every single feature of his handsome face, and my original relief was quickly replaced by trepidation at what would happen next.

The folder crashed to the ground with a resounding, ominous *thud*.

Phoenix stormed towards me, closing the distance between us in three furious steps. He never took his eyes off mine as he grabbed Chambers and wrenched him off me, ripping his shoulder clean out of his socket in one clinical, emotionless move.

He didn't say a word. He didn't look capable of it, letting his obvious fury speak for him instead.

Chambers howled in agony; howling that only grew louder and more acute as Phoenix dragged him across the floor and out of the conference room by his torn shoulder.

The second he was gone, I sagged against the table, grabbing onto the edges as I caught my breath and leveled out my racing heart rate.

I waited for my husband to come back, knowing that he would be beyond furious and agitated. Knowing that, like a caged animal, he would need the freedom to let his aggression out in some way.

But he never did.

Time ticked by and I eventually made my way back to my office and attempted to do some work.

I hadn't heard from him since. The only thing I knew for sure was that Chambers wouldn't be in any state to require future legal assistance after Phoenix was finished with him, except potentially of the estate management kind.

Unfortunately, that's one of the only services we don't currently offer at Sinclair Royal.

Even now as I finally face my husband, I can feel the rage coming off of him in waves.

I round the desk and walk up to Phoenix. When I'm standing before him, dwarfed by his height and daunted by the intensity of his gaze, I set a hand on his chest right over his heart. Its furious beat is evidence of the tumultuous emotions still crashing through him.

His hand comes to rest on top of mine, clamping my palm tightly over his heart.

I look up at him from beneath my lashes.

"Are you mad at me?"

A dangerous sounding rumble rolls loudly in his chest. His jaw twitches murderously.

"No."

I run my fingers up his torso and to his nape, imploring him softly, "Then stop glaring at me like that, please. It's not my fault he touched me."

Rough hands grab my hips and lift me. A small cry falls from my lips as he turns us both and drops me on his desk.

"Phoenix—"

He shoves my dress up my thighs and bunches it at my waist. With his stare still pinned on mine and his face still twisted in a scowl, he reaches between my legs and rips off my panties.

I'm already soaked. I always am when I'm around Phoenix, but it's especially true when he's being violently possessive like he is now. My body titters with excitement as I wait for him to act.

My arms go around his neck to pull him into me. I expect his fingers to dip between my folds, but I'm wrong.

Instead, I feel his thumb abrade the skin just above my pussy. The soft circles he's caressing on the area are in stark contrast to the aggression rolling off of him in waves.

His eyes drop to fixate on the spot he's touching.

The very same spot where he tattooed his name on me ten years ago in a not too dissimilar fit of jealousy and possessiveness.

Seeing his name branded on me reassures and calms him down, soothing him like a fidget toy might manage other people's anxiety.

He stares at it unwaveringly.

Unblinkingly, even.

"Who do you belong to?" he demands quietly.

I reach for his chin and tilt his face up so his gaze meets mine. With my other hand, I run my nails through his short hair. He still keeps it buzzed, his rough and dangerous appearance in complete opposition to the corporate man he pretends to be.

He shivers at my touch, his eyes fluttering momentarily shut.

"My husband."

157

They reopen, shining with arrogant satisfaction.

He rubs the tattoo again, then bends and licks the marked skin with a rough swipe of his tongue. "What's his name?"

"Nix," I whimper.

Another swipe of his tongue, designed to make me lose all my senses.

"Full name, wild girl," he orders.

His other hand slips beneath my dress to dance up my stomach towards my breasts. My eyes shut and I moan as he tweaks my nipple over my bra.

He insists that I wear padded coverage to hide the piercing at work. He won't let me take it out, but he also refuses to let anyone know of its existence.

Even through the thick material, my nipple responds to his touch. It hardens until the bud is so tight it's painful.

I gasp when he pinches it in a silent command to answer his question.

"Phoenix Sinclair."

He growls. "And what's your name?"

"Sixtine Sinclair," I breathe, arching into his touch.

"That's fucking *right*," he seethes, leaning over me.

With one swift thrust, he pushes two fingers inside me. He cups my nape with his other hand and tugs me forward. My eyes fly open to find him inches from my face, his gaze fixed heatedly on mine as he starts to thrust in tandem with his words.

"You bear my name, you wear my rings, you've had *my* baby, you sit right next to me in a building that has a twenty-foot sign that also has our last name on it, you're *my* wife—*my. fucking. wife*—and yet men still think they can touch you the second I turn my back," he snarls. "Why the fuck is that?"

Those black eyes of his hypnotize me. I lift my head ever so slightly and lick the underside of his jaw. He groans, his fingers driving ruthlessly into me. I try to clamp my legs closed around his hand but he shoves my thighs open, forcing me to take it.

"What is it going to take for them to understand that you're *mine*? What more do I have to do?"

I nip at his chin, my legs beginning to quake in response to his savage claiming.

"There will always be men in this world who think they're entitled to me just because they want me. Regardless of the fact that I don't want them, that they repulse me."

Phoenix slams his palm on the desk next to me, making me jump.

"How do I protect you from them?" he demands angrily. "It took less than two fucking minutes for him to put his hands on you. What about me says, "go ahead and touch my wife"? What is it, Six? Tell me if you can see it, because I'll cut it out of me right fucking now."

I'm breathing and panting heavily, my body twisting as I search for his touch and try to avoid it in equal measure, my orgasm like a looming shadow just out of reach.

He drives inside me with a vengeance that shows his anger. Every thrust of his fingers sends me to a higher plane until stars are shooting behind my eyes and I'm clutching desperately at him.

I nip his jaw and then his lips. I taste blood from where I bit him, as unhinged for him as he is for me.

There's nothing else to say except,

"I love you," I vow, clasping his face.

A rumble rolls up his chest and falls from his mouth. "And I love you. I obsess over you. I wake up and go to sleep and live and breathe solely for *you*."

His eyes close, his arm wraps around my waist, and his fingers curl inside me. I yelp when he rubs against the sensitive spot that makes me fall apart every single time.

"Sometimes I hate how much I love you, because I can't *stand it*, watching another man touch you," he murmurs. "I haven't been able to get any work done at all. Every time I close my eyes, the only thing I can see is his hand where mine usually is, so dangerously close to your ass that the visual of it imprinted into the backs of my eyelids might still give me a fucking aneurysm."

His grip tightens painfully on my waist like he's replaying those images in his mind.

"Erase his touch," I whisper. "I don't want him on me. You're the only man I want. Make us both forget he ever touched me."

I moan discontentedly when his fingers pull out of me, yanking me back from the brink of a climax and leaving me frustrated.

He rips his shirt off, revealing the tattooed torso beneath it. Over the years, the patchwork has evolved until not a single inch of free space remains.

"I made sure he'll never touch you again, wild girl. The last thing he'll ever feel against his skin is the cold, damp soil of the shallow hole his mangled body is being dumped into as we speak."

He shoves his trousers down past his hips, wraps a hand around his cock and presses the head against my entrance. He grabs my thighs and yanks me forward until my ass hangs off the desk. Then he drives into me with one thrust.

I gulp at the sudden intrusion, at the complete and utter stretch. My head falls back between my shoulder blades as a violent shudder rips through my body.

"Nix," I gasp.

He groans loudly and scoops me up into his arms, wrapping my legs around his waist. I'm impaled impossibly deep as my back hits the bay windows and a hand closes tightly around my throat.

"Tell me no one touches you."

He drives into me savagely, pinning me against the glass with every jealous thrust.

"No one touches me."

A satisfied noise rumbles deep in his chest. He bends his head and buries it into the crook of my neck. His teeth sink into the open skin there and then he's sucking it into his mouth. He holds me up easily with one hand on my ass as the other rubs my clit in tandem with his thrusts.

"I'm going to mark you," he announces hoarsely, barely lifting his mouth from my throat. "Right along the column of this pretty neck so no one misses it."

"You can't," I pant. "My clients—"

"I don't give a fuck," he grunts. "I won't have a repeat of today. You'll be marked and you'll wear it proudly so every man who looks at you understands exactly who you belong to. And if this still doesn't send the message, then next time I'll tattoo my name right on your throat so they can't miss it." His mouth moves up to breathe his next words against the shell of my ear. "They're lucky enough that I let them look. That's a kindness I'm extending only because I can't blame those poor fuckers for staring when you're the most beautiful woman in the whole fucking world. They should get to look, to appreciate how rare your beauty is.

But that's it," he growls. "If another man touches you again Six, I'll filet him alive. I'll make every last minute of his remaining existence as painful as humanly possible and then I'll bury his body with the others."

He punctuates the final words of his sentence with deep thrusts that send my pussy into overdrive. Before I know it, I'm clawing at his back, my nails digging into his flesh as I come. My muscles clamp down on him, spasming violently as pleasure takes me over the cliff.

Phoenix pulls out only long enough to set me down and turn me to face the windows. He pins me by the neck against the glass and pushes lazily back into me, drawing out every second of my orgasm. I'm so sensitive from my climax that his reentry makes my legs shake in agonized pleasure.

"Good girl," he purrs into my hair. He looms over me. I can see our reflection in the glass, see how he stands a full head taller than me as his hands wrap around my waist and he tugs my hips back. "Look out at the city. It belongs to us. And you belong to me."

It's madness, the way he makes me feel. The way he controls my body like a switchboard, tossing me around and doing whatever he wants to me, making me hear colors and pray to new deities.

His hands come around my front to palm my breasts and tweak my nipples. I drop my head back against his chest as ragged breath after ragged breath rips from my lips.

My eyes open to find him staring down at me with a stare so full of desire and demented possessiveness, it steals the oxygen from my lungs.

He keeps staring as he pinches my clit and watches my chin tilt up, my mouth part, and my eyes roll back into my head as I come with a scream so explosive I'm sure the rest of the floor hears us.

Phoenix doesn't let it stop him. He continues thrusting madly inside my tight pussy, kissing my mouth, and grabbing at every part of my body with greedy hands, until his own face screws up and I feel his hot cum spill inside me.

He slumps forward, trapping me against the wall. I feel his heart beating manically on my back, feel the warmth of his skin on mine.

I'm so delirious with love for this man that being pressed up against each other isn't enough.

I want to be able to crawl under his skin and into his body and make myself at home there for the rest of my life.

Gentle hands pull my dress down over my ass, but not before he slaps it once sharply, simply because he can never resist doing so. He turns me around and his hands come down next to my face.

He bends and claims my mouth, sucking my bottom lip between his as he groans erotically.

When he pulls away, his gaze falls to what I know will be a large red mark on my neck, and his eyes darken with fresh lust.

I get up on my toes and close my mouth around the flesh at the base of his neck. I suckle it deeply, feeling his hands come to my ass. For long seconds, I suck at his throat like a vampire and he lets me, doing nothing except panting and moaning carnally at the contact.

Finally, I release him and come down to my feet, staring smugly up at the matching mark I've left on him.

"You're mine," I tell him.

He nods without hesitation, the words having barely left my mouth before he agrees.

"Yes." His throat works as he licks his lips. "Yes, I am. I always have been."

***

Eleven years after graduation

Chapter Twenty

Rhys

I blow my whistle loudly and the shrill, piercing sound announces the end of play.

"Alright, half time," I call. "Good job everyone."

Excited squeals meet my declaration, followed by dozens of tiny feet pounding the grass as a horde of little girls descends on me.

"Did we play well?" seven-year-old Lila asks me.

Considering she shoulder checked a five-year-old on the opposing team and sent her off the pitch and out of the match crying, the question is hard to answer.

Is she effective? Yes.

Would her approach land her a red card and multi-game ejection in a non-children's league?

Also yes.

"You played phenomenally well."

I'm met with a chorus of excited cheers from the group of girls now standing before me and staring eagerly up at me. The vast majority of them don't even reach my navel so their chaotic display of enthusiasm is reminiscent of a dozen Minions jumping up and down in celebration. Girl chat is as equally indecipherable to me as the Minion language, so the comparison tracks in more ways than one.

We're down two-nil so my dubbing their performance as "phenomenal" is also debatable, however half of the team's roster is made up of younger girls who don't even understand the concept of scoring, so I have to manage my own expectations.

One of the older girls who does understand scoring, and doesn't enjoy the feeling of losing any more than I do, is marching towards me with a stormy expression on her face.

"Don't lie to them, Daddy. We're playing terribly."

Hayes stalks past me and plops down into one of the chairs on the sideline, a pronounced pout making a home for itself on her lips.

"Go get some snacks," I say to the girls who are still waiting expectantly for me to give them their next directive. They start to disperse when I call, "And Angie! Next time number eight yanks your braid on the pitch, you kick her in the shin. Heel to your bum first and then you release your foot right into her tibia. Got it?"

"Yes, Coach," she throws excitedly over her shoulder, running towards where her mother waits for her with orange slices.

I turn towards Hayes, offering words of encouragement. "There's still a half to go."

"Another embarrassing half if we keep playing the way we have been."

The girls play in a very informal seven-and-under mixed age league that holds games every Sunday in our neighborhood park. It's meant to be a non-serious, fun way to get kids off their screens and outside more, so I both coach one of the teams *and* officiate most of the games.

No parents have complained about the obvious conflict of interest in my double role yet, and I think that's probably because they come to the park to drink seltzers and hang out with their other parent friends as much as they do to watch the actual games.

To be fair, there's very little "game" involved — most of my time is spent gesticulating on the sidelines as I try to convince the preschool-aged girls to run. If by some miracle I manage to do that, then the next step is to eventually get them to run in the right direction for the entirety of the match.

This is about as far from the Champions League as you can imagine, but it's my favorite way to spend my Sundays, especially because it's time I have with my girls.

But none of that matters to my Hayes. She's the best — or some, like Rogue, would argue the worst — of her mother and I combined. Competitive to a fault with a touch of sore loser sprinkled on top.

It's not out of a love for football specifically. Everything she undertakes, whether it's a throwaway game in a kid's league, her math homework, or trying to read books beyond her level, she does with a stubborn determination and a hatred of failure.

She's studious and focused and I think when she grows older, instead of grounding her for catching her sneaking out at night, her mum and I will have to beg her to close her books and go to a party instead.

"We can come back from being down two-nil, Cloud."

Her features soften at the nickname. Hayes has beautiful, broody gray eyes, like a troubled sky after an afternoon of heavy rain, hence the moniker.

"Not if we score on ourselves again."

I sigh internally.

Yes, that really did happen.

Unfortunately, but quite hysterically, we're averaging about one goal scored on our own goalie per every three games we play, no matter how much I scream and wave my arms at them from the sidelines to turn around and go the other way. That can be frustrating for the older girls, but Hayes is always careful not to call out specific players.

Whichever little girl is the goal scorer is always thrilled at having put one in the net and comes running towards me for a high five, one I'm only too happy to give out because their little faces are so excited.

The own goals happen often enough that the *Daily Mail* even ran a piece about it with a front-page cover. Slow news day or not, coaching this little league may be severely hampering my chances of ever getting a legitimate professional coaching job once I retire as a player.

"Comeback victories taste the sweetest, little cloud. Believe me. We have something to play for and they don't," I tell her, coaching her like I would if this was a World Cup Final. "Now where's your sister?"

I turn and scan the pitch only to find my youngest crouching in the low grass, still in the middle of the pitch and seemingly unaware that halftime has started, her tiny hands plucking flowers out of the ground.

As much as Hayes's dismay is unsurprising, so is Ivy's disinterest. She's far more interested in examining the flora on the pitch than she is in touching the ball, for example. The number of times I've seen it fly

166

past her while she picked a dandelion or a daisy has done numbers on my blood pressure.

"Bow!" Ivy turns and gives me a brilliant, semi-toothless smile. "Come eat something."

"Okay, Daddy!" she calls, and then she's running towards me with all the uncoordinated excellence of a five-year-old.

I scoop her and the flowers she still holds clutched firmly in her fist into my arms and kiss her cheek. "Find anything good?"

"Look at this one," she says, showing me a purple flower as I settle her into a second foldable chair next to her sister.

"Very pretty," I say. "Not as pretty as you though."

She giggles, staring wide eyed at the petals. "Can I have hair this color?"

"Of course you can. Whatever color you want, Bow."

Since she's been old enough to start showing signs of her own personality, Ivy's had a fixation with bright colors. She shuns anything gray or black when it comes to clothing, she picked fuchsia as the wall color for her bedroom, and the drawings that come home with her from school use every single marker in the box and then some, earning her the nickname 'Rainbow'.

Over the years, 'Rainbow' became the diminutive 'Bow', and 'Raincloud' became 'Cloud'.

"Isn't she a little young to be dyeing her hair?" someone inquires.

I turn towards the snooty voice of the stranger and find a woman with thin lips and even thinner mental abilities, if the obvious judgment in her tone is anything to go by.

Straightening to my full height, I glare at her.

"Jog on, lady. No one asked you," I bark crisply.

"She can do whatever she wants," Hayes adds, ever her baby sister's defender.

The woman pales, not at my daughter's words but at recognizing who I am.

"I'm s-sorry," she mutters before slithering away.

"I can't change my hair?" Ivy asks with a devastating lip tremble that makes me want to go after the woman and force her to apologize.

"Of course you can, bow." Crouching, I cup her chubby cheeks and rub my nose against hers, making her giggle. "You're your mother's daughter. You were born to have different colored hair," I add, running my fingers through her messy blonde locks.

"What are we talking about?"

This voice, I welcome with a huge fucking grin. Standing and spinning around, I find my wife looking up at me with a smile tugging at her lips.

I'm reaching for and kissing her in the same breath, indifferent to the dozens of watching eyes I know are on us. A picture of this moment will be in the papers tomorrow, but I don't care. In fact, I welcome the press acting as my own personal megaphone to broadcast to the nation just how obsessed I am with my wife.

"Hi, Silver," I say huskily, pulling away but keeping her close to hide my now obvious erection, a terrible thing to be sporting at this particular event.

"Hi, Mackley," she answers, equally breathless.

I hear the girls call for her from behind me, but I ignore them. A displeased rumble sounds in my chest instead.

"You know how I feel about you calling me that," I warn.

She laughs, the sound as clear as a bell.

"Even now?"

"Even now," I confirm. "The only time you should say our name is when you're introducing yourself or the girls. But I don't want you calling me that."

It reminds me of a time when Thayer would refuse to say my name, all in an effort to keep her emotional distance from me.

No such distance is allowed now or ever again.

She strokes the hair away from my face, her eyes softening as she touches me. "Yes, Rhys."

"Better." I smack a kiss on her lips. "How was Pilates?"

"Exhausting and fun. How's the game?"

"We're down two-nil."

"Ouch. Hayes must be thrilled."

"Ding ding ding."

"And Ivy?"

"Well she hasn't touched the ball once, but she's picked quite the special bouquet of flowers."

Thayer laughs again. The sound slides beneath my skin and goes straight to the organ in my chest. She tilts her head and looks past my arm and over to our daughters.

"Hey, girls," she calls warmly.

"Mummy!" Hayes gets up and grabs her hand, pulling her over to her chair. "We're down two."

"I heard, baby."

"What if we lose?" she asks anxiously.

"What if you win?" Thayer challenges. "Think of what's possible and try to reach for that. Plus, those are the best victories because you really earn them," she adds, unknowingly echoing my words.

God, I fucking love her.

"Okay," Hayes says, fresh determination etching itself on her face. "I just need to get better at dribbling, I think."

"Your Mum can teach you, Cloud. She's always had superior ball handling skills, even to this day."

"Rhys," Thayer cuts in, her eyes narrowing on me even as she fails to hide the mirth in them.

"What?" I ask innocently.

"Don't be cheeky." She turns towards our other daughter. "What about you Ivy Bell? Are you trying to win?"

"Whatever Hazy wants," she answers, using her nickname for her sister. She thrusts her small flowers into her mum's face. "Daddy said I could change my hair color like this."

Thayer sits on the ground in between her daughters, her back to me. Her silver hair is tied in a ponytail, so I can clearly see that she's wearing yet another t-shirt with our last name printed on it.

"That's a great idea," she answers, immediately on board. "We can get some dye from *Boots* on the way home. Which color are you thinking?"

As half-time draws to an end, the three of them whisper and plot what color they'll dye Ivy's hair when the match is over.

"Alright, girls," I boom, drawing all the players' attention back over to me. "Second half starts in two minutes." The girls leave their parents and start running past me and onto the field as I shout directions. "Carla, I want your eyes glued to the pitch. No watching for planes in the sky, I promise you they'll still be up there when we're done. Ivy, no stopping to pick flowers unless play itself is stopped. Your goal is to touch the ball at least once this half. Bruna, I understand the impulse, I really do, but you can't just pick up the ball and run with it towards the goal, you have to use your feet. Lucie. *Lucie*! No eating on the pitch, for fuc— I mean, go throw those fruit snacks onto the sidelines, please. And Angie, remember what I said — we're kicking shins this half. I want to see explosiveness with those kicks, alright? Now let's go and win this match, girls!"

Fifteen minutes later, the second half is over and the match ends in a draw, which I consider a win. Hayes comes up big, as does a girl on the other team, both of them scoring a goal in our favor.

Thayer is the loudest supporter on our side, cheering and screaming from the sidelines and running onto the pitch to hug Hayes when she scores. I'm only too happy to have to go tell my wife to get back on the sidelines so play can continue.

***

That night, we put both of the girls to bed in Hayes's room, Ivy opting to sleep with her big sister as she so often does. Her freshly dyed lavender-colored locks shine against the white of the pillowcase beneath her head as I sit on the bed and tuck them in.

"Great job today, girls."

"Soccer is fun!" Ivy calls, pumping up a fist.

Thayer smothers a laugh when I glare at her.

"*Football*, love. Don't let your mother Americanize you on this subject. Your Daddy plays for the national team, you have to call it football."

"Alright, Daddy. Can we come see you at a game soon?" Hayes asks.

"Of course, little cloud. Whenever you want. How about tomorrow?"

"It's a school night, Rhys," Thayer chides.

"Please, Mummy?" Hayes asks, widening those depthless eyes of hers. Thayer is as powerless to resist as I am.

She mollifies, whispering, "Just this once then."

"Yay!"

"Alright, girls. Time for bed." I lean over and kiss both their foreheads. "What are our mantras?"

"I am brave," the girls answer in unison. "I am smart."

"I am special," Hayes says.

Thayer and I speak the words along with them, the same words we say every night before turning off the lights and leaving them to their dreams. We're raising our girls to be confident in knowing how special they are so that no one ever makes them feel less than.

"I am kind," Ivy adds.

"I am beautiful," they say together. "I am compassionate." The word gets garbled by Ivy's missing baby teeth. "I am…"

They falter, both of them momentarily forgetting the next part as their eyes flutter shut, heavy with sleep.

"I am fearless," Thayer and I fill in for them.

"I am fearless," they repeat.

"And?" I prompt.

Thayer rolls her eyes.

"And no boy will ever deserve the air I breathe or the ground I walk on," they parrot back to me.

"Keep going," I say with an encouraging move of my hand.

"And if ever one of them is mean to me or tries something on with me, my Daddy will kill them and bury them in an unsparked grave," they crow back happily as I mouth the words alongside them.

"*Unmarked* grave," I correct, adding with a proud smile to my wife, "That's my girls."

"You're incorrigible."

She shakes her head but her words carry no heat.

"Goodnight, darlings," she says, bending to kiss each of their cheeks.

"Night, Mummy."

I give Ivy an Eskimo kiss. "Goodnight, little bow."

She giggles. "Night, Daddy."

Leaning over her, I give Hayes a butterfly kiss. "Goodnight, little cloud."

She cups my face and kisses my cheek. "*Bonne nuit,* Daddy." She's been learning French at daycare to surprise her aunt Six and likes to practice when she can.

"Love you," I call, as I put an arm around Thayer's shoulders and turn the light off with my other hand.

"Love you, Daddy," they answer together. It's immediately followed by the sound of them burrowing deeper into their beds.

Thayer and I leave their room, closing the door softly behind us.

"Those two are Daddy's little girls through and through," she says, hooking her arms around my neck.

I hoist her into mine, wrapping her legs around my waist. "Definitely. But why don't I remind you who my favorite girl is?"

She laughs as I carry her into our bedroom and kick the door closed behind us.

***

Twelve years after graduation

Chapter Twenty-One

Rogue

I get out of the car and walk over to the other side to open the curbside door. A pair of legs appears, followed immediately by a body as Suki jumps out. Ivy emerges next, then Astra, all three of them wrapped in pink tutus as they hit the pavement.

"Thanks, Uncle Roro."

I grunt in acknowledgement and close the door behind them. Crossing the sidewalk, I open the door to *Fantasy Froyo* next, holding it open as they walk past in a single file line.

With military-like precision, they disperse once in the shop, each of them going to stand in front of different dispensers as they consider which flavor of froyo they're getting this time.

This all started one random Saturday in June a year ago. Sixtine was called in for an emergency at work and Phoenix was out of town so neither one of them could go pick up the girls from their ballet class as they typically did.

Six had tried calling Nera who was sick, then Thayer who didn't answer because she was at Pilates, then Bellamy who was so hungover from a dinner we'd had the previous evening that she didn't feel comfortable driving.

With all three of them out of commission, the task had fallen to me to get the girls.

Being suddenly saddled with three excitable five-year-olds, an overflowing amount of tulle and no idea how to handle speaking to this particular demographic—especially when they traveled in a pack formation—I'd been at a loss for what to do with them.

My solution had been to take them for post-ballet froyo, hoping that a sweet treat would distract them until Six made it home. Instead, I'd found myself sitting on one side of a table, faced with the three of them on the other, being pelted with rapid-fire questions ranging from "why are boys stinky?" to "is Santa real?"

Not famed for my tact in handling delicate situations that might shatter childhood illusions, I'd skirted the Santa question and instead focused my diatribe on much safer territory — why boys sucked and should be avoided at all costs.

I'd been met with expressions ranging from solemn to thoughtful, all of them listening intently to what I was saying like I was imparting philosophical wisdom the likes of which Europe hadn't seen since the days of ancient Greece.

When Six had called me that night, I'd expected and had been poised for the verbal lashing of the century.

Instead, she told me the girls had rebaptized me "Uncle Roro" and that they deemed me "cool".

Prior to that phone call, if you'd asked me how much time I spent thinking about getting the approval of three five-year-old girls, my answer would have been zero. Now it occupies an inordinate amount of my brain power. Bellamy likes to joke that I'm like a politician checking polling data in the run up to my election.

Rain or shine, post-ballet froyo has been a tradition since. I pick them up every Saturday, watch them spend an ungodly amount of time debating which flavor they should get before they inevitably pick the same one they always do, and then we gossip.

Those three are inseparable, their bond as strong as their mothers' and I rue the day they're unleashed on the world as fully blown adults.

They'll likely bring it to its knees.

"What's it going to be this time?" I ask Astra. She always gets a plain yogurt base and a million toppings.

"Maybe mint chocolate?"

I scoff. "Abysmal flavor combination. Only wankers like mint chocolate."

"My Daddy loves mint chocolate, Uncle Roro."

I pinch her cheek. "You're not exactly disproving my point, princess."

A line appears between her brows just as I walk over to Ivy.

"Can I get chocolate sprinkles on top?" she asks.

"You can get whatever you want. Are you getting strawberry froyo?"

Her mouth drops. "How did you know?"

I've only watched her order it sixty-one times.

"Lucky guess."

Suki walks up to me with a cup in each hand. "Smores for me." Handing me the second, "And peanut butter for you."

The girls alternate picking my flavor for me every week.

"Great choice."

She heads to the till and pulls out a pint-sized wallet. Following, I ask, "What do you think you're doing?"

"We're buying you froyo this time, Uncle Roro. With our pocket money," she announces proudly.

I snatch the bill out of her hand before the cashier can grab it. "I don't think so. Put this back in your wallet."

"But—"

"Instead of buying me froyo, why don't you tell me if that little bitch Sarah is still being a cunt?" The cashier gasps at my word choice. I shove my black card her way to shut her up. "Piss off."

Sarah is a girl in their ballet class. When I'd picked them up last week, Astra had been in tears because Sarah The Cunt had thought it a funny prank to hide my goddaughter's tutu.

Her parents' home address has been imprinted in the back of my eyelids since, waiting only for a greenlight from the girls for me to pay them a little visit.

"Uncle Roro," she giggles. "You can't say that."

I take my card back with a glare to the nosy cashier and usher the three of them out onto a patio and to one of the tables. "Why not?"

"Mum says it's a bad word," Astra answers.

"Your mum is too stuck up sometimes."

"Hey, that's mean."

I shrug. "Anyway, I can say it when she's messing with my favorite girl."

Astra gives me a delighted smile, my slight against her mother easily forgotten. "You're so silly."

"I spilled cranberry juice on her tutu when no one was looking," Suki says easily, scooping some froyo into her mouth, "So she was too busy crying to be messing with Astra."

"Now that's what I like to hear," I praise her. "Initiative. Revenge. Creative retribution approach. I love it. Very well done. What else?"

"Hmm, I stuck my gum under her shoe."

"Excellent. If you sneak in a pair of scissors, next time you can cut a big hole in her tutu."

Suki's eyes widen. "Oooh."

Froyo time isn't just fun and games. The girls learn valuable, real-world lessons and advice from their Uncle Roro.

"We look after each other," Ivy says proudly. "We'll look after Rowan when she's old enough too, don't you worry."

The heat that powers through my veins at the mention of my daughter's name nearly burns me alive from the inside.

She's three now, with a head of jet-black hair and green eyes, and spends her time running into things or tripping over them in ways that get more comical with every passing day. To say that I'm obsessed is an understatement.

And I'm not the only one.

"She's already well protected. I don't think her three brothers are going to let anything happen to her."

"Yes, but they can't be everywhere. We're girls. We can."

A very valid point I'd never even considered. I look over at the girls where they sit on their side of the table like their very own little council of elders dispensing advice to me.

"She's the youngest with Hana, so she needs us," Suki adds.

"You're right." I nod thoughtfully. "You'll tell me if Sarah gives you any more trouble?"

"What are you going to do if she does?" Ivy asks.

I smile innocently. I think it comes out as a grimace. "Talk to her."

"Mummy says it's bad to lie," Suki points out.

"I'm not lying. There'll be *some* talking involved."

Astra gives me a look that says she doesn't believe me while Suki gives me one that says she can protect her friend if it comes to it.

"Anyway, how's Rhodes? I, uh, haven't seen him in a while," Astra adds conversationally.

That piques my interest. "Why are you asking?"

Her gaze flicks over to Ivy who flushes tomato red. Color explodes on her cheeks, contrasting with the currently pale green hue of her hair.

"Just wondering," Suki interjects. "So, uh, how's everyone's froyo?"

"Strawberry is so good. I'll definitely change it up next week though."

That's what Ivy says every week and she always sticks faithfully by her favorite flavor. We continue eating and talking, the girls giggling and telling me the latest about their fellow classmates.

The information I gather during these froyo sessions rivals the kind CIA operatives spend years in deep cover to get. I file it all away for later, not missing a single morsel.

Not even how they asked about my oldest son before smoothly changing the conversation.

***

I've parked the car in our ten-space garage but am still sitting behind the wheel when the door opens and Rhodes bursts in.

His gaze moves swiftly over the cars and lands on me in the front seat of the Range.

He makes his way over to me, glancing with affected nonchalance into the back seat. The windows are tinted so he can't see through them, but he tries his best, squinting like an old man.

"What are you doing?" I ask, intrigued.

"Are you…" he clears his throat. "Did you drop them off back home already?"

"Obviously. Did you think I was bringing them here for a sleepover?"

Rhodes's ears turn a light shade of pink and his lips thin into a straight line.

Interesting.

"No," he mumbles.

I get out and shut the door, locking the car behind me with a loud double beep. "Anyone in particular you wanted to speak to?"

His ears go pinker. "No."

He turns on his heels and walks back down the garage and away from me before I speak again.

"Not even Ivy?"

That stops him. My six-year-old son stiffens and spins back around to face me. "Can I keep her, Dad?"

I laugh at his blunt word choice, caught off guard by the contradiction of his youth and the vehemence in his tone. He misunderstands my reaction and looks like he's about to cry, clearly thinking I'm making fun of him.

He's started to run away when I stop him.

"Rhodes, wait." I walk up to him and place a hand on his shoulder, thinking through what to say to him. I'm not exactly one to encourage restraint. "You can't keep her just yet," I tell him honestly.

"Why not?"

The question is asked so earnestly, my stomach pinches. It's clear my son doesn't understand why he's not allowed to keep Ivy when he likes her.

It's so simple to him.

"When you're older and assuming you still feel the same way, *then* you can keep her."

His brow furrows, his expression confused and uncomprehending as to why it can't happen *now*. He gets his impatience from me.

"I will still feel the same way," he vows, determination etched on his features. "Why do I not get to keep her now?"

"You're too young. You don't know if you really like her just yet."

"Uncle Nix knew with Aunt Six," he counters.

The twerp may be young, but he's inherited my debating skills. The lad is six going on sixteen.

I already know that Bell and I are going to have our work cut out for us with this one.

"That's true," I acquiesce. "That's how you feel?"

He nods vigorously. "She's cool, Dad. She likes bugs, and not the lame ones like other people pretend. Snails and cockroaches and even snakes. And I like her hair. She's not like other girls."

I bite back a laugh at the list of criteria he's identified that make Ivy a match for him. I'm about to try to dissuade him again but then I look down at his face. At the determined and stubborn expression on his features. The very same I see reflected on my own face every single day.

He's mine. Me in every way, except maybe worse because his obsession has already started. If it's anything like the one I have with his mother, then there's no changing his mind or stopping him.

"Then hold onto her tight and make sure you never let her go."

He nods, his expression more serious than a six-year-old's should be. "That's what I'm going to do."

I ruffle his hair affectionately. "Where are your siblings and your mother?"

"Inside. Mummy is making Lebanese food for dinner."

After being together for almost fourteen years, you'd think my reaction to my wife would have dulled by now. If anything, the heat that blows through my chest is hotter than ever, carried forward by obsession and possession. I'm sure Rhodes accidentally spilled the beans and Bell meant to surprise me by cooking food from my mum's country. She does it every so often, always upping herself from the previous time by learning new, more complicated dishes.

It's her way of keeping me connected to my mum. It's her way of showing love and unwavering support, exactly as she has since we first met. I'll never understand what I did to deserve her, but I won't question it either.

"Did you know your Mum is the best person in the entire world?"

"Yes," he answers proudly. "You're not ever letting her go right?" he asks, echoing the words I just said to him back to me.

"I decided to keep your mum a long, long time ago." Crouching so we're eye to eye, I grab his shoulders and whisper vehemently, "I'm *never* letting her go."

Rhodes smiles, showing me the many gaps where adult teeth are still growing in. "Me neither."

"Go inside and tell her I'll be right there. I just need to finish one thing quickly."

He does as he's told, skipping back into the house as I pull out my phone and text the lads.

Rogue: Rhys, my son just informed me that he wants to keep your daughter.

Rhys: I don't even need to ask which of your degenerate offspring is interested in which of my angelic daughters, I already know.

Rhys: Interest declined.

Rhys: He's been a menace since the day he was born and he will be dealt with.

Rogue: Do you think threatening my son is a good idea?

Phoenix: Rogue, what did you say when he told you that?

Rogue: That he couldn't.

Rogue: Not yet.

Rhys: Not ever!

Tristan: Has Rhodes considered that Ivy might not even want him back?

Rogue: Why wouldn't she?

Tristan: Sigh.

Phoenix: Maybe because — and I know this is going to be hard for you to hear, let alone understand — you and your sons are not God's gift to the Earth.

Rogue: Says who?

Rhys: Oh, for fuck's sake.

Rhys: Says me.

Rhys: And Ivy.

Rhys: Not that it matters because they're too young to even be discussing this, but she won't be interested in him.

Rhys: I won't let her be.

Rhys: She'll say no.

Rogue: Can you stop blowing up my phone like a preteen girl? You text the way a rabbit shits; a lot, all at once. It's embarrassing.

Rogue: And if we'd each listened to what our wives wanted in secondary school, the four of us would still be single.

Tristan: True.

Phoenix: Not me *smirking emoji*

Phoenix: Six always loved me.

Rogue: Rhodes actually brought you two up as the reason he knows Ivy is his.

Phoenix: Fuck.

Phoenix: Sorry, Rhys.

Rhys: Don't say it.

Phoenix: I have to. I think I ship Rhodes and Ivy now.

Rhys: Traitor.

Rhys: I'll remember this when it's your turn.

Phoenix: There won't be a 'my turn' because Astra is never leaving the house.

Rhys: Lol good luck with that plan.

Rhys: Tristan? Have my back here.

Tristan: I'm staying out of it.

Tristan: But no one bulldozed past more nos from their wife than me, so…

Rhys: Wankers, the lot of you.

Rhys: Mark my words, I'll get myself transferred overseas.

Rhys: I'll leave Arsenal if it means keeping your son away from my daughter.

Smirking down at my phone, I type out one final text.

Rogue: Do it. Make it a bit harder for him, it'll be more entertaining for us to watch.

***

Thirteen years after graduation

Chapter Twenty-Two

Tristan

"Kids," I bellow into the intercom service that connects the different levels and wings of the house. "Dinner's ready."

No answer comes through the line, but I hear the movement of bodies and the shuffling of feet as the children make their way down towards the kitchen.

Kiza appears first. She walks up to me where I'm standing at the stove and wraps her arms around my waist, burrowing her face into my back.

"Hi, Dad," she says, voice muffled against me.

Earlier this year, she started calling me 'Dad' instead of 'Daddy', telling me that only kids called their fathers that and proudly announcing that she wasn't a kid anymore.

Plunging a knife six inches deep into my chest might have been less painful, but I'd simply smiled, said 'okay', and kissed her forehead.

It felt like my little girl grew up overnight. Even though I knew it was a natural part of her getting older, I feared it meant that we'd lose the special connection that had always made us close.

I was thrilled to find nothing else changed, her hugs the moment I come home still as tight as they always were. Those hugs mean the world to me.

"Hi, sweet girl." I turn and drop a kiss on her forehead. "How was your day?"

"Great." She grabs one of the plates and brings it to the dining table as Cato walks in carrying Hana.

"Hey, Dad."

"Hey, little man. Missed you." I ruffle his hair then bend so I'm eye level with my youngest child. "And missed *you*, little darling."

Hana launches herself into my arms with a delighted laugh. I press a thousand kisses to her cheeks, then place her on my hip and go back to the stove, stirring the bacon so it doesn't burn.

Plating two more sandwiches, I hand them to Cato who follows Kiza into the dining room.

Suki and Juno walk in together, bickering loudly and the latter in tears.

"What's wrong, bud?"

"S-she t-took my caaar," he stutters through thick sobs, pointing an accusing finger.

"It's *my* car."

"No, it's not!" he roars, hitting her arm.

Just last month, we opened a new restaurant in Florence. I'd handled the entire process remotely, from design to build to the opening, pushing off having to travel there as much as possible since I didn't want to be separated from my family.

I finally had to make a trip out for an investors' meeting and had kept the visit short, only spending one night — last night — away from my wife and kids.

As always, it'd felt like an eternity.

Being back in the chaos of a full house of five bickering kids might be overwhelming to some — if not most — but it's heaven to me.

"Su, give your brother back his toy. You can have it after dinner. Juno, don't hit your sister."

"Not fair, Daddy," she pouts, handing him the toy anyway.

"You'll get your turn." I set Hana down and place her hand in Juno's. "Take your sister to the table please."

He leaves and I crouch in front of Suki who turns her head away. I love my children equally but there's something about my middle daughter; she has me completely wrapped around her little finger.

It might have to do with the five beauty marks on her nose and cheeks, the exact same ones that dust Nera's face. Like with her mother before her, I'm powerless to resist them.

"Su," I coax.

I smile when she refuses to look at me. Stubborn, that one. Gets it from her mother.

Reaching into my pocket, I pull out a Bacci chocolate and hide it in one of my fists. Holding them both up in front of her, I say, "Pick one."

Unable to resist the prospect of a present, she glances at my hands, then taps my left fist. I turn it over and spread out my fingers, revealing the chocolate snuggly held in my palm.

She grabs it with greedy fingers and throws her arms around my neck. "Thanks, Daddy!"

I wrap her in a big hug. "Missed you, lovebug."

"Me too," she answers, cheek against my chest.

"Grab your plate and go sit down. I'll be right there."

"Okay," she answers happily, storing the chocolate in her pocket for later.

I turn off the stove and finish plating the last two sandwiches, then head into the dining room where I find my kids and my wife sitting around the table, waiting for me.

"Eat, eat," I order. "It's better warm." I place a plate in front of Nera and bend to capture her lips. "Dinner for my beautiful wife."

She cups my neck, her dark eyes shining as she looks up at me. "Thank you, baby."

"I made us something special tonight. I wonder if you'll remember it."

She glances down at the plate and her hand tightens on me. Her gaze flicks back up to mine. "Is this the BLT you made me when we were first dating?"

I nod, humming, and add, "Technically we weren't dating yet. Mummy made me work for it, kiddos," I say to them as they look on at us, biting silently into their sandwiches. "Daddy suffered. Girls, take notes."

186

Cato and Kiza, who are both old enough to start asking difficult questions look at each other and then the latter asks, "How did you meet?"

"Um..."

"Uhhhh," I say, laughing uncomfortably as I meet Nera's panicked eyes. Bending so my next words are whispered against the shell of her ear, I add, "I guess we haven't discussed how we answer that question."

"I didn't even think about the fact that it would come up one day," she whispers back. "We can't tell them I slept with my professor."

"Or that I slept with my student. They'll think you're a daredevil, but they'll think *I'm* a predator."

She chews her lower lip, pulling my attention from the issue at hand and to her very delectable mouth. I imagine those very same lips wrapped around my cock tonight once the kids are in bed. I imagine them parted in pleasure as I sink into h—

She snaps her fingers, her eyes widening. "We met in a bar," she offers in a whisper. "Technically not a lie, right?"

"Brilliant. Aligned."

Nera turns towards Kiza and gives her the same answer. Thankfully, our daughter only nods thoughtfully and takes another bite of her sandwich.

I'm about to breathe a sigh of relief and sit down, when Cato speaks next.

"Daddy, what's a MILF?"

Silence descends on the room. I freeze, certain that I've misheard him. Nera's eyes bulge, her hand flying to her mouth.

Turning my head slowly towards my eldest, I try to keep a rein on the disbelief coursing through me.

"I beg your pardon?"

"What's a MILF?" he repeats, seemingly unaware of how my eyelid twitches.

I'd rather face a hundred more questions about how his mother and I met and started dating than wondering for a moment longer about why Cato knows the existence of the word MILF.

He can only have heard it spoken in one context and that context makes me want to put my fist through a wall.

"Where did you hear that word?"

Nera's hand tightens around mine, squeezing my palm to settle me down when she hears my throttled tone.

"Stephen's older brother Justin said it at school the other day. When Mum came to pick us up, he said a bad word and then he said she was a 'Hall of Fame-worthy MILF'." He frowns and scrunches his nose, his expression confused. "What is that? Does that mean she's on time for pickup? Because his mum wasn't there yet."

Beside me, I hear Nera choke back a laugh.

A vein throbs dangerously in my temple, my heartbeat strangled within its walls. It feels so close to bursting that I have to take deep, steadying breaths to keep from passing out.

My fist closes tightly around the back of Nera's chair. The wood screams its distress in response.

"Tell me," I ask, my tone pleasant. "Where does Justin live?"

Correctly interpreting my underlying tone, Nera places a hand on my forearm. "Tristan, no."

The thought that some thirteen-year-old ogled my wife and called her a *Hall of Fame-worthy MILF* to his friends, to my *son*, makes me want to reinstate the lost art of drawing and quartering people in public.

"Can you get me his address, Cato?"

"Sure, I mean, it's where Stephen lives. So, 97 Stu—"

Nera interjects, speaking over him so I miss the street name. "That's great, darling, thank you. Tristan, a word in the kitchen?"

She stands, forcing me to release my grip on her chair to let her pass, and walks back to the kitchen.

"Keep eating," I instruct, following after her.

I'm on her before she's even fully turned around, a surprised gasp ripping from her lips. Trapping her against the island, I bury my face in her neck and suck at her throat like a vampire.

She moans loudly, then slaps a hand over her mouth to muffle the sound. "What are you doing?" she whispers distractedly.

I maul her like an animal, capturing the skin between my lips and suckling at it.

"Not only are the fathers at school ogling you, but now so are their preteen boys?" I mutter angrily against her neck. "That's fucking bullshit."

Nera cups the back of my neck, shoving my face deeper into her throat instead of pushing me away. "I think it's a compliment."

"It means Mum I'd Like to Fuck," I churn out.

"Y-yes," she breathes.

"I'm the only one who fucks you. The only one who should even *think* about fucking you."

Not a question, not even a demand. Just a fact.

She knows it so she doesn't answer.

I suck and bite viciously at her skin until it's red and raw. Lapping at it soothingly with my tongue, I growl as I revel in the way I've marked her.

"Wear your hair up when you pick up the kids tomorrow."

This time it is an order.

"Make sure they see these." I trace the red traces with my thumb. "I want everyone talking. All the mums whispering and gossiping about it. All the dads jealous that I get to own you. *Everyone.*"

I slam my mouth down on hers, stealing the breath from her lips. Pushing her up onto the counter, I spread her legs and nestle myself between them, rubbing my hard cock against her center. I fist her hair and control the speed, intensity, and violence of the kiss.

Nera must sense I'm seconds away from ripping her clothes off because she places a hand on my chest and pushes me back softly, panting for breath.

"We can't. The kids. If you fuck me here, we're going to have to answer a lot more questions than we're ready for."

I groan in frustration and drop my forehead to hers.

"Fine." I breathe heavily, my chest rising and falling with every ragged inhale and exhale. "But I want you naked and on your knees for me the second they're in bed."

She licks my lips teasingly so I smack her ass in warning. Her eyes turn heavy.

"I can do that," she whispers coyly.

"Careful," I warn. "I only have so much control."

She grins. "I know."

I purr contentedly. "You really are a MILF. But for my eyes only."

Running her hand through my hair, she asks. "What are you going to tell Cato it means?"

"Mum who's In Love with Fencing," I grumble.

She bursts out laughing, my favorite sound in the world. "That doesn't exactly line up."

"It's the best I can do on such short notice."

She presses a kiss to my lips. "You're ridiculous and I love you."

"Fuck, I hope you do. Because I'm never going to love anyone else the way I love you."

***

The following week, I'm in my study when I hear Nera come home with the kids. The sound of her making them a snack is followed by that of her feet on the stairs as she comes to me.

Dropping my head back against my chair, I watch as my wife walks in. She's wearing fashionable grey linen trousers with a built-in flap that falls just above mid-thigh and a tight black halter top. Her hair is piled high on her head, her eyes framed by mascara and her lips darkened with red lipstick. Small gold hoops complete the look.

"Hey, baby," I call out.

She crosses the room and comes to my side of the desk. Resting her hips against the edge, she bends and presses a quick kiss to my lips, brushing the lipstick off my mouth with her thumb.

"Hi," she says, then straightens and crosses her arms. "Anything you want to tell me?"

"Not specifically, no."

"I ran into Stephen's parents during pickup today." She quirks a brow when my expression remains stoic. "Tell me why they informed me they've suddenly and unexpectedly decided to send him and his brother to boarding school in the United States?"

I put on my best surprised expression, although I'd have better luck trying to sell her sand in the desert than getting her to buy my innocence.

"Not sure. That being said, I commend them for their decision. I think it's a wonderful idea. Justin, specifically, might learn a thing or two while he's there."

"Tristan."

"In fact, he might have been heartily encouraged to learn a thing or two before ever setting foot back here."

"You banished a thirteen-year-old because he called me a MILF?"

"I didn't do a thing," I say innocently. "His parents made a great decision based on empirical facts that may or may not have been presented to them by a concerned third party."

She shakes her head but a smile tugs at her lips. "And what are you going to do when Cato goes to secondary school? Assuming we send him to RCA, you remember what it was like there. You know how teenage boys are. The hormones. What are you going to do then?"

"Plenty of open spots at that American boarding school. Justin will enjoy having friends with common interests, I'm sure."

***

Fourteen years after graduation

Chapter Twenty-Three

Sixtine

Opening the door and pushing aside the flap that keeps the heat inside, I duct my head and walk into the glamping-style tent we have set up in our backyard.

"Here you go, *ma chérie*," I say, handing Astra a steaming cup of hot cocoa. "Be careful, it's very hot. Blow on it before taking a sip."

Astra reaches for the mug with small, excited hands and blows at the steam as instructed, a large smile stretching across her face. "*Merci, Maman.*"

Like my parents did with me, Phoenix and I are raising Astra in a bicultural household. Even though she's never lived in France, she's completely fluent and embraces her Frenchness as much as I do, much to my own Mum's delight.

It helps that her dad is fluent as well. I found out when I was in the hospital after an allergic reaction to peanut oil. I had witnessed Phoenix conversing easily back and forth with the nurse. It's only later that he told me he spent years learning it as a way to stay close to me when he couldn't keep me out of his head.

He's always been that way; as secretive and quiet in his obsession with me as some of his friends are loud and boastful with their wives. Phoenix has given me more than I could ever dream of over the years, but the best thing by far is the ability to raise our daughter in the language of my heart. I didn't realize the significance of that gift until she was here and the words of love that came most naturally to me were in French.

"Are you comfortable?" I ask her, fluffing the pillows behind her before motioning for her to lie back down.

"Yes. Are you?"

I snuggle in beside her and bring the thick down blanket up to cover us both.

"Very. Only one thing is missing…" I reach for my mug and bring it up to my lips, taking a hearty sip of the rich cocoa and humming appreciatively. *"Parfait."*

She giggles happily and burrows into the crook of my arm as we both look up towards the heavens. Astra has been obsessed with stars since she was two when she was first gifted a coloring book of the galaxy. It might have been spurred by the origins of her name or the fact that her father and I talk to her about the stars, but her obsession has grown independently since.

For her eighth birthday last weekend, we rented out the Royal Observatory and had two astronauts attend in full costume. She'd watched and listened to them with wide-eyed astonishment, barely moving from her spot for the two hours they were there.

Later that night, she came to our room and announced that she was going to be the first woman to walk on the Moon.

As a present, Phoenix had this tent custom made for her. It's your classic rigid structure with a few notable upgrades; namely, built-in heating to ward off the cold and a translucent ceiling for optimal stargazing.

The day after her party, Phoenix had to leave on a business trip with my dad. He'll only be back tonight, so he had a specialized team come over this afternoon to set the tent up for our first night outside.

I'm not sure who was most blown away when we first set foot in the tent, me or Astra. Phoenix went above and beyond in setting up the coziest sleepover possible, featuring hundreds of individual star nightlights, a massive fluffy mattress with an overabundance of pillows and throw blankets, a mountain of snacks, and even a telescope.

"When is Daddy coming home?"

I look down at my watch. "Soon. He should have landed already."

"I hope I'm still awake," she says dreamily.

"Don't worry, *chérie*, he'll wake you up if you're asleep."

Astra has her dad wrapped around her little finger. He's more protective of her than he is of me, if that's even possible, and it's only getting more pronounced as she starts to approach the age Astor was when he died.

She looks a lot like him.

While Phoenix and Astor were twins, they were also complete opposites in coloring. The former is dark haired with equally black eyes whereas the latter was fair haired with blue eyes.

Astra inherited Astor's exact hair, a deep golden color that shines brightly in the sun with red undertones she got from me. Her face has his same shape and the dimples she flashes at anyone who's earned her smile are the ghost of his.

She's as beautiful as he was.

There are times I've had to do a double take when glancing at her because she looks so much like Astor, so I can't imagine what it must be like for Phoenix. Sometimes I catch him staring at her while she's playing in the back fields of our country house and I know he's seeing his brother running through those same footsteps.

The only major difference in her features from Astor's are her eyes. I like to believe they couldn't decide which brothers' color to go with so they decided to split and represent them both. Her right eye is black, as obsidian as her father's, while her left eye is light blue.

The heterochromia is at once stunning and startling, making most people do a double take when they look at her. She's gotten used to it over the years but I fear it'll get more pronounced as she grows older and starts to attract attention of a different kind.

I swallow a choked laugh at the thought of her bringing a boyfriend home. Her father is going to have a coronary the second she mentions a boy's name.

"Look!" She points excitedly at the sky. "A shooting star. Did you see it Mummy?"

I turn my head away from my examination of her face and towards the sky just in time to catch the tail end of the shooting star as it burns out.

"I did. You know those are signs of good luck, right? You have to make a wish now."

Astra scrunches up her face in concentration, her eyes moving frantically behind her eyelids as she thinks of something to wish for.

"Quickly!"

Her eyes burst open, wide with ebullient excitement.

"I got it!"

"Good. Keep it close to your heart. You can't tell anyone else, otherwise it won't come true."

"I won't," she vows.

Lifting a brow at her, I add, "You can't even tell your Dad."

Her face falls. "But what if he asks?"

I laugh softly. "You have to keep this one secret from him."

"Will he be mad?"

I brush back her hair and kiss her forehead gently. "No, little star. He won't."

She doesn't look convinced. "Okay then."

The air is crisp and the sky is clear, not a cloud in sight. A perfect night for stargazing. As we look up at the black canopy of the skies, I see stars that I haven't seen in a long time.

"Do you see that little star right there? Just off to the side of the Big Dipper?"

"Yeah."

"That's my star."

Astra looks at me with a face full of childhood wonder. "*Your* star?"

I nod. "Do you know how many stars I own?"

She shakes her head vigorously back and forth. Looking down into her small face, I can see the sky reflected in her one black iris, almost as if it's tattooed there.

Conspiratorially, I whisper, "Five thousand."

"Five *thousand?*"

"Well, five thousand and sixteen to be exact." I grin. "Your father can be sentimental."

"Daddy bought you the stars?" I can hear it in her voice, that her awe of her father is growing even wider with this revelation.

"He did. He buys them for me all the time, for the little milestones like the big ones. I think he'd buy me a planet if it was possible to purchase those."

The sound of a flap being thrown back echoes, followed by, "Make no mistake, I'll get you a planet if you want one, wild girl."

196

My husband appears as if I conjured him by wishing for him upon that shooting star.

And maybe I did.

Maybe I did.

Phoenix is shedding his coat and striding across the tent in the same breath, and then he's lifting the covers back and sliding in besides me, wrapping his warm arms around my middle and burying his face in the crook of my neck with a throttled, almost pained-sounding groan.

"Back home at last," he mumbles into my throat, inhaling deeply.

I reach back and cup his nape as my heart settles, running my nails up and down the slope of his head and neck just the way he likes.

"Nix," I sigh.

"Daddy, come over here!" Astra demands on the other side of me.

"In a moment, little star." He licks my throat and nibbles my ear. "I have to say hi to your mum first."

She pouts discontentedly but I barely register it. Phoenix's hand slides underneath my sweater, runs up the expanse of my stomach and cups my breast.

"Fuck, baby," he mutters against my skin.

"Missed you," I breathe.

"You have no idea." His hands are everywhere. Feeling me. Caressing me. Reacquainting himself with me as if a couple nights away has made him forget my curves. "I'm buying you a planet next."

I gasp softly and turn into him, my back facing Astra. She's used to witnessing lengthy reunions between us so she doesn't interrupt further, merely clutching her stuffed astronaut to her chest and continuing to stare up at the sky.

Phoenix grabs my hip and pulls me against him, hooking one of my legs over his and palming my ass.

"No— Nix, you can't buy me a planet."

His brow furrows, that deep line he gets when he doesn't understand emerging between his eyes.

"Why not?" He fingers strands of my red hair, wrapping them possessively around his fist and staring at them with dark, obsessed eyes. "You're the sun," he whispers. "Every planet orbits you, desperate to bask in a moment of your attention, just like the rest of us. It's only fitting that they should also belong to you."

When my father walked me down the aisle on our wedding day, he hesitated when handing me off to Phoenix. He wouldn't release my hand, asking me one final time if I was sure, if I knew what I was doing, if Phoenix really could make me happy.

Back then, I simply assured him that he could and would.

Today, I'd tell him that my husband is a man who would reach into the heavens and pull down the stars from the sky just to give them to me. A man who would steal the moon itself just to see me smile. A man who would stand between me and the most violent of storms just to protect me.

When your husband looks at you the way a sunflower looks at the sun—turning every which way in desperate attempt to follow its journey, to bask in its light—you can't help but feel like you might actually be the sun; bright and burning and beautiful.

I knew it back then, but I couldn't articulate it to my father.

I can now.

Phoenix loves me more than he loves the breath in his lungs.

I cup his face and seal my lips to his, relishing in his taste after a couple days of separation.

"Leave some of the sky for others, Nix. I'm happy with my five thousand and sixteen stars."

His eyes are lowered to my mouth, pupils blown. His thumb brushes across my bottom lip.

"Five thousand and seventeen."

I kiss his thumb, then his words register. "What?"

His gaze remains fixed steadfastly on mine as he reaches into his back pocket. "I'm sorry it took so long; they were stubborn as fuck at the IAU." He unfolds a piece of paper and hands it to me. "It took me every day of ten years, but I won in the end."

I peruse the document in my hands.

The deed of sale.

The date of purchase.

The name of the star.

Sirius.

Sirius, who we first looked up at when I wasn't sure we would make it. Sirius, who we've watched countless times and has been our guiding light these past fifteen years. Sirius, who Phoenix promised he would get for me even though it didn't seem possible.

And he did.

"How?" My hands shake, as does my voice. "I-I thought it was impossible."

He's satisfied by my reaction, his grin as arrogant as I've seen it. "Impossible is nothing when it comes to you."

I smash my lips against his, my arms wrapping around his neck in my desperation to be closer, infinitely closer, to him. He rolls over onto his back with an appreciative groan, taking me with him. One hand palms my ass greedily while the other cups my nape, keeping me pinned to him.

"Nix—" I rip my lips from his with difficulty, breathing heavily. "We have to keep it PG-13… *Astra.*"

The way he pulls air into his lungs reveals his breathing is equally affected. "We'll finish this later," he promises or warns, I'm not sure which. "I'm not going anywhere."

He throws back the covers and stands, walking over to where he hastily discarded his coat and picking it up off the floor.

I take advantage of his momentary distraction and turn back towards Astra, murmuring so only she can hear me, "In a few years, you'll probably have your first crush. Then your first boyfriend or girlfriend. Remember, never settle. Don't date anyone who doesn't treat you exactly like your Daddy treats me, okay?"

"Someone who buys me things?" she whispers back.

"Not necessarily. Money isn't what's important because not everyone has it. We're extremely fortunate," I explain. "No, someone who will give you their whole heart without any reservations."

"I'll try."

Squeezing her hand, I say, "I'll help you, if you want."

She shrugs. "Maybe. Boys are gross anyway."

"*Exactly,*" Phoenix interjects, getting into the bed on her side this time. "Boys are horrific creatures who cannot be trusted and should be avoided with the same abject horror as the bubonic plague."

I roll my eyes but don't put up a fight. Astra has already moved on from this conversation, too busy showing her dad exactly what she's discovered in the night sky.

***

Later, Astra is sound asleep in the crook of her dad's arm. Her face rests on his chest and moves up and down with the rhythm of his breathing. Phoenix stares down at her in wonder, much more taken by her than he is the stars. He brushes his fingers through her hair quietly, content to spend his night this way.

Picking back up where we left off, I say, "I know we're years away from this yet, but she's never going to meet anyone if you helicopter parent her like this."

He throws a narrowed look my way. "First of all, no man will ever be good enough for my little girl. Secondly, she'll never date anyone. Ever." His hand tightens around her. "I challenge any man to come after her when she's not allowed to leave the house."

With a loose smile on my lips, I shake my head. There's a battle ahead, of that I'm sure. "Poor girl," I whisper thoughtfully. "She won't ever be able to leave her tower. Some brave person is going to have to get behind the walls of your fortress to get to her."

He growls in warning, a deep sound that rumbles in his chest and curls his lip into a snarl. I laugh in the face of it, not easily cowed by his theatrics when I'm used to defusing him before he detonates.

The sound of my laughter alone is enough to ease the tension in his shoulders. For a few minutes, we simply watch our daughter sleep.

"Do you want another one?"

The question is whispered softly, inquisitively, the same way as the two other times he's asked it. I know him well enough to understand that he's not asking because he wants to press the topic or because he has a particular opinion on the matter. He asks because, as always, he's checking in on what I want. Making sure that he's not passing by a desire of mine that I might be keeping secret simply because he hasn't asked.

So he asks.

And my answer is the same.

"No." I reach over to them and drag my knuckles in a soft caress down Astra's pink cheek. "But maybe one day."

I would tell him if I was ready to adopt.

***

Fifteen years after graduation

Chapter Twenty-Four

Thayer

I've been in the kitchen all afternoon, working on perfecting dinner. I'm not particularly renowned for my cooking and typically let our chef handle all of our meals, but I chose to dismiss her for the evening.

It would have been easier to let her handle this bit so I could focus on the upcoming confrontation, but part of me—a foolish, irrational part of me—thought that if I cooked a perfect dinner, then maybe everything would be alright.

I place two plates on the dining room table and sit down, anxiously wringing my hands. Then I wait for my husband to come home to me.

Bile sits heavy and sour in the back of my throat. My heart races and my hands are clammy. I tell myself it's the heat from the stove causing this reaction in my body, but I know it's not. I'm shaking, hoping against hope that there's a good explanation for what I discovered.

That my world isn't going to be ripped from under me again, like it last was at RCA.

I'm used to sharing my husband. He's the biggest star in England, the most iconic footballer and cultural icon since David Beckham. He has millions of adoring fans of both sexes throwing themselves at his feet wherever he goes. I'm used to only getting pieces and watching others claim parts of him for themselves.

But not *this*.

Never this.

The front door opens. It's immediately followed by indecipherable muttering as Rhys greets our butler, James, and then he's in the dining room with me.

"Honey, I'm home!" he exclaims, putting on a jovial American accent.

His *business trip* must have gone very well.

Acid swells once more in my stomach, causing painful cramps.

My back is to the doorway so I don't get a look at him before he wraps me in a hug from behind and buries his face in my neck.

"I'm so happy to be home, love." He inhales deeply then grumbles appreciatively. "One hit of your scent and I'm drunk. Love drunk." I can hear the grin in his voice without turning around.

"How was New York?"

"It was great, minus the fact that I thought about you the entire time."

If he notices how stiff I am in his arms, he doesn't comment on it. He sounds like himself. Happy, carefree, easygoing.

My husband, exactly as I know him.

Not a liar.

"It smells amazing. Did Trudy cook?"

"No, I sent her home." There's no hiding the hollow note in my voice now. "I cooked tonight. Chickpea curry."

Rhys stiffens and releases me slowly. I hear him unfold himself to his full height behind me, his hands leaving my body. Then he's rounding the table to where his plate waits for him, getting his first look at my face when he comes to stand opposite me.

Our gazes connect and his eyes narrow slightly. He rubs his hand across his jaw thoughtfully as he takes in my tight expression and the harsh line of my lips.

"My favorite," he comments. There's a reason I chose to make that specific dish tonight; to remind him of what an amazing wife he has at home, even as he betrays me. "What a great welcome home." His tone is cautious, the lightness from moments earlier now gone. "Where are the kids?"

"They're sleeping over at Nera's." I take a sip from my wine glass, taking a moment to equally savor the dry red and measure my words. "I didn't want them here for this."

Rhys swallows thickly. His eyes narrow further, then scrape down the length of me like he's going to find the answer to an unsolvable riddle in my body language.

"Didn't want them here for what?" he finally asks. "What's wrong?"

There's genuine worry on his face, a promise that he'll fight whatever battle I need him to etched on his features.

This is my husband.

This man right here.

The same man who rescued me not one month ago when I got stuck in an elevator for the second time in my life.

He and I were meeting our friends at Sinclair Royal to discuss the status of our portfolio, then heading out to lunch. I arrived minutes before him and rode up the elevator alone to the twentieth floor.

Somewhere between the seventeenth and the eighteenth, there was a loud, screeching noise and then the cage came to an abrupt, jolting stop.

The force of the elevator coming to a sudden halt sent me sprawling to my hands and knees.

It took the length of time of pushing my hair out of my face to realize that I was stuck.

It took far less time to realize I was terrified and on the brink of blacking out.

Past experiences hiding from my mother's many dangerous boyfriends made me petrified of tight spaces. I avoid them with ease so as not to trigger my claustrophobia or the inevitable ensuing panic, but faulty elevators seem drawn to me.

The first time I was stuck in one, I was lucky because Rhys was in the elevator with me.

This time he wasn't. I cursed myself for being impatient and not waiting those few extra minutes to have him with me.

Being alone while scared out of my mind made the experience that much more terrifying.

I sat on the floor, in the corner, my legs drawn up to my chest, my eyes closed, and my hands pressed tightly over my ears to try to drown out the sensory overload. If I couldn't see it or hear it, maybe I'd believe the elevator wasn't there. Maybe I wouldn't feel like the walls were closing in on me.

Try as I might, I couldn't shut out the noise, or the lack thereof.

Not the eerie silence, which scared me just as much as the screeching brakes, and not the subsequent sound of screaming metal followed by a loud *thunk* above my head.

I only had time to look up, lifting my hands a couple of cautious inches off of my ears, before a ceiling panel crashed to the floor at my feet with a decided *thump*.

My scream of terror was prepped in my throat but I never got a chance to release it. I blinked and suddenly Rhys was in the cage with me.

Convinced the claustrophobia was making me hallucinate my greatest wish, I didn't react to my husband's impossible appearance.

Not until he gave me a familiar crooked grin set below a concerned and searching pair of eyes. His hands reached for me in the same breath, wrapping me into his arms as he whispered "hi, love" into my hair.

Later, I'd learn from Bellamy that when he learned I was stuck in the elevator, he raced up the emergency flights of stairs in one go, emerging on the eighteenth floor barely winded and storming towards the elevator, determined to destroy the machine that held me trapped. He'd pried the doors open with his bare hands and, in an impressive feat of athleticism, had jumped down the ten feet that separated where he stood from where the elevator was stuck between the two floors, landing smoothly on top of the cage. He'd kicked in the panel and dropped in next to me like *Spider-Man* himself.

He knew that when he jumped into the elevator shaft and down into the cage below, he would be trapping himself with me for as long as it took the firefighters to come rescue us. He did it without thinking twice, flinging himself off the landing before Bellamy could even put out a hand to attempt to stop him, and he held me for two hours while we waited, his presence instantly calming.

Once we were free, word of his heroics spread like wildfire. It came as no surprise to find him gracing the cover of the London Times the following morning.

That's Rhys. That's my husband.

That was him barely a month ago.

And now we're here, staring at each other, tipping perilously close to the edge with a much steeper drop below us and no cage there to catch our fall.

"What's going on?" he asks.

"We need to talk."

"Sounds ominous." He chuckles as he lowers his big frame into his seat. When I don't laugh in return, he freezes halfway down, his smile wiping instantly off his face. "Silver?"

There are tears in my eyes but I blink them away. If I start crying now, I'll lose my nerve. I'll choose the easier road, the one I hesitated between for days, agonizing over whether to confront him or live in blissful ignorance.

We're happy. What I don't know won't hurt me, right?

Wrong.

I fiddle with the jewelry on my left hand. The massive engagement ring and the wedding band Rhys slid onto my finger ten years ago. He asks me a question but I don't hear him over the roaring in my ears.

I slide the rings off and set them on the table.

The sound of them quietly touching the wooden surface echoes as loudly as a gunshot in the tense, deafening silence that hangs between us.

The low-ball glass in Rhys's hand freezes halfway to his mouth. His brows draw together, his gaze remaining fixed unflinchingly on the rings. He's sitting now, which is good. I couldn't do this if he loomed over me, intimidating me with his presence.

So slowly it's almost unbearable, he sets the glass down without taking a drink. The confused look on his face is only overshadowed by the swiftly darkening color of his eyes.

He's never quick to anger, my husband.

Never.

Not unless he feels like his claim over me is being threatened. There is no clearer indication of that than me taking off my rings, and if his face is anything to go by, he fucking *hates* it.

Hypocrite.

"What do you think you're doing?"

The carefully controlled anger in his question weakens my bravery until I feel like I'll bend beneath the force of his gaze.

I gather my wits about me and steel my spine.

"When you put these rings on my finger, you took a vow. We both did. To be faithful for the rest of our lives."

The muscle beneath his left eye twitches. "Yeah."

I push the rings towards him. I don't mean for them to scrape across the wood, but they do and he flinches. The hand he has laying nonchalantly on the table balls into a tight, brutal fist. Throttled veins bulge from beneath his skin and run down the length of his wrist.

I nod at the rings before meeting his gaze. "Then do I still have a reason to be wearing these?"

An angry hiss whistles sharply past his lips.

He leans forward, eating the distance between us across the table and easily dwarfing me into the back of my seat. This close, I can see the rage in his eyes.

"Put them back on."

Every word is twisted with fury.

He's seconds away from a catastrophic explosion when it's *my* anger that should be driving this, *my* heart that's broken.

I open my mouth to say something since he doesn't seem inclined to actually answer my question.

Whatever words I was about to utter, they're cut off by the sound of his fist slamming down viciously hard on the table.

So hard that the plates, cutlery, and even the candlesticks lift an inch off the surface before landing back down in a cluttered mess.

Chickpea curry splatters everywhere.

Unlike him, I don't flinch.

I didn't know how Rhys was going to react, but I'd been prepared for anything.

Anger doesn't surprise me.

"Put the rings back on now, Thayer," he seethes. "How dare you even ask me that?"

"Did you have a good work trip?" I ask, my tone pleasant. "Did you get everything you needed done?"

He eyes me cautiously. "Yes…"

"Where were you, Rhys?"

"You know where I was. I was in—"

It's the affected look of confusion on his face like *I'm* the one lying through my teeth that makes me snap, finally shattering the charade.

"Before you lie to me again, I know you weren't in New York."

Rhys's fist relaxes, the veins disappearing back beneath his skin as before. He deflates, slumping into his chair as if overcome with exhaustion, his face suddenly pale. With the distance reestablished between us, I feel like I can breathe again.

Last week, Rhys had announced that he and Seymour were traveling to New York City for a few days to help recruit a young, very sought after American talent to come play for Arsenal. Using your stars to woo emerging players is pretty commonplace so I believed him without a second thought.

Honestly, even if he'd given me a ludicrous excuse like he was going to New York for a haircut, I would have believed him without question. That's how much I trusted him.

But he'd *lied*, and we don't lie to each other in this family.

Not since RCA.

That's our golden rule.

"Hayes broke her wrist at school. I tried calling several times but you weren't answering your cell so I called Seymour to see if he could put you on the phone. Imagine my surprise when I found out he was in London and not New York as you'd made me believe. There was no work trip." I laugh humorlessly. "He tried his best to cover for you but he was wholly unprepared to lie, poor guy." Clearing my throat of the tears that are lodged there, I add, "Given this elaborate cover story you concocted and all the lies you've told, including since you sat down, I'm assuming you flew somewhere to meet up with another woman."

It's my turn to close the distance between us this time. When I lean, my mouth is set in an angry rictus, twisted by anger and betrayal. I turn to humor as my defense mechanism to shield myself from the worst of my emotions as I've always done.

"Pro-tip for when you inevitably cheat on your second wife—make sure you let your friend know he's your alibi before you involve him in your lies. You might actually get away with it next time."

Rhys holds my gaze after I'm done with my tirade, letting the silence stretch for poisonously long seconds. His eyes are inscrutable, the emotion in them deeply guarded. Where there was anger just moments ago, there's nothing now.

We sit there with my rage brewing and building between us, and then he abruptly cuts off the eye contact. He may as well have ripped out my heart.

He sighs heavily and his eyes drop to his hands where they rest in his lap.

Like a needle brought to a balloon, my anger explodes into nothingness. It doesn't erupt out of me, it simply… disappears.

And I wish it would come back because it leaves all the hurt behind, now without the much-needed protection of my fury. I feel alone and vulnerable and scared, except this time Rhys isn't there to jump into the elevator to save me.

He's the walls closing in on me.

As angry as I was, part of me—that same foolish, irrational part from before—had hoped there was another explanation.

His averted gaze does away with that futile hope as quickly as wiping marker off a blackboard.

There's me and my hurt left, and nothing else.

"Oh, god… Rhys…"

The brokenness in my voice is evident to the both of us.

I didn't think he would actually cheat on me.

I really didn't.

Since we broke up our senior year, he hasn't lied to me. Not once. I truly didn't think he'd ever hurt me like this again.

Stupid, stupid, me.

The tears are back and this time there's no stopping them. They roll down my face, evidence of my heartbreak.

"How long?" I ask. My voice is brittle. Like hand blown glass easily broken by a passing breeze.

I don't know why I ask.

I don't care.

I need to know, but I don't care. *I don't care.*

Maybe if I say it enough times, I'll believe it.

Maybe I can wish it into existence.

His continued silence is starting to hurt as much as the confirmation of his infidelity. After fifteen years together, I thought he'd at least have the decency to be honest with me if he'd made a mistake.

I wouldn't forgive him, but I'd have a little more respect for him than I do now.

There's a violence in my hands as I push back from the table. I stand and my momentum sends my chair crashing to the ground at my feet with a cacophonous bang.

I can't look at this, this… this *stranger* I've shared my house and bed with for almost half my life. I can't bear to be in the same room as him.

I don't know him at all.

I'm halfway to the door when his hand closes around my elbow and he yanks me violently back into his chest. He traps me so tightly against him that I can feel his heart thrashing through his clothes. My head tucks easily under the painfully stiff line of his jaw, even as I try to shove off of him.

"I'm not letting you walk away from me again," he bites out, irate.

"Let me go!"

James comes to investigate the source of the loud bang, his timing unfortunate.

My husband whirls on him next.

"*Get the fuck out,*" Rhys snarls at him, hand tightening on my elbow as the ugly roar rips from his lips.

James scurries away with a respectful dip of his head, averting his eyes from the scene. Once he's gone, Rhys's glare slides from the door and down to me. He stares daggers into me, the blades of his eyes so sharp they cut actual wounds into my body.

The air is so thin between us, it's unbreathable. Still, his chest heaves furiously, up and down and up and down, managing to drag in oxygen I can't seem to find.

"How long have you been cheating on me for?"

His jaw grinds so tightly together, I'm surprised he doesn't come up with a mouthful of crushed teeth. "I'm not cheating on you."

"Who is she?" I barely recognize my voice. It's small and shaky with no hint of my usual confidence. "What's her name?"

"I'm not fucking cheating on you, Silver."

With one last stern look in my direction, he shakes his head and reaches for the fallen chair. He releases my elbow and traps my wrist in his fist instead. When the chair is back on its legs, he pushes me into it.

I try shaking his hold loose but his hand only tightens around me, an animalistic growl leaving his lips warning me to stay put.

He kneels between my legs and tugs my wrist towards him. Without looking up at me, he opens his other palm, revealing the rings he has clutched in his fist. He must have swiped them off the table before he came after me.

210

Rhys pushes the wedding band back on my fourth finger, followed immediately by my engagement ring.

"I really don't like it when you take these off, love," he warns, voice tight.

His words would be no more obvious a threat than if he'd held an actual gun to my head when he said them. His voice shakes under the strain of his barely controlled temper but he kisses the back of my palm as if to soften the anger in his words.

"You're right, I wasn't in New York." His eyes lift to mine, deep, dark, enticing blue. "I lied." The remaining air dies a quick death in my lungs at his admission but he doesn't let it stand. "I was in Chicago."

I freeze.

My hometown.

"Why?"

"I got a call that your mum relapsed last week. I was there to help her get admitted back into rehab."

A cold drift washes through my body, robbing me of my words. I can't even process what he's just said to me. It's so far from the truth I'd manufactured in my head and shocking in so many different ways that I find I'm capable of no more eloquent a response than, "What?"

He remains kneeling between my legs, his hand squeezing mine. "I lied to you and I'm sorry. If I'm being honest, I never intended for you to find out. I was going to take this secret to the grave with me." He brings my hand up to his mouth and kisses the tips of my fingers. "I know how it affects you every time she relapses—how you suffer. I couldn't stand the thought of seeing you get hurt like that again. I couldn't let that happen."

After my mom's ninth attempt at getting clean since Rhys and I started dating, I had hope that things had changed for the better. This time, she'd been sober for over a year. She had a consistent job in a diner, a new apartment, and she attended meetings. We were in regular contact via FaceTime and she looked well. Better than she had in a long time.

It wasn't the first time I thought things would be different. It had happened before, countless times. But I felt this time was *the* time. She'd taken steps she never had before and I was older, wiser, more adept at spotting the lies if they were there, more guarded against the hurt if it came. Or so I thought.

I'd let my guard down and put my trust forward.

She'd made me pay for that gullibility in spectacular fashion by showing up to Ivy's birthday high as a kite and stinking of cheap vodka.

I'd cried for days afterwards, absolutely shattered by this newest betrayal. Rhys had seen me through that particular heartbreak like he had every other before it, steadfast and loyal as ever. But I'd seen how my pain had hardened him, chiseling his anger to stone inside him.

That was a year ago and I'd barely talked to my mom since. I heard from Nolan that she'd gotten clean again in that time, but I no longer believed it.

Given the context, I can understand why Rhys would seek to distance me from a tenth relapse.

He stares at me with eyes gauging for my reaction and a softness on his features that completely undoes me.

"I didn't want you carrying that burden anymore. I've helped her through every relapse before this one and I'll continue to do so until it sticks, because one day it will. There's no reason for you to put yourself through that pain over and over again when I can take it on for you." He reaches up to cup my face, brushing a fresh tear off my cheek like it was never there. "I was with her for three days making sure her intake was done correctly. She's well taken care of. She's safe."

He pulls out his phone and shows me a picture he took of her room. I can't help but spot the fresh flowers on the bedside table.

Lilies, her favorite.

It's not hard to guess whose thoughtful attention resulted in those flowers being in her room.

"We've done this before, her and I. We have a bit of a routine. But that was before. She hurt you and she could have hurt our daughters so she needs to change. I didn't go easy on her. I think this time it'll be different." The corners of his eyes tighten. "I'm sorry for lying to you," he repeats. "You're loud and you're funny and you're joyful and when she makes you quiet and sad and mournful, I see red. I only wanted to take all your pain away, not inadvertently cause you more hurt." He reaches up and laces my throat in a possessive gesture, his pupils flaring. "What I didn't lie about is the fact that I thought about you the entire time I was gone. I understand that my lies made me look suspicious, but cheating?" His hand tightens around my throat. "What do you imagine I'd have been looking for when you've already given me *everything*? I'd sooner cut off a limb than ever touch anybody else. And I'd sooner never make another sound again than laugh with someone else. I'm wholly devoted to you—I have been for the last fifteen years and I will be for the next sixty, until we're old and wrinkly and watching our great-grandchildren grow up together."

I dig my palms into my eyes, hoping the pressure will stop the tears from flowing freely like they have been the entire time he's been speaking. It's a useless endeavor — they keep streaming down my face no matter how hard I try to stop them.

I can't see him but I can feel his anxiety. His uncertainty. It ripples off him in thick waves that crash against me.

"Are you angry with me for lying to you?" His hands come down on my thighs and run up and down my flesh soothingly. "You have every right to be. I promised you I would never lie to you again."

I shake my head vehemently, still crying.

I've been so stupid. And the relief is so fucking monumental, I can't seem to control my emotions.

We don't have to break up. I don't have to learn to live without him. Thank *god*.

A fresh sob rips from my mouth.

"No." I hear his breath catch on his lips. "Thank you for always protecting me." Wiping my eyes with the back of my sleeves, I finally look at him once more. He's where I left him, kneeling before me like a priest would get on his knees before God, every inch of him attuned to and waiting for my reactions. "I feel foolish for accusing you now. I really thought you were cheating on me. I–I couldn't believe it, but you lied... and then you said nothing when I confronted you."

His hands tighten painfully on my thighs. "I didn't speak because I physically couldn't. I couldn't get around the shock jamming my throat closed that you'd believe I would *ever* cheat on you." His voice deepens with fresh anger. "And the second wife dig? That was vicious," he growls. His fingers find my rings, pushing them down until the metal digs painfully into the webbing. "Take these off one more time, Silver, and I'll be forced to intervene so you can never do it again. I'll find a doctor who'll fuse them directly to the bone of your finger for me." He pulls me towards him until my ass is hanging off the edge of the chair, his hands caressing my skin back and forth in a vaguely threatening fashion. "I'm nice, love, but push me again and we'll see how much you like my reaction to your provocation."

The guilt eats at me. I'm the one who fucked up this time, accusing him of the worst betrayal when the whole time he was acting as my biggest protector.

Softening at the expression on my face, he adds, "You're my family and I love you."

"How I'll ever get you to forgive me, I don't know. I'm s—"

"Forgiven."

His interruption slices through my words before I can even get the apology out.

"But—"

"You're forgiven."

It's a statement of facts, clearly not up for discussion.

"I don't deserve—"

"I would have thought the exact same thing." He gathers me into his arms, pulling me down into his lap on the floor. An arrogant smirk curves his lips, pulling an immensely relieved sigh from me that we're seemingly getting back to normal so quickly. "All it means is that you love me and that you can't stand the thought of me being with anyone else. How could I ever be mad about that?"

With a choked sob I throw my arms around his neck and crush my mouth to his. The kiss screams of desperation and wholehearted apologies. It roars of love and loyalty, the kind that most people could only ever dream of.

I'm lucky and I won't forget it or doubt it again.

Rhys pulls back only just far enough to break the kiss, but his lips remain hovering over mine. "I'm going to fuck you quick and then we're going to go pick up the girls and bring them back here. I don't care how late it is, I'm not letting my family be fractured away from me for even one night over this. We're sleeping together under one roof tonight." He fists my hair and yanks my head back. I wince at the sting in my scalp but my eyes widen when he shifts his face to loom over mine. The anger is back in his gaze for a moment, just long enough to issue one final warning. "No more talk of leaving me. No more second wife jokes. If you're no longer my wife, it means I'm already dead. Now lay back on the table and spread your legs."

***

Sixteen years after graduation

Chapter Twenty-Five

Bellamy

There's a loud commotion on the other side of the door. Angry, raised voices filter in through the wall, although what they're saying remains indecipherable. I'm about to go investigate the matter for myself when the door to my office flies open. It bounces violently against the wall and almost shatters in the process.

Quick to gather both my wits and my jaw from off the floor, I shift my gaze over to the man storming my way, groaning internally when I recognize him.

I'm not shocked he's here to confront me, only surprised at how long it took him.

"Peter," I say coolly. "I see you've decided to treat my door with as much regard as you did your wife."

My words stop him dead in his tracks.

He's not used to me being this blunt with him but I don't need to pretend to tolerate him anymore now that he's been convicted.

"You stupid *bitch*," he spits. "You were supposed to get me off."

Rachel, my assistant, rushes in, wide-eyed and concerned. "Should I call the police?"

I smile at her. "It's alright. Looks like Peter has decided to give me his feedback in person rather than via our survey. I'll handle it, thanks Rach."

She hesitates at the door, loath to leave me with him. It's brave of her given that she's all of five feet tall. I give her another reassuring smile and this time she ducks out, leaving me with him.

With a world-weary sigh, I stand and pick a loose piece of lint from off my dress. "I'm good at my job, Peter. Great, actually. No, *spectacular*. But I'm not a miracle worker. You beat up your wife in the middle of a public street, in broad daylight, in front of three witnesses. And that's not even accounting for the Ring camera footage which broadcasted a 4K replay of your assault for the jury. Even Muhammad Ali couldn't have won this fight."

He storms to my desk and slams his palms down on the surface. "Then why the fuck did I pay you hundreds of thousands of pounds if you couldn't get me acquitted?"

Unflappable, I reply, "I'm glad you brought up payment actually, Peter. Accounting tells me you have an outstanding balance of eighty thousand pounds. Since you were kind enough to come visit me in person today, I'm happy to escort you to our CFO's office so we can get that all squared away."

He slams a fist down on my desk. "I'm not paying you a fucking dime. You *lost*."

Men like Peter Gingrinch make me want to quit this job and never look back. I thought there was something noble in being a criminal defense attorney — in representing the wrongfully accused or in helping everyone get equal representation under the law. But these days, I find myself almost universally representing men like him — spoiled, selfish, privileged assholes who hurt those closest to them the second they don't get their way.

They were taught the world revolves around them and that there are no consequences to their actions. Well, in the adult world, there are. And when those consequences have come calling, I've yet to see one of those men rise to the occasion and bear them with accountability.

This tantrum is just another example and reminder of the weakness of the man before me.

I give him a placid smile, not rising to his level.

Or, in his case, abasing myself down into the pits of Hell where his level is, in fitting company with the rapists and pedophiles.

"You're paying me for my legal advice. And my consistent advice to you starting a year ago was to plead guilty in exchange for a lighter sentence. You ignored me repeatedly, even when I told you time and time again that this case was unwinnable and the jury would hate you." His face gets progressively redder the more I speak. A vein pops out in his forehead, tracing a line down to the bridge of his nose. "But that's the issue with you, Peter. You think you're smarter than every woman you meet, which is exactly why when your wife kindly informed you that you'd gotten the time of your meeting wrong, your knee jerk, instinctual response was not to thank her for her help, but to beat her to within an inch of her life for her perceived impertinence."

The vein looks like it's going to explode out of his head now. Staring into his eyes, I see the moment he tips over into madness.

With a furious roar, he uses his forearms to sweep the contents of my desk to the ground.

Despite the violent outburst and the ensuing loud crash, my heart rate is still even.

That is, until I look down and see the framed picture of my family shattered on the floor. It's a photo of Rogue and I and the kids from a day we spent at a county fair while we were on a trip in Cornwall. He's standing, holding a pigtailed and smiling Rowan in his arms, and I'm crouching, gathering Rhodes, Riot and River in a group hug to my chest.

The boys are struggling to see who can be the closest to me and I'm laughing at how adorable their in-fighting is.

A stranger snapped the candid moment and then sent it to us.

I love that picture.

The glass is cracked in the middle, the spidering fissures reaching all the way across the edges of the frame, obscuring everyone's face in the process.

Crouching, I reach for it, absentmindedly dusting off the glass like that'll fix the problem.

"What's going on here?"

Glancing up, I find Rogue in my doorway. His hands are buried casually in the pockets of his suit, his stance nonthreatening.

But his expression is black and his dead stare is pinned unflinchingly on the man who stands on the other side of the desk, his face still tomato red from screaming at me.

His eyes move slowly from Peter, to me, to the mess at my feet, taking in the scene with an expression that grows progressively darker and more volatile with everything he sees.

Finally, his gaze comes back to me. He watches me closely, getting a read on my brewing emotions. "You need me, sweetheart?"

I place the cracked frame back on my desk, returning it to its pride of place, and shake my head. "No, I can handle this."

"Sounds good," he purrs, going over to the couch that lines the left wall of my office. He drops onto it and lies down, casually crossing his ankles over the side of the armrest. "Tag me in if you change your mind."

"Who the fuck are you?" Peter asks.

Rogue reaches into the breast pocket of his suit and brings out an energy bar. Lately, Rogue has been dropping the children off at the gym with Phoenix who's teaching them martial arts, then going weightlifting while they train, so he's eating more than ever. At thirty-four, my husband has never been more attractive. He's grown into his body, his sinewy muscles rippling beneath his suit, and it's all I can do but to openly stare.

Focus.

"Who am I? Oh, that's easy." He grins easily in response, a sharp smile full of teeth that would warn a man smarter than Peter to be careful, then tips his chin at me. "Her husband." He unwraps the energy bar and takes a bite. "Don't mind me. I'm just here as a casual observer to your public execution." He waves a hand in my direction. "Proceed."

"Peter," I say, bringing his attention back to me. "Your sentencing is tomorrow. I suggest you go home, shower, eat an expensive cut of steak, and enjoy last night breathing free air before they lock you up to rot in a dark hole for the next ten years. As tomorrow is the last day I'll ever have to lay eyes on you again, there are a few things I'd like to say." I round my desk, stepping over the discarded memorabilia from my desk until I come to stand before him. "You are a despicable, *despicable* man. I've never seen such a disproportionately sized ego to ability ratio in my life and that's saying something considering I represent failed criminals for a living. Your lack of class is outmatched only by your total absence of intelligence. I've known rocks with more critical thinking skills than you, but even that will go over your head. You'll walk into prison cloaked in your belief that your wealth and privilege make you superior to your fellow inmates and they'll teach you a lesson for it that you won't see coming." I take a step closer.

Slowly, I drop my gaze down the length of his body, taking the measure of him and finding him woefully wanting.

My pointed perusal done, I lift my eyes back up to meet his. Over his shoulder, I catch Rogue grinning at me.

"You didn't listen to my advice the last time I offered it, but maybe you will now. Don't worry, this one's on the house given your obvious financial issues. Are you ready?" I swipe a nonexistent piece of lint off his shoulder and look back up at him. "Learn how to make a shiv, you're going to need it. The only thing inmates hate more than child abusers are wealthy white men who beat their wives." Smiling politely, I add, "You belong in prison, Peter. I'm sad to add a loss to my record, but knowing you'll be rubbing elbows with London's finest murderers *does* feel like a win."

Peter is hardly breathing, the air remaining trapped inside him and puffing out his chest until he looks like he's going to blow.

With a labored exhale, his words hiss out at me in a venomous explosion. "You fucking *cunt*."

Spittle flies from his lips and hits my cheeks.

A tired sigh comes from over his shoulder. Rogue stands, buttoning his suit jacket as he shakes his head.

"See, now you've crossed the line."

"Rogue—"

"Sorry, sweetheart. He's mine now." He casually tosses the energy bar wrapper into my trash can as he walks up to Peter. His hand comes up to grip the back of his neck. I can tell based on the way Peter pales that Rogue is squeezing the life out of him. "And, Peter, you'll find that my approach is a lot less diplomatic than my wife's."

With that, he uses his grip to slam Peter's head into my desk.

The sound of his face colliding with the hard surface is chilling, bone breaking and cartilage twisting loudly in my office. I jump, my hands flying to my mouth in shock.

"She's a peacemaker, that's why I love her," Rogue adds with a smile, talking about me with ease while his prey groans in pain. "And I'm more than happy to be the bad guy in the relationship. Balance, you know?" He pulls Peter back up to standing. "Now that we've been introduced, let me make something clear." At their full height, Rogue stands four inches taller than the other man. He looks down at him, taking in his mangled nose, bleeding cheekbones, and bruised jaw. "Insult my wife again and you'll be picking the pieces of your teeth off her office floor with a pair of tweezers and a magnifying glass. Do you understand me?"

Peter nods frantically, his expression still twisted with rage and a promise of retribution. Rogue's expression goes from outwardly friendly to downright mean in the blink of an eye. Peter's skin takes on a ghostly pallor as he swallows thickly.

"See, I don't think you do. Let me give you a taster to make sure the message really sinks in."

Peter doesn't have time to react.

Rogue pushes down on his neck and brings his knee up in the same move. It slams brutally into his jaw and I hear in real time as at least ten of Peter's teeth shatter. He howls in pain and drops to his knees, his hands closing over his mouth in agony.

Rogue leans over him until his face is level with Peter's. "*Bon appétit.* That's French, if you didn't know," he informs him. "My friend taught me." Straightening, he positions himself between me and Peter, shielding my body away from him. "Get the fuck out of here while I'm still in the mood to let you leave alive and in one piece. Well, more or less. Have you ever picked your teeth off the floor with broken fingers? I haven't, but I've been told it's not fun." Rogue places his shoe on the back of Peter's hand. He adds slight pressure and the man whimpers. "You have two minutes before I change my mind and give you a go."

Peter scrambles to his feet as best he can, dazed by the pain and dripping blood onto the floor in a zigzagging line to the door. Before he can slip out and disappear, I call to him.

"Peter."

He turns and I step out from behind Rogue's body, coming to stand shoulder to shoulder with my husband.

"Would it surprise you to know I have friends at Belmarsh Prison? Not everyone thinks so lowly of my legal services. You'd be shocked how many of them would be willing to do me a favor if I simply asked." Steeling my spine, I hiss, "Come to my office again to threaten me and I won't need my husband to defend me. I'll handle you myself. For Lydia and the many other women I'm sure you've hurt in the past."

I don't stay to watch him go. I turn away and face Rogue. He doesn't take his eyes off the door until he's sure the threat is gone and no danger is imminent. Only then does he look at me, his features softening and his mouth relaxing into a real smile, not the awful grimace he gave Peter.

My arms cross over my chest and I lift a brow at him. "You're paying for a cleaning service to get the blood and teeth out of my floors."

He grins, his hand wrapping around my hip and pulling me into him. "I can afford it."

I snort, my palms finding his chest. I stare at and play with the buttons of his dress shirt absentmindedly for a moment before I murmur, "I could have handled him myself, you know."

"Of that, I have no doubt. But you'd have had better luck convincing me to run buck naked through Siberia in the dregs of winter than asking me to sit quietly by like a good boy while he insulted you."

I laugh at the visual.

"Fine. I suppose I would have reacted the same way if the roles were reversed."

Rogue sobers, his expression turning serious in a heartbeat. "Be careful with him, Bell. I know the rage I saw in his face well. I don't think we've seen the last of him."

"He's going to prison tomorrow, hopefully for a long time."

"Money and power open a lot of doors, we know that better than anyone," he warns. "Just like those things bought him his temporary release on bail instead of remand which he should have gotten based on his crime, they may very well buy him a reduced sentence. You've made an enemy there, one who hates women. I'm asking you to please be careful."

Something in my chest softens immeasurably at his tone and at the clear worry in his face. Reaching up, I palm his cheek. "I will, I promise."

"Let me get you a security guard."

"No."

"Bell—"

"No, Rogue. I'm not some popstar with a stalker who needs to be protected. That's overkill — nothing's going to happen to me. I'll be careful and pay attention, but I'm not getting a bodyguard."

He makes a discontented noise but doesn't argue, correctly reading the expression on my face that tells him he's not going to win this one. "Fine. But you need to tell me the second you feel threatened or scared in any way, okay?"

"Yes. And if it comes to that, then we can revisit the bodyguard question."

His charming smile is back, the one he keeps only for me. He holds me tighter. "Look at us compromising. We're so good at this marriage thing, sweetheart."

I laugh loudly, my hands moving to close around the back of his neck. "What are you doing here anyway? Did Rachel call you?"

"No, but as it happens, she was very relieved when I appeared. I understand why now." He dips his head and seals his mouth to mine in a sweet kiss. "I wanted to see you."

I cup his cheek fondly. "You're in my office more than you are your own, you know."

"We can easily remedy that if you come work at CKI." His hands tighten on my waist. "Be my chief counsel. I need your brilliant mind to keep my ass out of jail."

Rogue has been trying to get me to come work for Crowned King Industries almost as long as I've been a licensed solicitor. I've always refused, preferring to have a separation of church and state in our household, but these days my refusals are getting less and less staunch.

"That's getting more tempting with every spoiled, rich asshole I represent."

"Exactly," he says, nodding. "At CKI, the only spoiled, rich asshole you'll have to represent is me. And I'm pretty sure you like me so that's half the battle won already," he adds with a pleased smirk.

"Like you?" His eyes narrow. "Baby, I *love* you."

A sound of pure male satisfaction rumbles up his chest and he releases me. My brows pull together when he heads for the door, but he closes and locks it, then comes right back to me.

"There's another reason I came to see you, but it'll have to wait."

"What do you m—"

My words cut off when his mouth slams down on mine. The force of his kiss pushes me back into the wall. He cups the side of my neck and rubs circles over my pulse point with his thumb as his mouth moves over mine.

Fire ignites low in my gut at the way he touches me, his hands as worshipful as they've always been. I'm pressed against the wall, trapped beneath his massive body, the heat of him engulfing me and there's nowhere else in the world I'd rather be. I arch into his touch and he groans low in his throat.

"Do you know how fucking hard watching you verbally eviscerate that wanker made me?" When I shake my head, breathless and incapable of words, he cups my ass. "Do you want me to show you?"

I nod and he uses his hold on my ass to press me into his very hard cock.

"You're blushing," he murmurs, brushing his thumb over my cheek. "Seventeen years since we first slept together and you're still blushing." He buries his face in my neck, his tongue coming out to lick the skin at my throat. "Could you be any more perfect?"

"A good singing voice and I'd be unstoppable."

He laughs and his lips find mine again, his entire frame shaking from his laughter.

Palming my thigh, he runs his hand up the length of my leg and to my hip where his fingers toy with the line of my thong. He hooks his index under it and slowly starts pulling it down, his mouth still claiming mine.

I'm panting wantonly into the kiss, my hands gripping his hair as I pull him closer, always closer. When my panties are off, he lifts me into his arms. My legs wrap around him and he groans loudly, the sound almost pained. He paws at my ass, greedy fingers digging into my flesh, and walks us over to my desk chair.

He sits, bringing me down onto his lap. For a couple minutes, all we do is kiss. I grind my pussy into him, rocking my hips back and forth over the length of him until he's making near feral sounds of pleasure. Hearing the way I affect him even after all this time and after four babies heats my blood to dangerous degrees.

It takes all my strength, both mental and physical, to rip my lips from his, push off his chest and stand. Rogue leans forward immediately and reaches for me blindly, his eyes still closed.

He's so lust-addled, he's stuttering, barely able to string two words together as he finally manages to peel his eyes open. "What the– What are you… Where are you going?" His pupils are dazed, his voice thick with desire, his hair disheveled, his lips shining from my lipgloss.

"Nowhere," I answer. Then I spread his legs and drop to my knees between them.

"Fuck," he groans when I unbuckle his belt and unbutton his trousers with practiced expertise.

I pull his cock out, wrapping my hand around him as best I can, and go in for the kill. I run my tongue up the underside of his shaft from the base up. When I get to the tip, I close my mouth around him and push down his length, taking his entire cock into my mouth.

"*Jesus*," he gasps. "You're a dream, you know that? My favorite fucking fantasy."

I hum in acknowledgement of his praise even as I continue bobbing up and down his cock. I loosen my jaw and relax my throat, taking him as far back as I can until my nose is pressed against his stomach. He fists my hair with both hands and guides my head up and down. He's muttering unintelligibly; filthy, heated words of love and lust.

When I cup his balls and roll them between my fingers, his head falls back and he curses loudly. I hollow my cheeks and suction just the tip into my mouth and his entire body shudders, goosebumps erupting across his stomach.

"Fuck this," Rogue grunts, leaning forward and pushing me off him. "I'm not going to last and I need inside you."

I release him with an audible *pop* and fall back onto my ass. His hand on my shoulder pushes me further still until I'm lying on the floor on my back, and then he's on me.

His body drapes over mine as he pins me to the floor. One palm comes down next to my head as the other reaches down to part my legs. He doesn't even bother to pull his trousers down further than right beneath his cock and suddenly he's pressing against my entrance.

He finds my lips once more, tasting himself on my tongue and moaning with abandon as he pushes inside me.

The strangled noise that rips from his lips makes me smile against his mouth.

"How are you always this wet for me, sweetheart?"

I laugh softly and wrap my arms around his neck, pulling him closer. He starts pumping and I arch into him, searching for deeper thrusts.

"Right there," I pant.

"Yeah?" He thrusts again, a savage drive of his hips that moves me up the floor. "Here?"

"Mhmm," I confirm, stars shooting behind my eyes when he hits that soft spot inside me.

His voice drips with arrogance as he does it again. And again. And again. "Like that?"

"Yes... yes... yes... Oh, *god*." Pleasure coils, dark and delicious inside me, growing and burning until it feels like my entire body is on fire.

A violent shudder rips through him at my loud moans and his thrusts turn brutal. His hips slam into me, the sound of flesh against flesh resounding loudly in my office as both of us build towards an impossible climax.

"Tell me you love me," I beg, my head thrown back in exquisite pleasure.

He growls, the sound angry. "If you have to ask then I've been failing as a husband." He rolls onto his back and takes me with him so that I'm sitting on top of him with him buried impossibly deep inside me. I gasp. "I love you." He drives up inside me, spearing me almost to my stomach. "I fucking *love you*. Every waking moment of every day is consumed with thoughts of you." He grunts, his words turning almost pained. "I don't know how it's possible that my obsession with you still gets stronger with every passing day."

His frantic confession is all it takes. I come with a loud, throat-ripping cry. My legs shake uncontrollably, the muscles in revolt at the assault of pleasure hitting me. I'm still screaming my release and clamping down on him when he follows me over the edge with his own sounds of demented rapture. Rope after rope of his cum floods my walls as I slump over him, boneless.

His arms close around me and he holds me, his fingers drifting aimlessly over my lower back in a familiar caress. The companionable silence stretches for comfortably long minutes as we hold each other.

"Do you ever think about how close we came to never meeting or meaning anything to each other?" I ask him, burrowing my face into the crook of his neck. I listen to the reassuring beat of his heart against my right ear. "If Thayer hadn't applied for the scholarship behind my back, if I hadn't gone to *Bella's* at that exact time on that exact day, if we'd never gotten detention..."

He cups my cheek and looks down into my face. "No, sweetheart. I don't." He stares at me like he's taking inventory of all my features to draw me from memory. "Meeting you wasn't random chance, it was fate. I would always have found my way home to you eventually, no matter how long it took."

A slow smile stretches across my face.

"Good answer, baby."

I sigh happily and snuggle back into his throat, intent on spending at least the next few minutes enjoying the feel of my husband beneath me.

He almost immediately stirs.

"Shit. The kids."

Startled, I sit up, eliciting a groan from him and shiver from myself when I drive back down his length. "What?"

"Your surprise. I swear, you're lethal to me, Bell. I get distracted the moment I see you." He lifts me off him with ease, tucks himself away and stands. Fishing my panties from his back pocket, he gets down on one knee and helps me put them back on. When he's done, he grabs my hand and tugs me after him. "Come on."

"Where are we going?" I ask as he throws the door to my office open and drags me down the hall.

Rachel isn't at her desk, which means she mercifully must not have heard our rather enthusiastic floor gymnastics routine.

"You'll see."

Rogue doesn't say anything else. He simply pulls me past rows of my employees who all smile at me. When he arrives in front of our largest conference room, he stops.

He tips his chin at the door. "After you."

"Okay…" I move past him and grab the handle. With one last suspicious look over my shoulder at him, I push the door open and walk in.

"Congratulations, Mummy!"

Someone blows into a party horn at the same time as a confetti cannon erupts, both of them startling me.

My hand goes to my mouth in surprise as I see all four of my children before me, with Rachel smiling just off to the side. They're honking their party horns or holding up signs as they clap excitedly for me.

Next to them, the table is laid out with trays and trays of food and more bottles of champagne than I've ever seen.

Rogue wraps his arms around me from behind, his chin coming to rest on my shoulder as he holds me.

"Congratulations on your milestone business anniversary, sweetheart. Ten years ago today, you started Sinclair Royal. Look at everything you've accomplished in that time." He presses a kiss to my cheek. "I'm so incredibly proud of you."

Tears pool in my eyes as I watch the scene before me, overcome with emotion. "The kids?"

"They wanted to be a part of this. They're as proud of their mum as I am. Except Rowan, I'm not sure she understands what's happening quite yet, but she's happy as a clam to be on party horn duty. We might have a musician on our hands. Or a tone-deaf daughter, it's hard to know which at this point."

It still shocks me that Rogue ever doubted himself as a parent. He was born to be a father and he's embraced that role like a second skin. If anything, he's *too* protective of a parent. We routinely have to have conversations about how he's not allowed to 'get rid of' anyone who so much as blinks wrong at one of his children.

"This is amazing," I tell him, wiping my tears away and going up to my kids with a big smile on my face. "*You guys* are amazing. Thank you so much for the surprise," I say, gathering them all up in a hug.

"Are you happy, Mummy?" Riot asks. It still bewilders me that my kids have British accents and call me "Mummy", but somehow it makes them even cuter than they already are.

"*So* happy."

"Can we join the party?"

I look over my shoulder to find Sixtine and Phoenix hovering at the door with equally big smiles on their faces.

Well, *Sixtine's* face. Phoenix's is set in his usual mask of cool disinterest.

"Of course! This is *our* anniversary after all."

Rogue grumbles grumpily from behind me. "Not sure I like you sharing an anniversary with my wife, Sinclair."

Phoenix shrugs but avoids giving me a celebratory hug nonetheless.

We stay in the conference room for hours, inviting the rest of the London employees to join us and cheers to the last ten years and the next ten. When it comes to the second half of the toast, I hold back my glass and glance over at where my husband is now standing on the opposite side of the room.

He senses my gaze. His eyes find mine immediately and an arrogant smirk curls his lips when he sees that my glass isn't lifted with the others'.

He knows that having played the long game may well pay off for him very soon and that victory is near.

Only time will tell how much longer I stay at Sinclair Royal and when I leave to go join him at CKI.

***

Eighteen years after graduation

Chapter Twenty-Six

Nera

"What time is the event tonight?" I ask Tristan.

He and I are sitting alone around our vast dining table, having just finished a late lunch. The kids are all out of the house — Cato is at a movie with his friends, Kiza is at Thayer's with Hayes, Suki is at gymnastics practice, and Juno and Hana are both at Bellamy's to hang out with Riot and Rowan.

It's a rare moment of peace in our otherwise bustling household and we're savoring the calm. It'll be over before we know it — Suki should be home sometime in the next fifteen minutes and the others won't be far behind.

Tonight, we're attending the hundredth anniversary party for Crowned King Industries, Rogue's company. It's a black-tie event guaranteed to be full of pomp and circumstance.

I'm looking forward to it—it's been too long since I danced with my husband.

"Hmm, I'm not sure. Let me check." He pulls out his phone and scrolls through his emails until he tracks down the invite. "Starts at…" He groans. "Ten pm."

I laugh softly at his ill-tempered exclamation and give him a teasing smile. "Are you getting too old for ten pm starts, grandpa?"

His eyes flick to me and he lifts an unimpressed brow. "No."

"Is this when we finally start to feel the dreaded age gap between us?" I sigh. "I knew you were too good to be true."

"Nera…"

"It starts with complaining about how late parties start, and next thing you know you're popping two Viagra just to perform. It's a shame to think you could deteriorate so quickly, babe."

Tristan chuckles easily, a laugh that tells me he'll make me pay for baiting him. He stands and rounds the table over to my side. Grabbing the seat of my chair with one hand, he yanks it backwards and turns me towards him.

His face comes down inches from my own, his lips brushing against mine as he speaks. My breaths falter even as my heart starts beating faster, excitement thrumming to life in my blood. I love how easy he is to rile up.

"If you're questioning my stamina, I'm more than happy to prove myself to you right now." His hand cuffs my throat, his fingers caressing the sensitive skin there. He makes a soft sound of satisfaction when he sees me shiver beneath his touch. "You'll regret provoking me when I fuck you for five hours uninterrupted."

Without giving me a chance to answer, his mouth crashes down on mine. His hand moves from my throat to cup the back of my neck as his tongue thrusts past my lips, searching for mine with a desperation that makes it seem like the last time he had me was weeks ago and not less than twelve hours ago.

I'm about to lose myself in the moment, in the mindless lust, when an arrow of lucidity pierces through, reminding me that if I don't stop this, Tristan and I may very well end up traumatizing at least one of our children.

"Tris," I gasp, pushing against his chest.

His lips rip from mine against their will, his heaving chest evidence of how I affect him. Tristan immediately reaches for me again, his face coming towards me, intent on recapturing my lips.

"Tristan, stop." Only my resolved shove keeps him from claiming my mouth again. His settles into an unhappy line as he lifts his eyes to mine.

"We can't… Suki," I pant, catching my breath. "Suki's going to be home soon."

"Fuck," he groans, dropping his forehead to mine and closing his eyes. "*Fuck.*"

When I notice the way his hard length tents his trousers, I can't help but giggle. "Maybe you should walk that off before she gets home."

He grunts grumpily, adjusting his cock with a pained sound of unmet need. With a heavy breath, he pulls himself away from me. "Don't start something you can't finish again."

"Technically, you—"

"*You* started it," he interrupts, gritting his teeth in agony. "And your ass will suffer for it later."

I shiver at his ominous promise and he doesn't miss it, his eyes darkening until they're nothing more than two black disks.

He takes a step towards me, then stops himself.

"No." He turns on his heels and away from me, chastising himself beneath his breath. "*No.*"

"Down boy," I call out with another laugh.

Tristan looks over his shoulder at me. His eyes flash, then narrow in a promise of upcoming retribution. I know what that look means and I swallow thickly in anticipation.

"Bend over the table."

"We don't h—"

"We have time for this. Bend over the table," he orders. "*Now,* Nera."

I stand on shaky legs and do as he says, as powerless to resist him when he uses that deeply authoritative tone of voice as I've ever been. There's no view of the dining room table from the front door so if Suki does come home, I'll have time to move before she ever sees what her father is about to do to her mother.

A strangled noise of arousal leaves Tristan's throat as I lay on our table and arch my ass up. He closes the distance between us slowly, his eyes pinned on me.

"This isn't doing anything to help calm my throbbing cock," he murmurs.

His fingers graze the skin at the back of my thigh, making me jump at the contact. They trail up my leg, lifting the hem of my dress with them until my ass is bared in my undies. There's nothing particularly sexy about them and yet Tristan reacts like he just uncovered incredibly provocative lingerie.

His touch raises goosebumps on my flesh, causing an electrifying shiver to rack through my body.

These half touches are driving me insane. He's wasting time. "Get on wit—"

Slap.

I keen loudly.

"What was that, baby?" he coos, rubbing a possessive palm over the heated skin he just spanked.

I shake my head and he smacks my ass again. My hips jerk into the edge of the table, adding a new dimension to the pain rippling through me.

"Cat got your tongue?"

I blow out a throttled exhale just in time for him to bring his palm down on me again. And again. The whimper that rips from my throat is soaked with lust.

"Not so mouthy when you're submitting your ass to my hand, are you, wifey?" Pride and satisfaction drip from every word, especially the last one. He leans over me until his chest is pressed against my back. "I hope you know a spanking isn't what I was talking about when I said your ass would suffer later." His fingers dig beneath my undies and dip between the valley of my cheeks, dancing down to find my tight hole. He rims me skillfully with his index until a powerful ache pulses between my legs and my shoulder blades bunch together in the middle of my back. "No, baby, that would be too easy."

I should tell him no, not now, not when our kids could walk in at any point, but it's beyond my abilities when he's touching me like this. Thankfully, he straightens and pulls his fingers away himself, making me sag against the table in something that's more disappointment than relief.

I have only seconds to gather myself before his hand comes down on my ass once more.

He smacks my cheeks with an assuredness that speaks to the eighteen years he's spent exacting this particular punishment out of my flesh anytime he's deemed it necessary.

He loves playing with my ass, in any and every way that he can, whether it's touching it, groping it, smacking it, or simply fucking it.

And, I... Well, I never say no.

I bend over like a good girl and let my husband do whatever he wants to me, coming with explosive screams every single time.

234

My ass is burning, my skin red and throbbing from his blows, but my pussy is wet and my blood is thrumming through my veins and demanding that I undress and claim my husband right this minute.

He spanks me again, this one the hardest yet, and I cry out. My scream is cut off by the sound of a key turning in a lock.

Tristan immediately rights my dress with one hand and grabs my arm with the other, guiding me up from the table and back down into my seat in the next breath.

I wince when my ass makes contact with the velvet of the chair and he smiles a sinfully dark smile.

As sensitive as the flesh of my ass is, the unmet, unsatisfied arousal in my pussy is worse. I rub my thighs together in search of a release, knowing I'm unlikely to get one for several hours yet.

His smile broadens when he sees my legs move and hears the tormented whimper that falls from my lips.

This was his plan, I realize. To make me as aroused and desperate for him as he was for me so we both suffer equally.

He's diabolical, my husband.

I moan and peer up at him. He thumbs my chin, tipping my face up towards his. "Are you horny for me, baby?"

I nod and he brushes his thumb across my lower lip.

"Join the fucking club," he growls. He leans forward and captures my mouth with his in a quick but intense kiss. When he pulls back, he whispers against my lips, "And for the record, I wasn't complaining about the start time because I'm tired. I groaned because a ten pm start means we won't get home until two am at the earliest and we have Hana's dance recital at eight tomorrow morning. I groaned because Rogue's damn anniversary party is cutting into the very few and extremely precious hours I have at night with my wife."

Tristan has a knack for always saying the most perfect thing. He never misses. Not once. Sometimes I wonder if he's rehearsed these lines because there's no way a *man* could be this romantic, but the openness in his face and the raw authenticity in his features tell me he's genuine.

I don't get to answer him because the door slams and Suki comes storming into the room. Tristan straightens, distancing himself from me, and turns towards our daughter.

He stiffens, and when I glance at Suki's face, I understand why.

Even through the haze of my arousal, I can tell something's wrong. Her features are tight, her face flushed red. Her eyes are shining in a way I've never seen from my ten-year-old.

"Darling, are you alrig—"

She comes to a dead stop, her fists clenched at her sides. "I want to stop gymnastics."

My brows pull together. "Why, you love—"

"Well, I hate it now!" she screams. "I *hate* it. I want to stop."

Her anger has an immediate cooling effect on the fiery lust burning through my veins, dousing them entirely. Suki's always had a strong character, it's what I love most about her. At such a young age, she already knows who she is and what she wants, and she's not about to let anyone tell her what she can and can't do.

But she's never raised her voice like this before.

Tristan takes a step forward. "Su—"

She turns on him. "*Don't* try to change my mind. I don't like it anymore and I'm never going back there again. If you force me, I'll run away." Her lower lip trembles as her eyes turn glassy.

I raise a calming hand and stand, rounding the table. "Of course we'd never force you, Su. If you want to stop gymnastics, then that's the end of it." I go to close the distance between us so I can hug her, but she flinches, freezing me in my tracks. "I want to make sure you're okay though. Are you?"

"I'm fine," she snaps. "Stop asking me if I'm alright, I'm *fine*." With those final hissed words, she spins on her heels and stalks out, slamming the door closed behind her.

I turn towards Tristan to find him blowing out a breath.

"Do you think that's a taster of what her teenage years are going to be like? Because that might *actually* kill my stamina."

I smile but my heart isn't in it. "She didn't seem like herself."

"No, she didn't," Tristan agrees. "But you know how she gets. She probably couldn't master one of the skills today and decided to give it up. It happened with ballet, it happened with archery, and now it's happened with gymnastics. She'll find something new soon and hopefully this one'll stick."

Tristan isn't wrong in his assessment. Suki is a bit of a perfectionist. She gets it from me and I know better than anyone how toxic the dark side of perfection can be. I'm sure he's right and her tantrum was informed by a bad practice.

We're close, she would tell me if it was something else.

***

Chapter Twenty-Seven

Nera

The centennial anniversary party for Crowned King Industries is held in the palatial Grand Ballroom of the Ritz, the most lavish hotel in London. The party itself is as equally grandiose as the chosen location.

The room is decorated with countless gold mesh floor lamps and lit with priceless and resplendent chandeliers. The subdued atmosphere of the lighting is luxurious and by no means the only sign of opulence. French art adorns the walls and champagne towers stand at all four corners of the room, two of the tables framing a makeshift stage. Acrobats in reflective gold uniforms hang from floating wheels, their bodies moving in slow, sultry dances above our heads as we walk in.

Clearly, CKI spared no expense to celebrate this landmark anniversary and the show takes my breath away.

My neck is craned, my face aimed at the sky as I watch the artists, when someone comes up from behind me and smacks my ass.

"Hey, hot stuff," a seductive voice whispers in my ear.

"Ow," I moan, gently rubbing at the still sore flesh to appease the stinging.

Thayer appears beside me with a sly smirk on her face. "Not the first time someone's done that to you today, is it, Nerita?"

I roll my eyes at her and don't fight the smile that pulls at my lips.

"Keep your hands off my wife's ass, Thayer," Tristan drawls, appearing on my other side and handing me a champagne flute. He presses a kiss to my temple and walks off to catch up with the guys.

"Didn't your mother ever teach you to *share*, Tristan?" Thayer calls after him. "How about you get one cheek and I get the other? No?"

We both laugh when he pretends to plug his ears with his fingers, not even bothering to look over his shoulder and back at her.

"They're so fun to mess with."

"Who is?" Sixtine asks, appearing next to me. "Hi," she says, kissing both of our cheeks.

"Our husbands," Thayer answers.

"Oof. A word of advice — don't mess with Phoenix tonight, he's not in the mood," Six replies.

"How come?"

"Wait, don't gossip without me!" We turn to find Bellamy holding the hem of her black gown and racing towards us as best she can in her high heels. "Hi, so glad you guys could make it," she says, flushed from the effort. "What are we talking about?"

"Apparently Phoenix is to be given a wide berth tonight," Thayer explains. "Six was about to tell us why."

"Astra came home from school with a Valentine's Day card from a boy." Six sighs. "Phoenix didn't take it well. He's been calling other schools all afternoon to try and get her enrolled in a new one by tomorrow."

I hid my laugh behind my flute and catch Thayer doing the same.

"I'm surprised he was unsuccessful," Bellamy comments.

"It's *Saturday*. He was pulling people away from their brunch plans or their children's activities, so they weren't exactly in the mood to do what he wanted. And since he was threatening them over the phone and not in person, it was easy for them to just hang up on him and face the consequences later. You can imagine how much that thrilled him."

"So where did you leave it?"

"I won in the end. I finally got him to agree to let her stay at her school," Six answers proudly. "Oh, and to only threaten people Monday through Friday, and not on weekends. It's common decency."

I lift a brow at her. "And what did that cost you?"

Six blushes the color of her red dress.

"Not another "horseback ride", I beg you," Thayer says, horrified.

"No!" she replies, swatting at her. "He wanted... Do y— Do you know what free use is?"

This time, the three of us don't bother hiding our laughter.

"Sounds like *he* won," Bellamy says with a grin.

Six nods. "He did. I'll be honest, I might not even make it a full day. He's... Well, it's only been seven hours and already *five times*. If he continues at this pace, you're going to have to cart whatever's left of my body around in a wheelchair by the time next Saturday rolls around. *J'en peux plus.*"

Bellamy looks over her shoulder at where our husbands are standing together on the other side of the room. Phoenix is speaking, hands buried in his pockets, looking as bored and unmoved as he usually does.

"Do you think he's introducing them to the concept of free use as we speak?" she questions thoughtfully.

"If he is, no need for him to talk to Tristan about it. He's already *very* familiar with the subject," I note, taking a demure sip of champagne.

Six rounds on me. "You've been holding out on us!"

"It was his anniversary present last year. Remember that week we went away to Florence just the two of us? I'd planned an entire itinerary full of museums, wineries, restaurants, you know, the best the city has to offer," I tell them. "We didn't leave the room once for those five days."

"I wondered why you didn't get me a souvenir."

"Yum," Thayer answers with a smile. "But he needs to keep that concept far away from Rhys."

"Really?" Bellamy asks, glancing at her. "I'd have thought this would be right up your alley."

"He's a *professional athlete*, B. Phoenix went five times in seven hours but if Rhys ever gets the greenlight from me on this, he'll go seven for seven plus an eighth and ninth time for good measure and a tenth just to gloat. For my and my vagina's sakes, let's keep him to his normal appetites."

"What about you, B?" I ask.

"Phoenix can feel free to gossip to Rogue about it whenever he wants," she answers with a sultry smile. "I'm intrigued."

Before we can say anything else, a woman in a sober black dress wearing an earpiece comes up to her and whispers something in her ear. Bellamy listens, nodding, then turns back towards us with a smile. "An

240

issue with the canapes, if you can believe it. I need to handle this — I'll see you guys in a bit."

"That's a mic drop exit if I've ever seen one," Thayer laughs.

Bellamy walks off with a wink. She's barely gone when a phone starts to ring.

Thayer grabs her clutch from where she has it held under her arm and pulls out her phone.

"I should take this, it's the babysitter," she explains, turning on her heels and walking off.

"*Et il n'en resta plus que deux,*" Six says, smiling at me.

I hook my arm in hers. "The OGs."

Together we move closer to the dancefloor and the countless couples who sway to the soft notes of classical music. We stand off to the side, near one of the pillars.

"Can you believe this is our life?" Six asks. "We met in Hong Kong, we went to school together in Switzerland, and now we live in London. We're godmothers to each other's children and our husbands are best friends. Can you believe we got this lucky?"

Truthfully, the answer is no. For so long everything in my life seemed to be going wrong. I had bad luck after bad encounter in a constantly repeating cycle.

That all changed almost overnight.

I often pinch myself to make sure the last eighteen years haven't been a dream.

I hold my breath before every pinch, scared this is going to be one time the result is different, but I've never woken up.

This is *actually* my life and I'm so grateful for it.

"I knew you were going to be by my side for the rest of my life the day I met you, but no, I never imagined that we could have everything else. I would have called myself unbelievably greedy if I'd even tried to ask for all of this."

She squeezes my hand. "Same."

I hesitate before I ask my next question, but only for a moment. "We haven't talked about it in a while, and maybe that's intentional, but I wanted to see if you had talked about adoption again? I know Astra is your entire world—have you guys closed the topic off entirely?"

"We talked about it recently, actually. We're both on the same page that we don't necessarily need any other children." Six gets a thoughtful look in her eye that tells me that even though she's taken a brief pause, she hasn't actually finished talking. "For me, the subject of adopting another baby is closed. But, I'll be honest — the more I work with high-risk families and see these abandoned kids going into the care system, the more it breaks my heart. If we were going to adopt, it would definitely be an older child."

Six is the definition of a bleeding heart. She's absolutely brilliant but that's only part of what makes her a formidable solicitor. She cares about everyone equally, whether friend or stranger, and with a fierce, relentless passion I've never seen in anyone else.

Time and time again, I've watched her go to war in defense of children and their families and win. She's truly the most selfless person I've ever met.

"I think that's a wonderful idea and it makes so much sense."

Her face softens. Relief crosses her features like maybe she thought I'd think otherwise. "Really?"

"Of course. There are so many children in care who need homes."

"There are!" she exclaims, her passions igniting. "Phoenix actually just surprised me by making a very sizable donation to this charity called *No Child Left Behind*. I'd mentioned it to him in passing and he... well, they called and let me know they're going to be able to open two new homes and house thirty kids full time until adulthood because of him."

"I think he lives exclusively to find ways to put a smile on your face."

"He's very good at it," she admits, the signature smile her husband loves to pull out of her blooming on her lips.

I look over at where the guys are standing and find Phoenix with his gaze pinned heatedly on his wife. She hasn't noticed yet, too busy telling me about how they're not rushing into adoption and 'they'll know' if and when the right child comes along. Phoenix tracks every movement of her lips the entire time she speaks. He's too far away to hear a word she says or even read her lips, but he stares anyway, his gaze unwavering. Rogue, Tristan, and Rhys talk animatedly around him but he pays them no mind.

When he sees me watching him, he tips his chin at me in a request to get his wife's attention.

"Um, Sixtine," I say, clearing my throat. The intensity of his gaze on her has me feeling flush via secondhand contact.

"Yeah?"

"I think Phoenix might be ready for round six."

"What?" She lifts her head and looks around until her gaze connects with his. He tilts his head to the side slowly, his face settling into a peaceful expression but his eyes turning smoldering with possession.

"Yeah, he's *definitely* ready for round six."

A blush creeps steadily up her neck. "Oh."

"*Go* before he causes a scene. We can talk later," I add with a laugh.

"Bye," she answers distractedly, her feet already carrying her across the room to him.

Phoenix doesn't let her do all the work—he leaves the trio behind and meets her halfway. He swallows her hand in his and tugs her after him, no doubt to find the nearest room with a locking door. This is a five-star hotel so one item this place has in excess is beds, but something tells me Phoenix isn't going to have the patience to go through the process of checking into a room before having his way with Six.

"I'm glad your friend finally left," a voice calls from behind me.

I turn to find an attractive man with blond hair and blue eyes, a lean build, wearing an expensive tux standing before me. He gives me a charming smile.

"I've been waiting all night for a chance to get you alone." His eyes rake languidly down the length of my body and back up. He hums appreciatively. "That's a very beautiful dress."

I'm wearing a burnt orange designer gown with an embellished illusion bodice. The peplum style top is crowned with a sweetheart neckline. It narrows at the waist and flares at my hips before dropping into a straight, floor-length skirt. With my pitch-black hair pinned away from my face and straightened into a glossy mane down my back, I know I look both elegant and beautiful.

"Thank you," I say, and because I'm not in the mood to extend this conversation any longer than is strictly necessary, I add with a decided lack of subtlety, "My husband is going to be ripping it off me later tonight. I'd wager with his teeth."

I get a real kick out of watching the man choke on a sip of champagne. He brings his glass down from his lips and coughs, wiping his mouth with the back of his hand.

"Well, that's certainly *one* way to tell me you're not interested."

"Would you like to hear another?" inquires a dark voice at my back.

A chest presses against me from behind and ignites a fire low in my gut with the barest of touches. The heat of his body envelops mine and makes my heart clench violently in response to his presence. I'm not surprised; Tristan is never far from me at these events, no matter what it may look like. He lurks close even when we're separated, always at the ready to intervene if needed.

And clearly, right now he feels it's needed.

My pulse flutters when I feel the dominant press of his hand on my waist. A wave of arousal washes over my skin, tightening my nipples and causing a raw ache to throb in my pussy.

He curls me territorially into his side and I can't help but moan softly at the feel of him against me, at the way he overtakes my senses.

Similarly affected, Tristan makes a quiet noise of pure male satisfaction when I lean closer still and daintily cover his left hand on my waist with mine.

The man's eyes drop down once more, this time registering the large diamond ring now visible on my fourth finger.

"Apologies." He inclines his head in a conciliatory manner, his tone amiable. "I didn't realize she was taken."

"My *wife* very much is," Tristan answers, not without bite. "And now you know, so leave."

The man puts his hands up in a universal sign of surrender and backs away, eventually disappearing into the crowd.

Tristan waits until he's gone before he spins me in his arms. His hands find my ass in a way that's completely inappropriate for polite company, but he's never been one to care much about society rules anyway.

"Good girl." He massages my flesh, taking in and enjoying the way I wince at the soreness. "You're such a good girl," he purrs approvingly.

The lowered pitch of his voice sends a tremor coursing through my body.

"Why?"

"You told him to fuck off so creatively."

He smirks, an arrogant smile that tells me he's going to take his time with me later, then releases my ass and steps back. He extends a hand towards me, smiling in a way that makes him look devilishly handsome.

"May I have this dance?"

"Always." I place my palm in his and he pulls me to the center of the dance floor. His arms circle my waist as mine do his neck and we turn about the room staring into each other's eyes.

244

"He was right about one thing." Tristan's wolfish eyes drag slowly down from my face to my body before coming back up to my eyes. "It's a beautiful dress. Can I really tear it off you later?"

I press closer until every inch of me is glued to him.

"I wore it for you."

He delivers a sharp swat to my ass in the middle of the dancefloor. "Behave," he orders. "We have to stay until the speeches are over."

I look up at him from beneath my lashes. "Yes, chef."

He groans and spins then dips me, eliciting a gasp from my lips. "You know what it reminds me of?"

"What?"

He pulls me back up and twirls me. When I'm held snugly back in his arms, he says, "The dress you wore to the Mackley Library grand opening all those years ago."

My mouth drops. "How do you still remember that?"

"It was a memorable night," he answers. "The dress. The forest. The chase." In an instant, his eyes turn smoky with arousal. "The moment I caught you."

The temperature of the room feels like it inches up ten unbearable degrees.

"*You* behave," I murmur.

"Impossible when you're in my arms, in that dress, and I have a movie of that night playing on loop in my head."

The sound of the music stopping and metal clinking on glass saves me from answering or finding whatever broom closet Phoenix and Sixtine went off to and getting our turn in next.

Fanning my face with my hand, I turn in Tristan's arms and look towards a makeshift stage at the far end of the ballroom.

Rogue holds a mic in one hand and a champagne flute in the other as the room comes steadily to a quiet. Bellamy stands next to him, smiling out into the crowd. Her eyes search for mine and twinkle when they find them.

"Did we miss anything?" Six asks, reappearing besides me with her hair decidedly more disheveled than the last time I saw her. Phoenix is on her other side, his hand clamped possessively on her waist.

"Nope," I answer, wetting my thumb and running it under her eye to clean up the smudge of mascara I see there.

"Thanks," she says with a laugh.

"Sorry about that," Thayer says, breathless. "Ivy wanted me to— Six, what the *hell* happened to you?" Her eyes move from our friend's rumpled appearance over to the proudly smug husband standing next to her and she puts two and two together. "Never mind. *Six times?*" she mouths at her, holding up that many fingers.

When Sixtine nods, Thayer gives her an impressed thumbs up then looks around helplessly.

"Where's my—"

"I'm right here, love," Rhys answers, coming up behind her. Thayer melts into his embrace, settling back into his chest the way I am with Tristan.

Rogue cuts an impressive, intimidating figure on stage. He's unsmiling, his sharp and cutting eyes without a trace of humor as he looks out coldly at the hundreds of people who've all gathered to worship at his altar.

"Thank you all for coming out tonight to celebrate Crowned King Industries' centennial anniversary." He pauses as the crowd breaks out into polite applause, many of the attendees, including ourselves, clients of the company. "It's been almost eighteen years since I took over the business and a lot has changed in that time." He smirks, the expression as ice cold as the rest of him. "Your portfolios are proof that change has been for the better. Most notably, I'm proud to announce that in tandem with our hundredth anniversary, we're also celebrating CKI crossing the one hundred and fifty *billion* pound threshold in revenue." This time, the applause is anything but polite. The crowd cheers loudly, whooping and praising the significant growth they've seen in their personal bank accounts.

Rogue looks unmoved by it all, sounding about as emotionally invested in his news as he would be reading out the specials menu at a random Mexican restaurant. He's a predator, no matter where he is or what he wears, and a tux does nothing to calm the violence that thrums off him in waves.

It's only when he glances over at Bellamy that the mask pulls back and his face softens. If I hadn't seen that very same look on his face almost every day for the past eighteen years, I would find the transformation unbelievable to witness. Even now as the crowd quiets, I can hear the titters of conversation from interested onlookers rippling around us.

246

"I'm far prouder to announce news that's infinitely more personal and important to me," he continues, extending his hand towards Bellamy who takes it. "And that's that after what feels like a lifetime of begging on my hands and knees, I've finally convinced my brilliant wife to join CKI as our Global Chief Counsel."

He tugs a smiling Bellamy into him and crashes his mouth to hers, kissing her in front of a roomful of people, seemingly unaware or uncaring of the fact that we all hear his happy moan because he's still holding the mic up.

They break apart and she wipes the lipstick off his mouth with her thumb.

"Cheers, sweetheart," he murmurs with charming sincerity, turning back towards the crowd with her hand still clasped in his. He starts talking about the value she'll bring to the company, but I don't listen.

I glance at Six to find her beaming at them.

"How do you feel about this?"

"Oh, I'm so happy for them both," she answers, grabbing my hand in hers before looking back at our friends. "I've had her for twelve years, it's his turn now. I mean look at him." She motions at Rogue with a tip of her chin. "Have you ever seen him so...content?"

Rogue's speech finished, he and Bellamy are walking down the few makeshift steps to rejoin their guests. Rogue goes first, looking back to help his wife down with a possessive hand on her hip. His eyes stay pinned on the stairs to make sure her feet don't get caught in her dress.

Once she's safe on the ballroom floor next to him, his gaze moves up to hers and he laughs. He laughs like I've only ever seen him do maybe a handful of times in my life, every past time in similar reaction to something his wife said. His face relaxes and transforms, all the demons and violence and anger wiping away like they were never there.

"See?" Six says, eyes twinkling. "He needs her more than I do."

"Are you going to rename the firm then?" Thayer asks.

"Definitely not. B wants to keep doing some pro bono work through us so she'll still be involved. Even so, we would never drop her name. We started it with her and nothing changes that."

"You're not?"

The six of us turn to find Bellamy and Rogue behind us. They worked their way down the sides of the ballroom to find us so we didn't see their approach.

"Course not," Phoenix answers in his usual straightforward fashion.

Tears well in Bellamy's eyes and she does her best to blink them away. "That... That means a lot to me. Thank you."

"Of course!" Six says sincerely before giving her one of her famous hugs.

Thayer doesn't wait to be invited; she joins in, her arms wrapping around the both of them. "Congrats, B!"

Never much of a hugger myself, I find I can't resist the pull. I'm the fourth to join and they open up their arms to make room for me. We hug for a long time and when I crack open an eye and peek over Thayer's shoulder, I find our four husbands staring fondly back at us.

***

Chapter Twenty-Eight

Thayer

The good spirits that follow the centennial anniversary party for CKI last for a blissful two weeks.

Two weeks where our time is spent in each other's company, where we laugh together and our kids play together, where life is *normal*. The same as it's always been, nothing more, nothing less than that.

We don't know it yet, but tomorrow is going to happen, and it's going to change *everything*.

After that, it's going to be a while before life is ever normal again.

***

Chapter Twenty-Nine

Bellamy

It's a beautiful May day in London. The sun is out and high in the sky, shining down on us and making all the colors around us seem brighter. After months of short, dreary days and gray or downright rainy skies, the city comes alive bathed under such spectacular weather.

I'm standing in the kitchen of our home, staring out of the bay of windows at our massive garden.

My phone rings.

I answer without bothering to look at the caller ID.

"You can't keep calling."

"Ugh, come *on*. I need to know all the deets," Thayer pleads. "What are they doing?"

I turn away from the window and the scene I was watching, walking further into the kitchen.

"I'm not going to *spy* on them, Thayer."

"And why not?"

"It's an invasion of their privacy!"

She makes an affronted noise. "See, this is why I knew we should have done this at my house."

"We couldn't do it at your house. Your husband is there."

"Okay, fine. But next time we do this, I'm finding a way to kick him out. Clearly you can't be trusted to be a good informant."

I roll my eyes. "Please, they're not even doing anything *that* interesting. Rhodes just has her sitting on his handlebars while he cycles arou—"

"Hold up. I thought you said you *weren't* spying."

"Well, I–I'm not," I sputter. "I can't help it if they're doing this stuff *in front of my window.*"

"Oh my god, you're totally spying. Fantastic, this is exactly the version of you I needed to show up today. Tell me everything," she asks excitedly. "Did you just say he was cycling around with Ivy on his handlebars? That's so cuuuuute."

I laugh into the phone, turning back towards the windows just in time to see the bike hit a rock. Rhodes brakes suddenly, hands squeezing the handlebars tightly, and Ivy goes flying off.

My heart momentarily stops in my chest as I watch her fall. Thankfully, she doesn't go far. She lands a foot away from where the bike abruptly stopped.

I'm about to tell Thayer what happened when Rhodes throws himself off the bicycle and tosses it aside like it personally offended him.

In an instant he's on his knees in front of Ivy, his face twisted with worry and his hands clutching her leg. She looks more startled than hurt, her gaze tracing over Rhodes as he caresses her knee.

"I mean, truly adorable behavior," Thayer continues, unaware of what I'm watching develop in front of me. "He must get it from you. Lord knows Rogue's cute side is limited on a good day and entirely suppressed on every other day."

The connection between Rhodes and Ivy has been evident to everyone in our friend group since they both learned how to walk. Who knows, it might actually have started before then had their inability to physically go to each other not been a barrier.

Rogue is a vocal supporter of this connection, finding quite a bit of humor in his son's obsession with his best friend's daughter. Rhys, on the other hand, has a decidedly frostier approach to the entire thing. Short of hissing at Rhodes when he gets within a ten-foot radius of his little girl, he's done everything else to keep them apart when they're not with the larger group.

A month ago, I asked Rhodes what he wanted for his upcoming twelfth birthday. I expected an extravagant request in line with what I'd heard other boys in his class had asked for. Instead, he'd looked up at me with those big green eyes, the same as his father's, and he'd told me the only thing he wanted was to invite Ivy over so they could play, just the two of them.

I thought my heart might burst with affection and pride. When I told Thayer, she'd had a similar reaction. I think the echoes of her cooed "aww" might have reached as far up as Scotland. Together, we'd maneuvered to set this playdate up without telling her husband—who would have outright refused— or mine—who wouldn't have been able to resist gloating in his best friend's face.

Rhys was told that Ivy was with Suki at Nera's and Rogue was dispatched to the movies and then the park with our other children.

"Don't hold out on me, B. What are they doing now?" Thayer asks.

I chuckle at her nosiness. It took firm negotiations on my part to keep Thayer at home instead of face glued to the windows of my veranda, hand buried in a bag of popcorn watching this afternoon unfold as she'd originally intended.

But I didn't want to make a show out of this, not when it was just a playdate and our husbands were already adding undue pressure. The children are young and they deserve the space to figure out what they mean to one another, whether that's just being friends or eventually more.

From my position closer to the windows now, I have a better view and can see that Ivy appears to have a bloody knee. Her lips are twisted in a soft grimace but she's not crying.

She's tough as nails, always has been.

"Ivy fell off the bike."

Thayer immediately shifts into protective mom mode. "What? Is she okay? Does she need me?"

"I think she's okay. She's— Oh." I gasp. "Oh, *wow*."

"What? What is it?"

"Hold on, let me take a picture. You are going to lose your mind."

"You're scaring me. Is she hurt?"

"That's not it. Just look at your phone."

"What— *Oh*." She shrieks.

"My eardrum, Thayer!"

"Girl, *swoon*."

"It's even cuter in real life," I tell her, watching as Rhodes marches towards the back of the house carrying a bemused Ivy cradled tightly in his arms.

He hasn't hit puberty yet so he's only a couple of inches taller than her. Carrying her must be costing him dearly, but he's making it look easy. His face is set in a severe expression that only momentarily softens when his gaze sweeps over Ivy's face, hardening once more when they catch on her bleeding knee.

His steps are determined as he makes the journey back to the house, never once flinching at the weight in his arms. When he's only a couple feet away from the back door, I say, "I have to go, Thayer. Ivy looks fine but I want to make sure she's okay."

"Thank you," she answers with a relieved sigh. "Keep me updated."

"I will," I promise, hanging up.

Walking up to the back door just as they reach it, I open it for them. "Hey, guys."

"Mum," Rhodes calls, an underlying frenetic note in his voice. "I hurt Ivy."

"You—"

"No, you didn't," Ivy cuts in, shaking her head firmly. "I fell off the bike, Aunt B. It's my fault, Rhodes shouldn't get in trouble."

"It was me." I hadn't noticed it before but Rhodes looks a couple shades paler than usual. "I wasn't careful."

"No one is getting in trouble," I assure them. "Is your leg okay, Ivy?"

"Perfectly fine."

Rhodes shakes his head. "She's not fine. She's... she's *bleeding*."

I place a comforting hand on my son's shoulder. "We're going to get it disinfected and patched up, don't worry, darling." I start to reach for her. "I can take her, I'm sure you're tire—"

He steps back, pulling her out of my reach. "I can carry her. Just show me where you want me to put her down."

"I can walk," Ivy offers.

He narrows his eyes at her. "No, you can't."

She blinks at him, her cheeks turning a pretty pink color, but doesn't argue.

"You're a good friend, Rhodes. Come on, you can put her down here," I say, tapping the counter with my palm.

It's Rhodes's turn to go red. It would go unnoticed by a stranger, but his loved ones know his ears turn red whenever he feels a strong emotion. Ivy's eyes move over to his ears as well, not missing a thing.

Rhodes marches up to the counter and sets her gently down. It's as he steps back that I notice the beads of sweat coursing down the back of his neck and his temple. He shakes out his arms surreptitiously. Ivy doesn't see it, but I do.

It's as I thought—carrying her took a physical toll on him.

I set about getting the first aid kit and taking out the necessary items to clean Ivy's wound as they continue talking to each other like I'm not there.

"I'm so sorry."

"I told you, it's not your fault. It was so fun, I'm getting right back on as soon as Aunt B is done cleaning me up."

Rhodes stiffens. "No, you're not."

She lifts her chin defiantly at him. "I want to."

"No."

"You're not the boss of me, Rhodes Royal. I'm getting back on that bike and you're going to take me around like befo— *ouch*."

Ivy winces when I apply the antiseptic to her cut. Rhodes takes a hacked step forward, his wild eyes pinned on her knee.

"That stings," she whispers softly.

I pull the soaked cotton pad away from the wound. Looking up into her eyes, I find them glassy for the first time since she was hurt.

I'm about to offer apologies when Rhodes takes her hand, clutching her fingers in his with determined strength. I watch as he squeezes her palm and glances back at her.

"You're the toughest girl I know. You've got this."

Ivy's tears disappear before they can fall, replaced with a smile that starts off small and grows until it stretches across her entire face.

She nods at me. "Go ahead, Aunt B. I'm ready."

I bite back a smile. This would absolutely *kill* Thayer and there's no way I'm going to do the story justice when I try to recreate it for her tonight.

I get back to work, disinfecting, drying, and eventually putting a Band-Aid over the cut on Ivy's knee. Rhodes holds her hand the entire time and doesn't say another word.

When I'm done, he looks up at her with those disarming eyes of his. "Can we watch a movie now? I'll let you pick," he adds, sweetening the deal. Then, softer, "Please."

Her eyes stroke silently over his face. She must see the same worry in it that I do because she swallows and nods her agreement.

I'd anticipated that the afternoon might end there, so I say, "I put snacks in the cinema room if you want to go watch the movie there."

"Thanks, Mum."

The doorbell rings, surprising all three of us.

Rhodes throws me a questioning look when I sigh and shake my head.

"I think that might be your mom, Ivy. I told her you hurt your knee, I'm sure she wants to check that you're okay."

More like she wants to snoop on how the afternoon is going, but I can't be mad. Having her here is going to make this experience that much more enjoyable. The woman is pure entertainment.

I head over to the door and open it without checking the cameras, already reprimanding her. "I knew you couldn't resist getting involv—"

My words cut off abruptly when I find myself looking down the barrel of a gun. Confusion sweeps over me first, the cognitive dissonance of opening my front door to find a weapon brandished in my face rendering me dumb for a moment.

Then my gaze moves past the gun to the man holding it. Understanding and fear replace the confusion in one terrifying second.

Peter Gingrinch.

Peter, who was supposed to be in prison for at least eight more years. Peter, whose wealth and influence bought him a reduced sentence and early release based on good behavior.

Rogue was right and I should have listened, but it's too late for that now.

I immediately bar the door with my arms, trying to close it behind me so he can't come in. There's no fear for myself, only for the two kids who are just inside. I don't believe in god, but I find myself praying that they'll go to the cinema room. That they won't come after me. That Peter will never know they're there.

"What the hell do you want?"

His jaw twitches, his face contorting in an angry rictus. Veins throb in his temple, rendering him even uglier than usual. "Nothing's changed. You're still the same entitled bitch I remember."

"And you're still the same spineless coward who can only pick fights with those more defenseless than them. Doesn't your back hurt from bending over to punch this low?"

I bite back a gasp when he presses the gun to the middle of my forehead. Bringing his face inches from mine, he sneers, "Doesn't your mouth hurt from saying stupid shit that'll get you killed?" He licks his lips, bringing his gaze down to mine. "There are so many better uses for it too."

Ice chills my spine and I have to repress a shiver. I'd rather he just kill me now then try and put his hands on me.

He pushes the barrel into my forehead to try to force me back into the house, but I won't go. Not when that'll bring me closer to the kids.

"*Move*," he orders.

"No."

"Do you think I won't do it? You think I won't shoot you in the fucking head?"

I don't know what to do. I don't know how to buy more time, how to get him away from my house, from my k—

"Mum?"

My eyes close. A garbled sound of defeat rolls up my throat. My stomach plummets and constricts, fear taking hold of my insides and squeezing with deadly intent.

Peter sneers. "*Mum*? Now that's an unexpected but exciting development."

"Go to the cinema room, Rhodes!" I shout without turning. Addressing Peter, I add, "Leave him alone. He has nothing to do with this."

The expression on his face contorts into a twisted, cruel smile. Before he can say anything, I feel the door open up further behind me.

I extend my arms to either side of me and place my body between Peter and my son, shielding Rhodes from his gaze.

"Go back inside," I hiss.

Peter moves so fast that I don't have time to brace myself before the gun is brought down on my temple. I cry out and fall to one knee, clutching my head.

Small hands grab my shoulders. "Mum!"

The terrified tenor of Rhodes's voice slices a wound inside me that's much more painful than the throbbing in my head.

I clutch my head, whimpering. "Leave, Rhodes. *Run*."

"Stay."

Blood trickles down my forehead and over my brow, dripping steadily onto my cheek. I lift my head and glare back at Peter. Horrifyingly, his eyes aren't on me.

They're on my son.

"Stay," he repeats. He raises his gun and points it at Rhodes who recoils. "You've just made my plans significantly more interesting, little boy."

"Let him go," I plead, fear icing the blood in my veins. "I'll do whatever you want, but please, *please* let my son go."

Instead of answering me, Peter watches as Rhodes comes out from behind me. He positions himself in front of where I've fallen, his shoulders rolled back and tight.

"I'm not a little boy and I'm not going to let you hurt my mum," he announces.

My brave Rhodes. As brave and protective of his father.

"Who are you and what do you want with her?"

I wrap my arms around him from behind and try to pull him down into me, but he won't let me.

"Rhodes… *Don't*."

The blow to my temple is making my head spin. I'm dizzy and my brain feels addled. Nausea rolls up the length of my throat until I feel like I'm going to be sick. A cold sweat breaks out on my forehead, my vision tunnels, and I have to fight the creeping oblivion.

"And who is *this*?"

I follow Peter's gaze where it's pinned somewhere above my left shoulder, instinctively knowing the situation is about to take yet another turn for the worst. I find Ivy standing in the doorway behind me, a look of shock twisting her features as she tries to make sense of the scene unfolding before her.

She stammers, her voice small and unsure. "Aunt B… What…"

Peter moves his gun from my son to Ivy and Rhodes goes crazy. "Let me go, Mum." He thrashes in my arms, throwing his body every which way to try to free himself from my hold. *"Mum!"* He rips at my hands, his fingers digging into my skin. "Stop, please. Let me *go.*"

I release him, hoping that he'll go to Ivy and run. He lunges for her, but Peter gets there first. With a shove of his hand, he pushes Rhodes out of the way, sending him flying down the front steps.

I scream, too weakened by the violent blow to be able to move. Stars appear before my eyes and I blink them away, bathing my eyes in blood in the process.

"Rhodes..." I call out weakly, trying to hold on to my consciousness.

Rhodes tumbles down to the fifth and final step and pops easily back to his feet, apparently unharmed. His face is determined, his expression angry as he immediately lunges up the stairs once more.

But it's too late.

Peter has Ivy in his hold before Rhodes has even cleared the first step. She cries as his hand wraps around her upper arm, his fingers digging mercilessly into her flesh. His hand is so large, it closes entirely around her small bicep.

She fights, kicking and screaming. When she feels cold metal touch the spot at the back of her neck, she freezes instantly. Her eyes widen, colliding with Rhodes's.

He stops in his tracks, his hands going up.

"Please don't hurt her." His eyes are wild, darting from Ivy to Peter and down to me, unsure where to focus is panic.

I try to stand so I can help him, hating how defenseless I am. Both of my palms are on the ground and I'm pushing myself up when Peter pistol whips me a second time.

There's nothing I can do to fight this blow.

I fall in a pile of bones, rolling onto my back.

Rhodes's terrified scream echoes in my ears. *"Mum!"*

Almost like they're weighted with anvils, my eyelids close against my will. I manage to blink them a few more times, but the effort to keep the void at bay is monumental.

"Let Ivy go," Rhodes demands.

"No."

Blink.

Rhodes shakes under the weight of his anger. "What do you want?"

"Revenge."

"Why?"

"Your dear old mum here ruined my life."

The fucking *liar*.

"I was going to kill her, but now I see there's something that'll destroy her and your family even more. And it's this little girl right here." He shakes a boneless Ivy who gives a pained whimper. "You both seem to care very much about her. She's coming with me."

"You can't take her!" Rhodes springs into action. He leaps forward but falls back when Peter kicks him in the chest.

"No..." I whisper, the one syllable barely intelligible.

I should have let this playdate happen at Thayer's house. I should never have opened the door. I should have checked the cameras. I should have immediately punched Peter in the face once I saw who it was.

I should have...

I failed. I failed. I failed.

Blink.

"Please..." I beg as Rhodes scrambles back up to his feet.

"*Shut up*," Peter hisses at me. "Shut the fuck up before I change my mind and put a bullet in your skull."

"You can't take her," Rhodes repeats more vehemently.

"Rhodes, I'm scared," Ivy whispers, tears streaming down her face.

Blink.

My eyelids feel like they weigh a hundred tons, my blinking getting progressively more frequent as darkness calls to me.

"I am taking her," Peter announces, voice devoid of all emotion.

Rhodes climbs the final step until he's standing in front of Peter. He doesn't flinch as the gun comes to him.

"If you're taking her, take me too."

Blink... Blink... Blink...

"Rhodes...*No*," I manage to utter.

He ignores me.

Blink.

His chin goes up. "I'm not letting you take her without taking me too."

Peter's cruel smile stretches sinisterly until he laughs, the sound spine-chilling.

Blink.

"If you want to die too, I can make it happen."

Blink.

"NO!" My scream sounds louder than what I'm capable of right now. I realize it's because Ivy's voice joined mine, horror at Rhodes's offer bleeding into her tone just like it did mine.

Peter waves the gun, urging Rhodes to follow him down the stairs.

"I'm sorry, Mum. I'm so sorry," Rhodes whispers as he walks past me.

I see he's not crying.

He's scared and determined and the combination destroys me.

"Please…"

Rhodes is at the bottom of the stairs when he turns around. His eyes are glassy now.

"Dad will save you. I know he will." He starts crying. "Please don't die."

Blink.

This time, my eyes don't reopen. Before I go, my last thoughts are whether I'll ever wake up again and, if I do, whether my son and my best friend's daughter will both be dead.

Darkness takes me and I lose consciousness

A single tear slips down my cheek.

***

Chapter Thirty

Bellamy

When I next open my eyes, I'm lying in a hospital room surrounded by my friends, their husbands and mine conspicuously absent. At first, I have no immediate memory of what happened. I wake and smile when I see my loved ones. That smile wipes off in the flutter of a heartbeat when I see the somber expressions on their faces.

And everything comes screaming back to me.

The abject horror. The gut-wrenching fear.

The heart-rending realization that my son was taken.

Tears flood my eyes. Six squeezes my hand in both of hers, an equally stricken look splashed across her features. She tries for me, a tremulous smile painting itself across her lips, but she can't manage to hold it up and it disappears as quickly as it materialized.

"Tell me it was a bad dream."

Her mouth opens and closes, words failing her. Her lips flatten into a tight line and her eyes water.

I look at Nera. "Please, Ner."

She shakes her head. "I wish I could. More than anything, I wish I could."

The tears spill over when I see Thayer huddled in the corner, her legs pulled into her body and her arms wrapped around herself.

"Thayer…" My mouth is suddenly as dry as my cheeks are wet. "I'm so sorry. I'm so, so, sorry. I—"

She stands and comes to the bed, flinging her arms around my body. I feel her tears fall onto the skin at the base of my neck.

"I'm glad you're okay, B," she whispers, even as her body racks with sobs.

"I'm so sor—"

"Stop. It's not your fault." She cups my face, careful to avoid the injury on my forehead. "It's not your fault."

I stare into her eyes, seeing my own despair and fear reflected in her gaze. It tells me everything I need to know, but I ask anyway.

"Ivy…" My voice breaks, the next syllable nothing more than a hopeless croak. "Rhodes?"

Her face fractures, as close to a Jenga tower falling and shattering to pieces as I've ever seen anyone's expression be. Her brows pull down and her lip trembles as she tries to swallow a fresh wave of tears. She shakes her head and releases me, turning away. Nera stands and goes after her, wrapping an arm around her shoulders.

"Oh, God… I should have stopped him. I should hav—"

"There's nothing you could have done, B," Six assures me. "We all saw the footage, he—" Her voice catches in her throat. She wipes a palm under her eye to catch a falling tear. "It nearly killed Rogue to watch it. The sounds he made when Gingrinch hit you, when he took the kids, when you were left there, unconscious and bleeding… It sounded like he was being physically ripped apart from the inside." She scrubs a hand over her mouth, an agitated shiver coursing through her. "I–I've never heard anything like it."

The throbbing in my head is nothing compared to the ache in my heart and the pure unadulterated fear in my belly. I wish I could go back in time and redo everything.

"Where is he?" I ask. "Where's Rogue?"

"He's with the others, tearing the city apart searching for the kids," Nera tells me.

Thayer wipes a tired hand over her face, drying her cheeks in the process and pulling on her endless reserves of strength as she explains what happened.

"I'm the one who found you. I got to your house only twenty minutes after it all happened. I couldn't bear to miss out on all the action and I wanted to make sure Ivy was ok— that Ivy was okay." She looks off to the side, a small smile cresting the corner of her lips. It disappears suddenly as the memory changes. "Finding you on your front steps, bleeding and unconscious, B... I think a part of me died and I'm not sure it's ever going to come back. I thought you were *dead*." Her voice cracks audibly. "I called Rogue and an ambulance immediately. I didn't think it could get worse and then I realized the children were missing," she explains. "I thought Rogue was going to go into cardiac arrest when he arrived and found you unconscious and Rhodes missing. He...He didn't take it well, B. He destroyed hundreds of thousands of pounds worth of equipment when he got here and you were taken away. He assaulted two of the cops who tried to kick him out. Phoenix managed to keep him from being arrested and thrown in jail, but he's completely lost it. It took Rhys, Tristan and Phoenix to be able to drag him away. The only thing that finally got him to calm down was refocusing him on finding the children."

"He didn't want to leave you. He didn't want you waking up without him," Six adds. "He said he'll spend the rest of his life begging you for your forgiveness for not being here. It was an impossible decision, his wife or his son."

"I need him to find Rhodes and Ivy," I sob.

Nera nods. "That's what we told him you'd say."

I can only imagine the state Rogue was in upon his discovery of my assault and his son's kidnapping. Peter set out to hurt me and I'm sure he has no idea how inadvertently true his blows struck.

There's no way to quantify the amount of pain Rogue must have been in upon finding that his family had been targeted, that I might die and that his son had disappeared much like his mother had. The similarities with his traumatic past triggered that reaction in him, except this time I couldn't be there to help him through it.

Peter hurting my husband to such an extent strikes a killer blow to my own psyche.

"How long?"

Sixtine shifts uncomfortably in her chair and looks away. Thayer starts crying again, still held in Nera's arms. Nera refuses to look into my eyes.

"Please," I beg, looking at them one after the other. "How long ago was the attack? How long have I been unconscious?" I sit up, wincing at the throbbing in my head. "How long have they been missing?"

It's Thayer who steps forward and clasps my hand in hers. Nera follows, wrapping her hand over both of ours. Six is the last to add her comforting touch to mine.

"Twenty-eight hours and thirty-seven minutes." Thayer's voice is dead. "That's how long they've been gone for."

***

It takes another fifty-one hours before Rogue and Rhys track down the children and rescue them. Fifty-one hours of mental torture and torment more painful than anything Peter could have inflicted on me physically.

Fifty-one hours spent holding onto Thayer as we take turns crying and attempting to be strong for each other. Fifty-one hours that stretch interminably, the grains of sands in the hourglass falling so unbearably slowly I think mistress time herself is taunting me personally for my many failures.

I don't see Rogue during that time. I know he and Rhys don't sleep or eat or even stop for a second as they turn the country over looking for our children.

Eventually, they track them down to a farmhouse under Gingrinch's sister-in-law's name. Thayer and I are on our way there when they call to tell us that Peter and his two accomplices, whom he met during his brief stay in prison, are dead.

We sit huddled over the phone, oxygen trapped in our airways and our lungs frozen stiff as we wait for them to confirm the words we so desperately need to hear.

"Are they…" I swallow. "Are they alive?"

"They're alive," Rhys croaks. "They're okay."

Thayer and I fall into each other's arms in relief at the news. They're *alive*, everything is going to be alright.

In retrospect, I should have asked if they were unharmed.

Rhys's answer to that question would have been incredibly more measured.

It would have been more indicative of what was to come.

When I see my son again, I instantly know things will never be the same. He'd told Peter back at the house that he wasn't a boy, but he *was*.

He was *my* boy.

And now he's gone.

In his place stands a twelve-year-old with dead eyes and a void where his heart used to be. Not quite a man yet, but definitely no longer a boy. The flat wasteland of his gaze as he stares back at me reminds me so much of his father's the day I met him that it stops me in my tracks.

The shock makes the breath dry up in my lungs.

The kind, innocent boy is gone.

I lost him that day and I would never get him back.

Peter took that from me, from all of us.

Rhodes was near despondent when questioned, refusing to utter a word about his ordeal or give a clue as to how he was feeling.

He was marble; cold and beautiful and impossible to penetrate.

The only time he expressed any emotion in the immediate aftermath of his rescue was when he saw Ivy.

And that was perhaps the greatest shock of all.

Where reverence and adoration had previously shone in his gaze every time he laid eyes on her, he'd snapped out of his near comatose state on first glance at her and his tongue had swung in her direction, wielded like the sharpest of swords cutting through the softest of targets.

"Get the *fuck* away from me," he'd hissed, jerking to his feet and getting in her face. She'd cowered back against the wall, her gaze pinned dutifully downwards, her entire body trembling and submissive. "I never want to see you again. I never want to hear your name or listen to your voice or smell your perfume. I fucking *hate* you."

He'd loomed over her, fists clenched and nostrils flared as the vitriol spewed unendingly from his lips. And she'd taken it, crying softly but not saying a word in rebuttal or defense of herself.

At first frozen in horror, the four parents had then leapt into action, separating them. Even as he was being dragged away, Rhodes continued screaming at her and Ivy kept crying. We stood, stunned, torn between stupefaction at this sudden emotionality from him and staggered at the depth of his anger and its chosen target.

Neither one of them would talk about what happened during those three days, no matter how many times we asked over the coming weeks and months. We tried waiting for the dust to settle and reintroducing them once some time had passed, but the results were always the same. Rhodes was cruel and Ivy took it without looking at him.

We might have gotten our children back alive, but they hadn't emerged unscathed. Far from it.

They'd both changed.

Whatever happened during those three days destroyed them both in their own way.

Life couldn't continue as before.

After months of navigating a new normal that didn't feel normal at all, Rogue and I made the difficult decision to leave London.

We needed a fresh start. An opportunity for Rhodes to start over, away from the trauma, away from the constant trigger that was Ivy, somewhere that was a clean slate.

We took our family back to Chicago, to be closer to my mom. Being with their grandmother helped my kids and my family as a whole, but being away from my friends was incredibly hard. It was the right decision, but I was homesick in a way I'd never been before, and although the girls and I spoke every day and tried to FaceTime each other often, it wasn't the same.

The ripples of that one afternoon cracked the very foundation of our found family. Those fissures kept pushing us further apart for a long time. It would take years and us parents getting out of the way for things to finally settle back into place.

We would all be happy again, but I didn't know it then.

***

Twenty years after graduation

Chapter Thirty-One

Rhys

We exit the main building and walk out into the warm June day, the various couples holding hands as we amble out onto the perfectly trimmed grass.

Turning back towards the building, Rogue wraps an arm around Bellamy's shoulders and looks at his son.

"What did you think of that, Rhodes?"

The boy in question shrugs, his face an unreadable mask.

"It fucking bored me," he answers dispassionately.

Bellamy frowns. "Language!"

Rhodes turns on his heels and walks away, taking a path that we all know will lead him to a fork in the road between the pond and forest.

I watch him go, realizing that the fourteen-year-old is more man than boy these days. He's already well over six feet tall, with a full head of chestnut brown hair and moody dark green eyes. He looks too much like his father for his own good.

I need to keep thinking about him as a boy, because if I let myself consider him a man, I'll want to rip his throat from his neck for what he's done to my daughter. It's not lost on anyone here that she's conspicuously absent from this reunion and that Rhodes is the sole reason for it.

Nera turns towards her daughter. "What about you? Any thoughts about the next four years of your life?"

Suki rolls her eyes at her mother. "Whatever."

With an insolent flick of her hair, she follows after Rhodes.

I remember a time when Suki was gregarious, funny, and kind, but that was before.

Almost overnight, she changed.

These days she's nearly unrecognizable from the little girl I watched grow up. She wraps herself in emotions ranging from indifference to downright spitefulness, her razor sharp tongue aimed at those closest to her, a pale imitation of the girl I used to know.

Her parents have tried intervening to get to the root of what's wrong, but the results have backfired. Once the apple of her father's eye and her mother's cherished middle daughter, she's now frosty with them on the best of days.

And I know it hurts them.

Astra watches her ex-best friend walk away with an expression that hovers between sadness and longing. She was another casualty in Suki's overnight volte-face. To my knowledge, there was never an official falling out between them; one day, Suki just started giving her the cold shoulder.

Phoenix puts a protective hand on his daughter's shoulder.

"You okay, star?"

She gives him a sweet smile, as constant in her personality as her friends' have changed.

"Yes, Daddy. I thought the orientation was very helpful."

Astra is being kind where the other kids weren't. Her mother's family has been coming to RCA almost since the day it was founded. She needs the orientation about as much as I need a *Football for Dummies* book.

It's not my first time back at Royal Crown Academy, but it's always a weird experience. Walking the grounds and the halls as a parent who has hopes and ambitions for his daughters comes with a sort of out of body experience when those halls are the very same I used to wreak havoc in.

Everywhere I turn, I have flashes of memories of my time here.

The good, the bad, the earth-shattering, like the closet we just walked past on our way out, the very same one where I touched Thayer for the same time. I'd looked down at my wife and the pretty pink flush of her cheeks had told me she'd been thinking the very same dirty thoughts that I was.

We'd definitely have to make time for a little pit stop back into the closet before we left.

Thankfully, neither one of our daughters is here, otherwise they'd be mortified. Hayes, like Cato and Kiza, has already been an RCA student for two years so we didn't bring her along.

And Ivy...

Enrolling her at RCA was out of the question. Like the Royals, we'd move away from London after her kidnapping to give her a much-needed fresh start. I'd signed a contract with Real Madrid and we'd relocated to Spain.

Progressively, Ivy had been coaxed out of the dark hole in which she'd buried herself after that ordeal. She was better now, but not completely. There was still something not quite right, something her mum and I couldn't quite put our finger on, almost like a tiny sliver of her was still missing.

She was prone to bouts of intense quietude that were unlike her, times where her gaze strayed off and she became unreachable.

I'd have given my entire fortune to know what she thought about in those moments, if she was mentally torturing herself like I imagined she might be.

As her dad, I wanted to take all of her pain away, and the obvious place to start seemed to be getting rid of Rhodes.

If I ever got him alone, I couldn't guarantee that I wouldn't kill him, his father be damned.

In the meantime, we'd decided to enroll Ivy in a local secondary school in Madrid to keep them apart, so she wasn't here either.

"Can you guys believe Thornton's still here?" Phoenix drawls.

Tristan grumbles. "Fuck no. Every time he sees Nera and I together, he looks on the verge of having an aneurysm though, so might not be too much longer," he adds with a hopeful note in his voice.

"Not in front of the children," Nera chides under her breath, tipping her head at Juno and Hana who are hanging out just off to the side of us.

"That's it for the orientations, right?" Six asks. "What should we do now?"

270

Rogue turns towards his wife with a shamelessly racy smile on his face. "Bell and I are going to go check out the library."

She flushes and Riot looks at him with a disgusted expression on his face. "Dad, please never look at Mum the way you just did in front of us again. I know we're rich, but there's no amount of money in the world that'll cover my therapy bill."

"Or mine," River adds crisply.

"What's in the library, Daddy?" Rowan asks.

"Your mum and I used to spend *a lot* of time there," he grins down at Bellamy who swats playfully at him. She still bears a faint scar on her forehead from the blows she suffered at Gingrich's hand. "I want to see if there's still the fist-shaped dent in one of the back shelves."

River scrunches his brow. "Why would there be?"

"I punched a hole in it after your mother threatened to move on with another man."

"Mum!"

"Hey, context! I was entitled to. Your father had pretended to cheat on me at the time."

Rowan turns on her father, aghast. "Dad!"

Rogue's face darkens. "I was an idiot," he mutters, wrapping an arm around Bellamy's shoulder and pulling her close. "I learned the consequences of my actions that day. Let's go, sweetheart," he adds, moving back towards the main building.

"Hey, what about us?" Riot asks.

"Entertain yourselves for a bit, darling," Bellamy answers. "We'll be back in ten—"

"Twenty," Rogue interjects.

"*Twenty* minutes."

Riot makes a disgusted sound and turns towards his best friend. "Come on, Juno, let's go check out the pond." He stalks off, the rest of the children following dutifully behind him.

"Be careful!" Six calls after them.

Tristan grabs Nera's hand. "Alone at last. We've got unfinished business with the forest, don't we, baby?"

He drags her away without a backwards glance.

Thayer glances up at me with a suggestive look on her face. I have her in my arms before she's even uttered a word.

"Soccer pitch?" she asks, wagging her eyebrows.

"Football," I correct in a throaty whisper, before claiming her lips with mine. "But, fuck yes."

I hear Six turn towards Phoenix. "And you? Where do you want to go?"

A contented rumble rolls up his chest as his hands find her waist. "Wherever you want. I've only ever wanted to be wherever you are."

As the four of us walk off in different directions, I can't help but think about the closing of one door and the opening of another. All of our children, together, starting where it all began for us, about to make their mark on the very same world we inhabited for years.

A new generation begins.

***

Epilogue / Twenty-four years after graduation

Chapter Thirty-Two

Phoenix

The room is so small, I could cross it from one wall to the other in three steps. The darkness stings my eyes, forcing them to readjust to the poorly lit space. The only light streams in from the room's single window, its three other walls unfenestrated and made up of dirty, cheap panels that emit a suffocatingly cheap smell of dust mites.

Not for the first time, I ask myself why I'm even here. I know the answer, but there's something therapeutic in keeping the question on a loop when the answer is only mildly satisfying.

The reality is, I'm here because my wife wants me here.

And what my wife asks me to do, I do, no questions asked.

That doesn't mean I'm particularly happy about it.

The woman in question is standing in front of the lone window, bathed in its harsh light, arms crossed as she takes in the scene before her.

I walk up until I'm standing just behind her, the warmth of my body sending a small shiver coursing down the length of her spine.

With difficulty, I rip my gaze away from Six's nape where I'd been admiring the soft elegance of her neck, and look up, my gaze following hers through the window.

My jaw twitches when I see the boy sitting opposite the two cops.

He's nowhere near a boy. He's a fully grown man, his size, obvious attitude, and the reason he's sitting in that room on the other side of the glass evidence of the fact that there's nothing childlike about him.

"Look at him, Six."

Her arms tighten across her chest. It's not often that she digs her heels in and becomes stubborn as a mule, but clearly this is one of those times.

I bite back a sigh.

I'd rather she stubbornly ask me to buy her a mansion on the Amalfi Coast than take this on.

"I am."

"*This* is who you want to adopt?"

She nods once. Her eyes never once move away from the boy-slash-man in question. She doesn't look at me and that in it of itself makes me want to bring down the blinds on the one-way window so she can't look at him any longer.

"Yes. I have a feeling, I can't explain it. I think he was meant to be in our lives."

"He's eighteen years old. He doesn't need us."

That makes her turn around.

Finally.

And now I regret the words, regret wanting her to look at me, because she faces me with a look of such dismay and disappointment on her features that I want to rewind time and undo the last thirty seconds.

"What eighteen-year-old doesn't need their parents? Who's going to house him, take care of him, push him to succeed?" Quieter, she adds, "Don't you wish your parents had been there for you?"

I scowl at her. "No, they didn't deserve to be."

"Well, he deserves to have parents capable of loving him." She turns away once more. "It's never too late to save someone."

Six faces the window, her eyes back on the boy.

He has no way of knowing there's anybody on the other side of the window, let alone her, and yet it's almost as if he senses her gaze. The moment her gaze finds him, his face turns away from the cops and his eyes connect unseeingly with hers through the glass.

He's undeniably handsome, even with the bruise forming on the right side of his face and the defiant sneer contorting his rather unique features. A straight, stiff jawline, marred by an angry scar that cuts from his ear diagonally down to the middle of his jaw. Eyes that burn so hotly with rage they're nearly vivid red. A nose that's been broken a few times. A smattering of beauty marks on his unblemished cheek.

His evident rage makes him striking.

"He's violent," I point out. "He's got issues."

"He needs to be loved," she argues.

Earlier in the year, Six had heard about his family's case through a couple of social workers she works with. Even though she'd already been swamped with her current workload, my wife had been unable to turn her back on someone who so clearly needed her, as was typical for her.

She'd decided to take the case on and had specifically worked with the boy's parents to try and rehabilitate them.

She'd gotten them jobs and access to resources to get clean. She'd gone above and beyond to help them.

Four months ago, she'd gotten a letter from both of them officially declaring their intent to terminate their parenting rights over the boy. She'd tried to track them down, but they'd disappeared back into the circles of vice they'd originally come from.

Two months later, today, she gets a call from the police department telling her the boy has been arrested for assaulting a homeless man and that her business card was found on him.

And now she wants us to adopt him.

After she almost died giving birth to Astra, I waited years for her to come to me and tell me she was ready to adopt another baby. When she never did, I grew tired of waiting and asked her about it myself.

Every time, the answer was the same.

I'm not ready. I'm happy with what we have.

It's not like I disagreed. I was happy with it being the three of us for the rest of time, I just wanted her to feel the same.

When it became clear she wasn't interested in adopting, I stopped asking. To say I was caught off guard when the request finally reemerged this morning after being dormant for eighteen years is an understatement.

Finding out that she wanted to adopt not a baby, not even a kid, but an actual man in the eyes of the law, had been another shock. Learning he needed to be picked up at the police station had been the third and final surprise, the one that had nearly finished me.

Six seems blind to reason, my very numerous and valid arguments falling on deaf ears.

I'm running out of time, so I pull out my final trump card.

If this doesn't work, nothing will.

And then I'll have to live with this stranger in my house.

"Do you really want this boy who beats up homeless people for fun to be around Astra?" I growl. "He'll be her stepbrother."

She stiffens and slides an angry look at me from between narrowed eyes. I know she's about to make me pay for that low blow.

"He reminds me a lot of you twenty-four years ago, Nix. Furious at the world, being eaten up from the inside out by your bitterness and resentment. I think we have a loving home to offer and if we don't open it up to someone so clearly in need, then we're failing each other. Astra will understand that." She turns back around to look at the still seething teenager. "And stop referring to him as "the boy" just to keep your distance from him. He has a name. Use it."

I grumble unhappily, annoyed at the situation, annoyed at the fact that Six is clearly upset with me.

That's not a position I'm used to being in.

And to get out of it, I know I'm just going to give her what she wants.

"Ares is mine, Nix. I know he is."

"Careful with the 'mine' shit, Six," I fume. "I'm not above killing an eighteen-year-old if I feel you getting too comfortable."

Six looks up at me. The harsh lighting does nothing to take away from her beauty. Her eyes shine softly as they look up at me with affection now, her anger never one to linger for too long.

"He's my son, I mean. I was meant to come into his life. That's why I think I waited so long — I was waiting for him. Astra will get used to it. She'll understand that we have to help him."

She blinks up at me, her hand finding my chest.

"Put those eyes away, wild girl," I groan. "You don't need to bring out the heavy artillery to convince me. If you want this, you'll have it."

A beaming smile breaks out across her face.

"Really?"

"Really. He can come home with us."

She claps her hands happily, and suddenly a memory of her flashes through my mind so powerfully that it takes my breath away. Her, eighteen years old, hair blowing in the wind, freckles dancing across her cheeks, clapping just as happily as she is now because I agreed to go sledding down Blind Hill with her.

Making her happy makes me happy.

It always has.

I rap my knuckles on the glass to get the cops' attention. They stand and the boy, Ares, scowls at the one-way window.

As the cops exit the room to come meet us, I say to Six, "Tell them we're taking him home with us. I'll make the charges go away. But I'm telling you wild girl, one wrong move and he's gone. I won't have him endanger you or Astra. Do we have an agreement?"

She hesitates, biting her lip. "Three."

"What?"

"Three strike policy. Come on, Nix, you can't expect him to adapt so quickly. He's been abandoned by his parents. He's angry. He's bound to lash out. One mistake isn't fair, it's setting him up to fail."

"Not my problem. One."

She crosses her arms, her lower lip jutting out stubbornly.

"Three."

I sigh. "Fine. Two, and I'm being generous here."

"Two and a half."

"Six…"

"Two and a half," she repeats.

"How do you even define a half here?"

She lifts a shoulder and shrugs. "It'll be a discretionary half. If he messes up, we'll discuss if it's big enough of an offense to count as a half or full strike."

I cross my own arms. "Two."

"Three," she counters.

I growl at her. "That's not how bartering works."

She smiles sweetly in response. "It is in my world."

"For fuck's sake, *fine*. Two and a half, as ridiculous as that is." Six shrieks happily and throws herself into my arms, her warm body coming to mine as her forearms close around the back of my neck. "Don't be so happy, wild girl. If he hits two and a half strikes, I'll kill him."

"You won't. And he won't." She pecks a quick series of kiss against my lips. "Thank you, baby."

I grumble a reply as the doors open and the cops walk in.

278

Releasing her back to the ground, we go about negotiating his release and discussing Ares's guardianship process.

In a month, Astra, Suki, and Rhodes will begin their first year at Royal Crown College, the private university Rogue and Bellamy opened four years ago. They created it when their oldest son first set foot on the grounds of RCA, in anticipation of his graduation one day and the continuation of his higher education.

Set on the other side of the pond from RCA, nestled in the woods only a few hundred feet from the main campus and now sharing some of the same facilities as the secondary school, the college has already earned a prestigious reputation.

Being accepted and enrolled into the start of this year would be impossible for anyone else, not just because of the timing but because students require a near perfect GPA to even be considered, something I'm sure Ares hasn't maintained, but I'm not worried.

I know Rogue will have the board make an exception for us.

One thing's for certain — the page is turning and it's the beginning of a new chapter for our children.

It's about to get interesting.

***

The end… for now.

The Families

The Royals

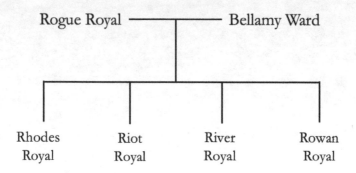

Rogue Royal —————— Bellamy Ward

Rhodes Royal | Riot Royal | River Royal | Rowan Royal

The Mackleys

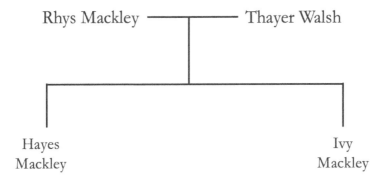

Rhys Mackley ——————— Thayer Walsh

Hayes
Mackley

Ivy
Mackley

The Sinclairs

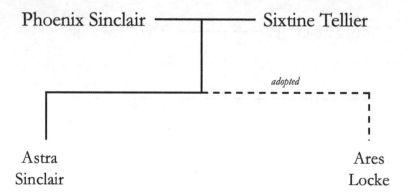

Phoenix Sinclair ——————— Sixtine Tellier

adopted

Astra
Sinclair

Ares
Locke

The Matsuokas

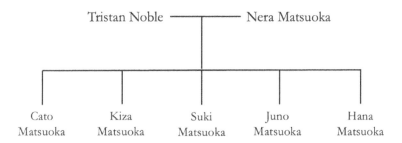

The Nobles

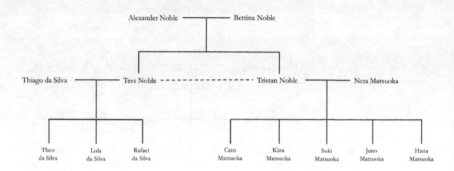

The Telliers

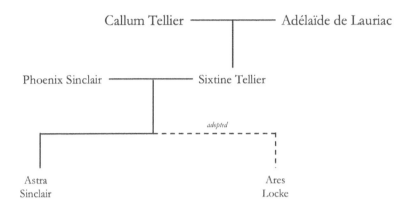

About The Author

Khai Hara

Khai Hara is an American author currently based out of New York City. An avid fan of the romance genre, 'It Must Be Fate' is her sixth novel and the conclusion of the Royal Crown Academy series. In her spare time, she enjoys traveling, hiking, reading and spending time with her boyfriend and their dog Thunder.

Follow her on IG at @authorkhaihara to stay up to date on upcoming releases.

Books In This Series

Royal Crown Academy

<u>Long Live The King</u>
Rogue & Bellamy

"Go ahead, scream for help." He taunts darkly as his hot breath tickles my ear. "No one here will save you from me."

When I get a scholarship to finish high school in Switzerland, I don't expect to meet a villain.

Rogue Royal.

He's the kind of gorgeous your mom tells you to stay away from, filthy rich and his family founded the school I just got accepted to.

Did I mention he makes my heart race?

Only because he hates me, of course. The first day we met, I accidentally spilled a milkshake on him and he's made my life hell ever since.

But this is my best chance for a better future for my mom and I– I won't let him break me.

Pay For Your Lies
Rhys & Thayer

Rhys
The moment I see her, I want her.
And what I want, I always get.
It's the competitive side of me.
Learning that she has a boyfriend already enrages me, but does nothing to deter me.
I know that eventually she'll submit to me and be mine.
I'm so sure of it that I bet my friends I can crack her in a month.
I just hope I don't come to regret it.

Thayer
From the moment I meet him, he's determined to have me.
He doesn't know that I'm just as competitive as he is and he's met his match.
I'm attending Royal Crown Academy on an athletic scholarship for my senior year; the only things I care about are good performances on the field and lots of fun off of it.
I'm not interested in any of the resident heartbreaker's games but find myself sucked in when the soccer star becomes my personal Coach.
As we spend more time together, I see a different side of him and find myself falling for him a bit more every day.
But can I really trust him?

Pay For Your Lies **is book two of the Royal Crown Academy series. It can be read as a standalone novel, but for better understanding of the universe, it's recommended that you start with the first book in the series,** *Long Live The King. This is a mature, mild slow burn, new adult romance with a jealous/possessive hero and lots of angst. It contains situations that some readers might find offensive.*

I Was Always Yours
Phoenix & Sixtine

We all know how the legend goes.
Girl meets boy.
They fall in love.
They get married.
And they live happily ever after.
The fairytale. The ending that every girl wants, that every girl dreams of.

For a brief moment there, I foolishly, naively, allowed myself to dream that's what our destiny was. That our friendship would evolve into something more and we'd be together forever.

The reality is that our story ended before it even began, with blood at my feet, tears on my cheeks and my broken heart held forever captive in the hands of someone who'd never wanted it.

I Was Always Yours **is book three of the Royal Crown Academy series. It can be read as a standalone novel, but for better understanding of the universe, it's recommended that you start with the first two books in the series,** *Long Live The King* **and** *Pay For Your Lies.*

This is a mature, new adult romance with a jealous and possessive hero, lots of angst and even more trigger warnings. It contains situations that some readers might find offensive.

Love In The Dark
Tristan & Nera

I've been banished to Switzerland with a fake name, forced by my father to spend a year teaching spoiled rich kids as punishment for humiliating him.

I'm supposed to stay out of trouble, to avoid scandals, to learn responsibility.

I'm not supposed to meet *her.*

I fucked up before I even set foot within the hallowed halls of RCA.

And there she is.

In my class.

In the halls.

In my veins.

Every fucking where.

She's going to be my downfall.

Or maybe, my salvation.

Love In The Dark is book four of the Royal Crown Academy series. It can be read as a standalone novel, but for better understanding of the universe, it's recommended that you start with the first three books in the series, *Long Live The King, Pay For Your Lies, and I Was Always Yours.*

Made in United States
Cleveland, OH
03 May 2025

16626430R00173